THE GEORGIA REGIONAL
LIBRARY FOR THE BLIND
AND PHYSICALLY
HANDICAPPED IS A FREE
SERVICE FOR INDIVIDUALS
UNABLE TO READ
STANDARD PRINT.

ASK AT OUR CIRCULATION
DESK HOW TO REGISTER
FOR THIS SERVICE, AS WELL
AS OTHER SERVICES
OFFERED BY THIS LIBRARY.

THE FIRST DAYS OF CHAOS

This Large Print Book carries the
Seal of Approval of N.A.V.H.

THE FIRST DAYS
OF CHAOS

ANNABEL JOHNSON

THORNDIKE PRESS

An imprint of Thomson Gale, a part of The Thomson Corporation

Detroit • New York • San Francisco • New Haven, Conn. • Waterville, Maine • London

THOMSON

GALE

Copyright © 2006 by Annabel Johnson.

Sequel to Last Days of a Toyshop.

Thomson Gale is part of The Thomson Corporation.

Thomson and Star Logo and Thorndike are trademarks and Gale is a registered trademark used herein under license.

Thorndike Press® Large Print Clean Reads.

The text of this Large Print edition is unabridged.

Other aspects of the book may vary from the original edition.

Set in 16 pt. Plantin.

LIBRARY OF CONGRESS CATALOGING-IN-PUBLICATION DATA

Johnson, Annabel, 1921–
    The first days of chaos / by Annabel Johnson.
      p. cm. — (Thorndike Press large print clean reads)
    "Sequel to Last days of a toyshop"—T.p. verso.
    ISBN-13: 978-0-7862-9755-9 (alk. paper)
    ISBN-10: 0-7862-9755-7 (alk. paper)
    1. Widows — Fiction. 2. Nineteen forties — Fiction. 3. New York (N.Y.) —
Fiction. 4. Large type books. I. Title.
PS3560.O37134F57 2007
813'.54—dc22   2007015654

Published in 2007 by arrangement with Annabel Johnson.

Printed in the United States of America on permanent paper
10 9 8 7 6 5 4 3 2 1

CONTENTS

This book is dedicated
To the City of New York, as it once was

The letter:

The words were printed in block form, paragraphs arranged down the page with mathematical precision, but the writing was shaky, as if it had cost a world of effort.

August 21, 1947
My Dearest Wife:

This is a hard one to write. I wish we could be together one more time. Some things are better said in person.

How can I help you? I ask myself.

First, understand that I am perfectly okay with the prospect of dying. It will be the most interesting experiment I've ever done. And living — for me — isn't all that great any more. I don't think I could enjoy a good life bearing the burden of guilt that will always be with me.

To understand that, you would have to

have seen what I have — a whole city and its inhabitants wiped off the face of the map.

Of course I am glad it was not one of ours.

I'm glad it ended the ruinous war.

I'm glad it saved lives.

But nothing can rationalize the fact that I share the responsibility for unleashing such evil power upon the world.

I believe what is troubling me most is that I don't know right from wrong any more.

I tried to find answers in the Bible, but I guess I'm not smart enough. I know the Lord made us all out of atoms, but why didn't He install a cut-out switch, to block our terrible inventiveness?

I think: Okay, I am sorry. But it doesn't bring back the days of innocence, when I was sure that my work would be a benefit to mankind. When I knew who I was.

I don't any more. So it's time to go. For me.

Not — repeat NOT — for you.

Somewhere in the Book it says: To everything there is a season. For you, this next year should be an equinox. You haven't ever had a life of your own. You have taken care of others, including me, for so long you haven't found out who you are. So let me tell you:

You are the toughest woman I ever knew.

You are the lovingest.

You are warm and gifted and I believe you will survive, if you can only find a little peace.

What worries me is your tendency to get impatient. Back in the days before we found each other, you were ready to go off in all directions. Five hard years made us grow up, You can make the difficult choices now by yourself. Just don't come to any decisions yet. I urge you not to be hasty.

If you still love me, promise me you will live. At least for one year, that's all I ask.

Go somewhere, do something, anything. Go to New York. Learn the city. You always had a yen to try it on — now's the time.

Look up Dixie. My sister loves you, no matter what you think of her. Forgive her problems.

Be the friends you once were.

Get a job. You haven't yet tapped the great mysterious potential that you were gifted with.

You got diverted from it when you were forced to concentrate on music. Now that you're free of pressure, don't discard the idea entirely. You've got a lot of music in you. forget being a concert pianist and have fun with it.

Meet people, women, men, don't be afraid to fall in love again. I won't mind. It can't take away anything from what we had.

Don't let me down, don't let yourself down. Give it your best shot, and know that I will be with you in every way that counts.

Never forget how much I have loved you, dear wife of mine.

Phin

August, 1947

She stood at the window and listened to the voice out there, an indistinct roar that pulsed with urgency, that almost articulated words of anger and need and excitement, the sound of a great city. Terra had never thought of a place as having a personality, much less a sort of communication. But there was no doubt that New York was broadcasting its nature for anyone who dared to live here: move fast or get out of the way. Cars honking feverishly, revving motors, tires spinning, voices yelling, pleading, cursing, whooping with laughter, chattering nervously. Someone blowing a whistle. Police? Doormen in their silly uniforms, standing at the portals of posh hotels? She had seen them as the taxi brought her here. There was no doorman at the YWCA.

Now, in this narrow cell on the tenth floor, with a view of an airshaft and beyond it a vacant brick wall, she could only listen, but the hovering roar stirred some feeling inside where she had been numb for a long time. A sense that she must activate some inner gears. Phin had asked her to live, and she had sworn to love, honor and obey. Until death. The vows didn't say anything about an extra year. But he'd asked for that and she owed him, even though he had deliberately left her, run out, deserted . . . the words percolated in her with a deep, abiding anger.

Maybe I can manage a year.

Terra turned back to the barren room that had been allotted to her. It was only temporary. The girl at the desk had been fiercely firm about it: "We need to put a strict limit on all stays. We have a waiting list. You have exactly two weeks to find other lodging." Then, with a touch of superiority, "I advise you not to plan to stay in the city. There simply aren't any apartments for rent. Everyone coming back from the war, you see."

Now as Terra walked out past the desk the clerk was making the same spiel to some newcomer, a girl in a shabby dress with a single small suitcase, who wasn't inclined to be patronized.

"Yeah," she snapped, "I heard about the war."

Stepping out onto the street Terra found herself part of that great sonorous entity she had heard from above. Caught in the stream of New Yorkers who rushed along the sidewalks, dodged the cars, these nameless people who had learned to adapt to the noise, the gas fumes, the smells of decay from the alleys, she was reminded of salmon fighting their way up the rapids. Terra found herself hurrying to keep up with the flow heading north.

Earlier she had studied a map of the city to get oriented on the directions — uptown, downtown, east side, west side. It was a very logical plan, Phin would have approved. She knew that the massive pile ahead was Grand Central Station. She had gotten off the train there yesterday afternoon. More elegant than the straight-edged buildings on either sides, it arrogantly blocked the street, traffic parting around it like a river. Before she got there she veered off to the west and found Fifth Avenue.

Heading uptown she moved past the great names, Saks, Lord and Taylor, Bonwit Teller. Full of fall colors the window displays were extravagantly handsome, bursting with the new look of longer skirts and higher heels, short upswept hair-dos on all the mannequins. Pausing, Terra saw her own reflection in the window glass, imposed on all that high style, and felt a vague amusement. She looked like a throw-back to war times in the blue gabardine suit, knee-length, with padded shoulders. She had bought it in 1942, part of her hasty trousseau. The dark hair had been shoulder-length then. Now it was braided into a coil at the nape of her neck. Phin had loved long hair. When she let it down, those rare nights when he hadn't been too exhausted . . .

First thing I'm going to do is get my hair cut.

No, that was not the top of her list. Getting a room had to take precedence. But even before that, one chore had to be faced. She strolled on, looking for 57th Street, found it and turned west again. Searching for a name among the art galleries, she almost missed it — up on the second floor of one of the buildings a broad window with a gold embellishment:

Galerie de la Coquette

Climbing the long flight of stairs she found herself in an anteroom dominated by a poster, of a woman larger than life size, rendered in quick black brushstrokes that

16

only sketched in the long arms and legs and face. The point was obviously her gown, flowing, saffron-colored, startling in its asymmetrical cut and suggestion of anatomy beneath. A handsome professional instant of art, it was signed in the lower corner with a signature flung down like a few loose sticks: **DIXI.**

It gave her a twinge of memory: "Phin says I should drop the 'e' off my name." Hard to realize that it was only five years since they had put his sister on the train in St. Louis, bound for a prestigious institute and a career in fashion. Terra had hated her best friend a little that day, for being so brave, going off to face the world. A sense of destiny had brought the glow of passion to a young girl's scrawny homely face. It had rendered Dixie strangely beautiful.

Shoving open the door Terra walked into the studio. It seemed to be deserted, a vast empty room only peopled by huge charcoal drawings pinned carelessly to the walls. Clever attention-getting designs, dresses, suits, slacks and jackets, they were all rendered in that powerful hand.

"Can I help you?" From side entrance at the rear Dixie moved forward into her own black-and-white exhibit, swathed in a silken cascade of colors that draped in loose profusion about her long skinny frame right on down to the ankles. Four inch heels in canary yellow — she came to a stop.

"Ohmagosh. Therissa Miller!"

"The name is Terra Berensen. Let me introduce myself, I'm your sister-in-law. Small detail, easy to overlook."

"I'm sorry. I just never have quite taken it in, the fact that you and Phin actually got married. You should have invited me to the wedding. Then I could have believed it." Dixie sounded flustered. Fluttering fingers with ruby red nails an inch long touched her sleek cap of black hair. It was plastered tight to her head, except for one arty tendril that curled past her ear, as if to emphasize her basic ugliness, the crooked face with the wide mouth. She went on nervously. "There's something weird about a childhood pal turning out to be your sister."

"There was no time for a wedding party," Terra said. "We were married by a Justice of the Peace in Oak Ridge, Tennessee, in a ten minute ceremony before we caught a train. Anyway, I wouldn't have wanted to interrupt you when you were in such an ecstasy at Pratt Institute. I see they didn't ruin your style." She glanced at the sketches with a nod. "You've got real paper now to draw on, no more butchers' wrap. I hope this gal-

18

lery is successful?"

"We're getting a reputation," Dixie hunched her bony shoulders. "It helps to have a friend who's rich enough to set up a show room here among the elite." In an old self-conscious gesture her long fingers revisited the short shingled black hair. "Zoey inherited a bundle from an aunt."

The name fell awkwardly into the empty space between them. *Take it or leave it,* the message was plain.

Bracing up, Terra said, "How is Zoey?"

"She's wonderful."

"I'm glad for you." The chasm was there, the thing that had separated them for five years. Now it had to be bridged. As Phin had said, they had all grown up. But both were wary.

With a defiant switch of hips Dixie wandered over to the window. "So, when did you hit town?"

"Yesterday — and it hit me first." Old habit of banter, it came back naturally.

"Where are you staying?"

"At the 'Y' temporarily. Got to find a place to live."

"You're here for good?" Surprise, a flash of joy?

"I'm here. Good — I don't know."

The sardonic air was back quickly.

" 'Good' could be better when it comes to style. Those braids, I'd like to take the scissors to them. And your clothes make me itch. I hope you'll let me deck you in something more modern. You look like a fugitive from a Lana Turner movie. That short skirt — egad! The war's over. We have plenty of cloth now, even getting some imported stuff from India, Scotland. It's great for a fashion designer. We can really swing."

"I guess I haven't kept up with fashions."

"No, I suppose there weren't any boutiques in that odd place where you lived, what was it called? Los Alamos?"

The words spoken aloud made Terra cringe. For so long they had been forbidden, the secrecy so deeply ordained that no one inside the place ever referred to the encampment by name. It had been simply The Hill. Now, of course, the public knew, or thought they did. *Oh yes, that's where they built the A-bomb.* She had heard it said right out in conversation, offhand, just another war-time episode, all over, thank heaven.

"Phin wrote me a few times," Dixie went on. "Never revealed much. His letters always looked like math theorems, sentences printed neatly down the page. But I could see him, with his cowlick and his elbows and his limp. Then of course he sent me the last one a few weeks ago. His handwriting was so shaky." All at once her eyes were jet-bright with tears.

Terra wished she could cry. She had tried, but the anger was too hot. It had dried her out. Dixie was trying not to let go, but her shoulders were heaving. In a rush she said, "I'll get us some tea. We always have a pot on in the back room." It was quite a while before she returned with a tray and two steaming cups. Setting them on a small ornate table by the window she pulled forward a couple of chairs, elegant with needlepoint on the seat-backs.

Terra enjoyed the smell of oolong. "You do your designing here?"

Dixie smiled. "Sketch 'em, sell 'em, cut and fit and stitch. I still do my own sewing."

"Really? I know you used to, but that was the Depression."

"No, that was me, being creative. Remember how I designed my own pajamas back in high school?" It was true, Dixie had always made up her own patterns. "I'll never forget how we dressed our paper dolls together, long rainy days, down on the floor in front of the fire place? How we made fudge in the kitchen, the three of us. Remember that time Phin tried to explain trigonometry when we were only ten years old?"

Silently Terra stared into her tea. For a minute she was back in the wonderful drafty old house. Then she put the memory from her furiously. Setting down her cup with a sharp clink she said "That was another world. It's long gone."

Dixie nodded silently. After a while, with effort, she said, "There's something I've just got to ask you. Sorry, I imagine you don't want to talk about it, but I need to know. What was Phin doing over in the Philippines? That last letter to me was from some hospital in Manila."

"He had been cleaning up the worst of the hot spots in Hiroshima, came down with radiation sickness. They shipped him off to the nearest American hospital. There wasn't much time, the thing works fast. Phin didn't even write me about it until it was too late. He didn't want me to rush over there."

"But why?"

"Don't ask me for answers. I don't have any. It was just something he had to do alone."

"I still don't understand why he had to go

to Japan? Did the government make him do it?"

"No, they didn't want it. They didn't fund it. It was his idea, the whole thing. He said he knew more about the properties of uranium and cobalt and strontium than anybody over there. He was trying to help the people of Hiroshima identify and isolate the worst of the hot spots. Ruining that city ruined him. Remember how he used to say he wanted to light up the world? Well, they took all that terrific brain power of his and used it to blow up the world instead."

The bitterness of her tone made Dixie sit silent.

Terra went on, "All through those years at Los Alamos I could see him getting thinner inside, stretching tighter. Then after the war was won, instead of feeling some kind of relief, he was bound to go over and see the results. A group of scientists went into Hiroshima and studied the effects for a month or so. When they came home, Phin wasn't with them. He was so appalled, he stayed to help people trying to clear away the debris. Personally, I think he wanted punishment. I think he was trying to atone for all that death the bomb caused. Anyway he stayed too long."

"But where were you?"

"Back in San Diego. I begged him to take me with him, but he couldn't, or wouldn't. I even warned him that if he died over there without me I would manage some way to follow him. I thought he didn't believe me, but I guess he did. His last letter . . ." She got it out. "He would want me to share this with you."

Dixie read it, slowly, and again. "And now you're — here."

Terra said, "I'm paying that one last debt. A year."

There was a silence that neither wanted to break. Finally, Dixie's chin came up in a gesture of acceptance. "You'll need a place to stay. And I happen to know a friend-of-a-friend who's getting married . . ."

The subway seemed unreal, like something out of a futuristic movie. The tight tunnel, the zombie passengers swaying to the rhythm of the train, the doors sliding silently open, then closing again, untouched by human hand, it was eerie. But efficient. Hurtling along so fast, Terra kept a tense watch as the stations raced past, ready to leap onto the platform at 86th Street.

Above ground again, she found that here Broadway was a street of small shops. Turning onto 88th Street she found herself in a canyon of old Victorian townhouses that streamed the length of the block, a flight of steps leading up to each entrance. No garages, no driveways, no alleys, the gray dowagers were shouldered up tight together. Called brownstones, according to Dixie they had been middle-class mansions in the days of the horse-drawn carriage. Now cut up into smaller components inside they had been converted into rooming houses.

Number 226 presented nothing to differentiate itself except the man sitting on the front steps. An indigent, to judge by his clothes, shabby and wrinkled and dirty, he sat slumped forward, elbows on knees, staring at his hands which were as filthy as if he'd just been cleaning out a sewer.

Hair of an indeterminate reddish gray was dusted with something like flour. It hung forward in a loose tuft over his eyes, which were now raised to stare back at her. Cautious eyes, rusty like his hair.

As she hesitated, he said, "Help you, ma'am?" in a voice so soft she could hardly hear it.

"I'm looking for a room. I was told there was a vacancy coming soon here."

"You want to talk to the super." His glance drifted away, toward the street. "That's me."

In the ensuing silence she recalled Dixie's

words: "You'll need to bribe the super, of course. Twenty-five bucks should do it. Maybe more, rooms are like gold these days."

But I've never bribed anyone in my life. How do I phrase it, so it doesn't sound insulting? "I'd be glad to pay the going commission for the rental."

His glance flicked back, looked her up and down, and he patted the stair beside him. "Have a seat."

Terra took a step up and sat down gingerly. When another several moments had passed, she fidgeted. "I'm staying at the YWCA for the moment, but I have to get out in exactly twelve days . . ."

"I can't show it to you yet," he muttered with a touch of impatience, still watching the street. As a taxi came prowling he straightened and stood. The driver double-parked beside the row of cars at the curb and leaned over to look out. The super gave him a small gesture: wait.

At the head of the stairs the outer door swung open and a girl came tripping forth, the click of her heels suddenly silent as she saw that her way was impeded. Perky in a pink traveling suit and straw boater, she was carrying two suitcases. The super moved up to take one of them from her.

"Let me help you with that." He set it behind him.

"Cutter!" she said, flustered. "What are you doing here?"

"Waiting for you, ma'am. Heard you order the taxi. Thought I'd save you the nuisance of looking me up to pay the three weeks' back rent you owe."

"Well, that's silly," she sputtered. "I put the check in the mail yesterday. You'll get it by tomorrow."

"No, ma'am. You know the rules. Cash only. That'll be forty-five dollars, please."

"Why, you . . . you . . ."

The driver gave a small impatient toot of the horn.

"And I won't even make you wait while I check your room for damage and theft." No touch of menace in his tone, but her eyes widened and she dug a wallet out of her handbag. As she forked over some bills, he handed her a receipt which he had ready in his shirt pocket. "There you go. Now all I need is your keys."

She slammed them into his hand. "You know you're a pig, Cutter. I feel sorry for anybody who lives in this dump." She had suddenly become aware of Terra. "If you're taking the room, better buy some rat poison."

"Let me help you to your taxi," he said amiably, picking up the suitcase. Ushering her into the cab he said, "Have a nice day."

As it rolled off along the street Terra stood up. "Does that mean the apartment is vacant now?"

"You might want to wait for me to go tidy it up first."

"I don't mind a mess." She led the way into the house, already picturing herself with a permanent address, set on it, even if the place turned out to be knee-deep in roaches. She saw one run as she mounted the stairs, didn't matter. She could bring her luggage over this afternoon.

Cutter caught up with her at the first floor landing and led the way down a long dim hallway where a radio could be heard behind a closed door. ". . . ball three, it's a full count . . ." An aroma of cabbage radiated from the front apartment as they made the turn onto the third flight.

"Is cooking allowed," she asked his retreating back.

"Gas hot plates." He said over his shoulder. "Got to be careful of 'em. Connections are old, go back to the turn of the Century. This is your key to the front door, and this one's Three-C." Unlocking the rear apartment, he glanced in. "As I said, you should have let me neaten the place up."

The room was what her mother would have called "all higglety-pigglety." A fairly large chamber across the back of the house, it had no partitions, only a curtain across the lavatory. To one side a double bed was shedding sheets in all directions and in an alcove the two-burner stove was stacked with dirty pans. Plates in the washbasin were being inspected by a large roach, and the floor was a clutter of trash, yesterday's newspaper, empty cigarette packs and soiled dish towels.

But Terra was looking past all that to a large window that opened onto a fire escape. The courtyard behind the house was about the size of a basketball court, clean of debris and paved with concrete. It gave the room breathing space. Across the way, from somewhere on the next street came sounds of a piano, somebody running scales, but it seemed twice-removed, impersonal like the noise of the city far away. Here within these walls was a place of privacy. A refuge.

Ready to lay claim to it she turned to Cutter, who was picking up the sheets. "I'll do that." She wanted to be rid of him, something about the man made her uncomfortable. "Where's the nearest laundry?"

"Chinaman's, over on Broadway, a block

north." He frowned. "Sure you don't mind?"

"Not at all. I want to move in at once. How much do I owe you?"

"It's fifteen a week, payable in advance. Cash."

She opened her purse where some bills were tucked in an inner pocket. Drawing forth three twenties she handed them over. "That ought to take care of the rent for a month. Now what about your — uh — commission?"

His blunt Irish face twitched, not quite a smile. "If you're going to do my job for me, I can't accept any grease." He got out a small notebook and scrawled a receipt, intoning in that soft voice. "Bath is down the hall. Be sure to lock the door, you have two other tenants using it. The fellow in Three-A is kind of randy, the old lady in Three-B tends to wander around. Refrigerator on the second floor, every apartment gets half a shelf. Signs on them. If your milk bottle disappears don't tell me about it, I don't settle squabbles."

"And I don't want any either," she said. "For your records, I'm Terra Berensen."

He looked at her outstretched hand, at his own mucky ones, and wiped them on his pants, which showed evidence of other wipings. Strong fingers clasped hers briefly. "Nehemiah Shanahan, they call me 'Cutter'. Sorry, I didn't take time to wash up. When I heard the young lady ordering a taxi I had to move on it. Pay phone's down on the first floor, got a loud ring. If you're expecting a call you'd better run down and get it. Chances are nobody else will. I don't usually answer it myself." As he turned away he added, "If you'll put all that junk in the wastebasket and leave it outside the door, I'll pick it up." Then, as an afterthought, he said, "If you need me for anything, you'll have to go out and down and under to the basement apartment. When they put in the oil burner they cut out the inside stairway to the cellar."

Terra closed the door and began to bundle the mess of sheets. Her instinct was to buy new ones, but who knew how long it would take to transfer her bank account from San Diego? She hadn't traveled with much cash. *Have to go out, today, find a bank. No, it's Saturday afternoon, I'll go Monday first thing. No, that's Labor Day. All I can do right now is get my clothes from the "Y".* She wanted her travels to be over. She wanted settle in, go out on that fire escape and sit in the sun. And vegetate for a year.

September, 1947

She repeated the directions in her mind: Take the 7th Avenue line to 42nd Street and catch the shuttle to Grand Central, then the Lexington down to Union Square. Or (the man at the subway change booth had said) just stay on the IRT down to 14th Street and walk over to Fourth Avenue. A walk, Terra decided, was just what she needed to get into the right frame of mind.

Her target was a publishing house. Presumably they would be looking for people with a literary background. Terra could claim to have worked in a library in younger days, if only as a shelver. And she had always been a good reader. Her vocabulary was better than most, thanks to the intensely educated people she had lived around these past four years. She thought she was probably as well qualified as the girl who had vacated the position.

Terra had been cleaning up the room last

weekend when a torn sheet of paper caught her attention, the draft of a letter. It was addressed to Oliver Manisch, President of Paragon Press. "This is to inform you I am quitting my job. I didn't give notice because you are a rotten boss and I don't need you for a reference anyways. I am leaving this lousy city forever, I just wanted you to know I contempt you." The page was ripped off and crumpled. After a momentary amusement Terra gave the address a second look. Somewhere down on Fourth Avenue there was an office that would be minus a worker on Tuesday morning. It seemed a good place to start her job search.

Now that she had arrived in front of the grimy building she had a moment of doubt. But the lobby was clean enough and the elevator moved efficiently upward to the sixth floor where she found herself in front of a door that bore golden words:

PARAGON PRESS.

In the foyer behind a large cluttered desk sat a tall woman with a stylish marcelled cap of very blond hair. Her rather handsome face was set in permanent planes of discontent as she concentrated on comparing one list against another, her pencil making sharp little check marks.

Glancing up with a frown she said impatiently, "Yes?"

"I'm looking for a job," Terra said. "I understand one has just come open here."

"Now how would you know that? Wait, I get it. You're a friend of Miss Sassypants."

"No. I inherited her room. I only know she was leaving town in a hurry. So it occurred —"

The woman had picked up the phone, punched a button. "Mr. Manisch, you've already got a job applicant. No, I didn't call in the ad to the paper yet. You want me to hold off?" She listened, then said, "Okay." And to Terra she jerked a thumb toward a hallway. "Back there, second door on the left."

The name on the frosted glass was Oliver Manisch, Pres. With a knock, she went in to find herself in a large office furnished in antiques — a grandfather clock in one corner, a delicate French table by the window, a print of race horses by Degas on one wall and opposite, a copy of van Gogh's "Starry Night." The visitor's chair before the desk was leather and low to the ground. Terra stayed standing in front of it waiting for the man to look up.

A scholarly sort, wire-rimmed glasses and

flourishing salt-and-pepper hair, he would be in his fifties, she judged. His desk was almost clean of clutter, just one double box with files neatly stacked, IN and OUT. Fountain pen poised over a sheet of paper, he was filling in a blank at the top. Reading upside down she saw it was today's date, time 10:03.

"Now then," he peered up at her with keen dark eyes under tufted gray brows. "You are — ?"

"Therissa Berensen. All 'e's."

He wrote. "Age?"

"Twenty-three years old."

"Married?"

"Widow."

"Divorced or — ?"

"My husband died in the war."

"Ah." The pen hesitated in mid-air. "How long ago was that, my dear?"

"One month, six days."

"I see." His tone was avuncular, his manner sympathetic. "I'm sorry for your loss. I take it he didn't die in battle then."

"No. But he was a casualty of the war."

"Well, it left some long-term scars on all of us. Now then, you want a job doing — what?"

"Whatever. I have stenographic skills, I know the mimeograph, the switchboard and the calculator. I'm a quick learner."

"And did our recent employee, Miss Crider, tell you what the job pays?"

"No, sir, I never met the girl. I was lucky enough to rent her apartment and when I was cleaning up I saw the draft of a letter she wrote, resigning her employment here. It occurred to me that there might be a vacancy."

His face brightened. "That was very alert of you, a good quality in any line of work. What college did you attend?"

"A small school down in Virginia, Gloucester College."

"That's a music academy, I believe." He made another note on the sheet before him.

"I'm surprised you've even heard of it, sir."

"Oh, yes, I know every educational institution in this country. We're a textbook house, you know. So you got your degree there?"

"No, sir. The war broke out in the middle of my freshman year. A lot of the teachers enlisted. My mother was deathly sick, so I went home."

"And how is she now?"

"She died, sir."

"Oh dear. I do seem to ask unfortunate questions." He gave her a quirky smile. "Where did you grow up, Mrs. Berensen?"

"St. Louis, Missouri." *And please don't ask me where I lived during the war years.* "Excuse me, but what does the job pay?"

"Forty-five dollars a week, which, I might add, is five dollars higher than the going rate for office workers here in New York. How long have you been in the city?"

"Five days. Counting today."

"Hmm. You don't waste time. Excellent. You may just fit in here. We are always under some deadline. You have been to a business school, then?"

"Yes, sir. The Complete Secretarial School in San Diego, California. Typing speed, seventy words a minute, shorthand one twenty." Learning the skills had been a lifesaver, demanding her concentration during those difficult months that she waited for Phin to come home.

"Have you ever applied your talents to an actual job?" He smiled to let her know he wasn't trying to be judgmental.

"I worked six months for an insurance company, mostly filing."

"Ah yes, lots of filing in insurance." The smile was broader now, his eyes warm as he regarded her thoughtfully. "How are you at handling people?"

"I once worked in a public library."

"I was thinking more — ah — one-on-one."

"I haven't had much practice, I don't know."

He smacked the desk with the flat of his hand. "That's a good answer. I like a person who can admit she doesn't know. Let's find out, shall we? I will introduce you to the man with whom you would be working." He stood and came around the desk, moving lightly, graceful as a dancer. She followed him out and down the hall again to another office, the door of which was open to reveal a narrow chamber cluttered with two desks and a huge library table, every surface awash with papers. Bent over the turbulence in the far corner, a wire-tight little man was peering through thick glasses at a tablet.

"Damned if I know," he said, "whether this is shorthand or not. I think the girl just scrawled — oh, sorry." He glanced over, took in Terra in a swift look — at least with one eye. The other was canted in a different direction, as if he were scanning the street beyond the window.

Manisch was saying, "Maybe Mrs. Berensen can figure out the notes of the late, unlamented Miss Crider. Theresa, this is Aaron Scheidler, our best and brightest editor. Ari, she's your new assistant. That is, if you two decide to like each other. Please try." He handed the man his sheet of notes and left them.

Terra felt uneasy, the oddly cocked eye disconcerting. As she floundered for words the editor grinned, aware that his defect was rattling her. Not the least self-conscious about his ugly face, with its big nose, broad mouth, a day's growth of beard on his jaw, he looked her over.

"So you want to be my — what's that awful term? — 'girl Friday?' "

"Whatever the job requires, sir."

"Oh, Gawd. Don't 'sir' me. My name is Ari, or Aaron, if you prefer. And you're —" he glanced at the employment form "— Theresa?"

"Terra."

"Thank heaven for that. One question: How do you spell the word 'physics?' Come on now, no dictionary."

She stared at him, wondering if he was kidding.

"Oh, all right, if you need to I guess you could use a —"

"P-h-y-s-i-c-s." Then, with a touch of irritation, she added, "A subject that includes electromagnetics, a field in which my late husband had considerable expertise."

His right eye impaled her with jet-black intensity. "Expertise." Then with a touch of bluster he said, "So you're literate. Is that why you want to work in publishing? Are you a great undiscovered author, think you'll make contacts here? If that's it, forget it. We deal only with textbooks. You'll spend your days writing letters to tenured professors who are dumber than a sack of hammers, pleading with them to get the galleys back because they're fouling up the schedule. Or you may be called on to ferret out our ad copy which is lost at the printer's and stand over them with a hatchet until they complete the order that they were supposed to deliver last week. That kind of thing. So don't come around with some half-baked manuscript you'd like an opinion on."

"If I baked a manuscript I wouldn't leave it underdone," she said, on a sudden hunch that he valued insubordination. If he didn't, she wouldn't mind being shown the door. Working in narrow confines with a cynic wasn't exactly what she had in mind. She went on, "I have no desire to be a writer. I just want a job, and I think I can probably do better than the lady who preceded me. The only time I saw her she was trying to run out on her back rent."

"Ah yes, sounds like our Miss Crider. All right, you passed, you're in. That's your desk there, somewhere under those heaps of manuscripts. Right now your assignment is to take each one, put it in an envelope and send it back to the author with a polite letter. Delete 'polite,' these fools are asking for rejection. Just say we don't take unsolicited material. But first, can you read these hen-tracks? They're all that's left of a blurb I dictated last week."

Terra glanced at the scrawl and said, "Sorry, sir, it certainly isn't Gregg. I think she was trying to write an abbreviated longhand, using her own symbols. She might have been able to read it back, but I can't."

"Damn! I'll have to dictate it again, but not right now. I've got to get this book in shape. We're already two weeks late. Go ahead with the slush pile."

A hard day. By five-thirty in the afternoon Terra's back was aching. She hadn't sat at a desk in weeks, even filing was less a strain. But she had managed to clear away all the rejected manuscripts, writing short refusals with a touch of sympathy. It must have taken a tremendous lot of work to write a book about how the Egyptians used mathematics four thousand years ago. She had the envelopes stacked, waiting for the letters to be inserted, hesitating to interrupt Ari for his signature.

He was working on a massive text devoted to quantum physics, red penciling whole paragraphs with angry strokes. Looked ready to go on with it all night if Manisch hadn't stopped by the office.

"Mrs. Berensen, don't let this fellow work you to death. Ari, it's quitting time."

"So go home." The editor waved at her distractedly. "Don't ask me to watch a clock for you."

"If you'll just sign these letters."

"You sign 'em," he snapped. "Editorial Assistant. I trust your expertise."

Tired, amused, a little proud of herself Terra dropped off the armload at the mail room. Now, as she walked out onto Fourth Avenue, she stretched her back and wriggled her neck to loosen the tightness. But this was only the tension of unfamiliarity. She realized that she was surprisingly comfortable with the job. All the old shyness, the fear of rejection, of hostility, had been left far back in the time before she went up The Hill.

It was hard to break the strictures of secrecy, to call it Los Alamos, even in her own mind. It all seemed like another world now, an enclave of such pressure, such brilliance, such a concentration of massive intellect that no ordinary man would ever again impress or frighten her. In the aftermath of that experience her only questions concerned her own untested abilities. For five years she had been a mere adjunct, like all the other wives, while the men threw their combined brain power into the deadly job at hand. Now, to be on her own for the first time in her life — it was unknown territory.

Which was exactly why Phin had wanted her to try it. He himself had reveled in challenges. He would like this place, the roar of the great city like a dare. *Okay, I will try taking the Lexington home.* It only made sense, to learn the subway system enough to use it without hesitation. She stepped into the human traffic flow heading for Union Square. A warm September evening, somewhere Fall was turning leaves diligently. Back home in Missouri the bittersweet would be hanging green, waiting for the first frost to pop the fruit open, sending clusters of red berries cascading down the shelving rocks of the Ozarks. The September sky would be a brilliant flag-blue. Here, the sky went unnoticed above the narrow canyons. Only if you looked up could you tell that a golden sunset was taking place somewhere. It glowed on the tops of the buildings, gilded the taller trees in the park.

Union Square was a utilitarian oasis, mostly concrete and trash cans and benches, a spot where people could congregate and protest. Even now, over to one side a man stood on a wooden box and harangued a small crowd in a gravelly voice. She couldn't hear the message, didn't want to. Turning the other way she saw a great brick warehouse with a two-story sign painted down its side:

**KLEIN'S
ON THE
SQUARE**

People were flocking toward it. Sheer curiosity propelled Terra in that direction.

A clothing store. Inside, she stopped, overwhelmed by the acres of racks, men's suits, coats, long ranks of identical housedresses, appallingly cheap. Hats were heaped in piles on tables, straw bonnets and fall styles in felt and feathers. The sign read: **$1.99 Each.**

"Well, you're on the right track." A casual voice at her elbow made Terra turn. It was the receptionist from the publishing house,

44

Gilda Sigmeir. Her long angular body had looked ungraceful behind the desk, but now there was a brash stylishness in the shoulder twitch and hip jut, a flicker of Dixie. Banana-yellow blouse and tweed skirt with matching jacket — she wore the bright colors to flaunt her tallness, rather than disguise it. That was Dixie's way, and she would have loved Gilda's decor. The large, cheap coral earrings matched the manicure and lipstick. Touching the wavy blond hair self-consciously, she was inclined to patronize. "I was hoping you'd shop for some new duds. Those clothes look like you nursed them through a war."

"I did," Terra admitted.

"Well, you've come to the right place to modernize yourself. Klein's has some great bargains if you know how to look for them."

"Really? It looks like it caters to the housewife. I was about to leave."

"You have to hunt to find the gold. Come on, kid, I'll show you."

Terra's instinct was to decline, but this was part of her assignment: to live, meet people, never mind why. Unprotesting, she followed down the aisle of wraparounds, house dresses. Gilda seemed to be searching, pulling out this one, that, browsing, moving on. Suddenly she stopped, and took

45

forth an evening gown.

"See this? It's an original Feona Marshall." The name meant nothing to Terra. "She's all the rage these days. Very high style, one-of-a-kind, right off the fashion runways. When a show's over, they send the designer models here. Maybe they've got a little crease in the seat, but who cares? Look at that price, $19.95. I'll bet the thing cost over a hundred on the show room floor. Good God, I wish I could wear it, but it would make me look like a sack of bones." She headed for another rack, her fingers rummaging rapidly through the cheap cotton dirndls, a whole bourgeoning of flowered skirts, Small, Medium and Large.

"Shades of June Allison," she muttered impatiently. Seizing a rag of magenta chiffon she held it up. "That's a beauty, but who could wear it except maybe Garbo?" She shoved it back on the rack. A few feet farther on she pounced again. "Now we're cookin'." It was a dark red wool suit cut with a subtle touch of elegance that set it apart from the crowd. "They took the label out, but it looks like Paris to me. Here, go try it on."

A half hour later Terra was laden with two dress boxes and a paper bag with a hat in it, a smart little felt with a pheasant feather that went perfectly with the suit. "But what about you? You didn't get anything?"

Gilda's eyebrow was a mobile penciled line in her pale skin. "I already spent my clothing allowance for this month. I just followed you in to make sure you found something. You really do need a new look. Hungry? I know a ratty little cellar café where they serve marvelous goulash. Nothing else, just goulash."

The city was plunged in twilight now, yellow windows hung like ornaments beyond the trees across the park. Traffic had slackened, the fumes had cleared somewhat. When they turned along a cross street, they found the sidewalks almost deserted. From a narrow doorway a wave of cookery greeted them, drawing them down a stairway to a basement room where a few people sat at small tables and ate a marvelously aromatic hash served with dark brown country bread. Terra realized that it was exactly what she wanted, pickles and all. It surprised her a little, she hadn't had much appetite for months.

And it came to her that she didn't mind the company either. Gilda's brusque manner was okay. There was a kind of go-to-hell air about her that Terra recognized. It was Dixie, all over again, swaggering amid the loneliness of rejection. She felt a twinge of curiosity, enough to make an effort to open the avenues of communication.

"Thanks for your help. I'd never have guessed there was elegance buried in all that cheap frou-frou. Have you lived in the city long?"

"About a year. I'm originally from Indiana. Don't you hear that Midwest twang in my voice? Little town you never heard of. Pass me the Tabasco sauce, I like my food hot."

Slathering butter on a slab of brown bread Terra relished the sensation. Real butter, none of the imitation stuff they had wrestled with for years now, squeezing the lardy margarine in a bag with a capsule of orange coloring to give it a semblance. This was cow-generated.

"So that's what makes me hate you," Gilda went on complacently. "You breeze into town and get yourself a room the first day, and here I am, been looking for a place for months now with no luck."

"Where are you staying then?"

"The Evangeline. It's a Salvation Army women's hotel a couple of blocks from here. Greatest people on earth, they never turn anybody away. But I'm bunking in a room with two other gals, one works the night shift at a movie house over on Broadway so she comes in at all hours. The other one snores. Not her fault. But I am just about ready to be committed to Belleview. That's our local booby-hatch. So what's your secret? How did you come by this room of yours so fast?"

"I knew somebody who knew somebody who knew Miss Crider was going to get married. I went over to her address last Saturday just as she tried to make a fast exit." Terra went on to sketch a picture of the scene on the stairs, the taxi, Cutter in all his grime standing carelessly between the girl and her suitcase. Gilda laughed out loud a farm-girl guffaw.

"Isn't it always those cute little baby-dolls who hook the eligible men and get 'em to the altar. Well, she'll probably spend all the poor guy's money and drop him, after she puts him through some misery. That girl has a tongue on her. You should have heard some of the fights that went on in that back room. Ari was ready to commit suicide . . ."

Later, as they walked up onto the street together the receptionist grew suddenly sober. "Listen, kid, I'm glad you came to work for us, but keep sharp. Don't let 'em fadoodle you. Manisch is as smart as the Devil and just about as holy. Forget I said

49

that, the guy pays my salary, I shouldn't bad-mouth him. Just take it easy and watch out for tricks. See you tomorrow."

Terra had a notion she knew what Gilda was talking about. There had been a cleverness about the boss, a sophistication as if he were the epitome of the word "New Yorker." She wondered idly if that's why he seemed so pleased with her: she looked like a country rube, somebody he could fadoodle.

Leaving the discovery of the Lexington line for another day, Terra began to walk westward through the darkening streets. And in the gloom she felt the loneliness fold back down over her like a blanket of some heavy material that weighed on her spirits. She should have got used to it by now. But this happenstance encounter, the new clothes, the impulsive goulash, had reminded her of what life used to feel like. It made the return of depression all the more acute.

As she passed a church she heard strains of music coming from within, a choir rehearsing, singing familiar words. "Whatever my lot, Thou has taught me to say: It is well, it is well with my soul . . ." She stood still, listening a minute. For five years she had rejected any contact with music, but once long ago, briefly, it had moved her to incredible joy. Never happen again, of course. She walked on.

By the time she reached the rooming house and climbed the long flight of stairs all she could think of was a hot tub. The communal bathroom was unoccupied and impeccably clean, down to its scuffed linoleum. Locking the door, she lay in the steaming water and reveled in blankness of mind, until someone tapped rudely.

"Hey, you, in there, you all right?" A man's voice.

"Yes. Fine. Be out in a minute." Hastily she toweled off and pulled a voluminous terrycloth robe around her. It had been one of Phin's and offered a world of concealment. Gathering her clothes she stepped out into the hall, almost bumping into the man who lounged against the wall out there. Must be Three-A she thought.

He was wearing a bathrobe that hung open to reveal a pallid paunch, rising to a chest thickly grown with black hair. Technically he was decent, pajamas beneath the robe, but the smirk was licentious. "Hello there. It's high time we met. I'm Jack Olander."

"Hello. Excuse me, I have to —"

"Hey, don't I get a name?"

"Mrs. Phineas Berensen. Good night."

He stepped aside, the self-satisfaction still in place. "See you around, sweetcakes."

Back in her room she bolted the door.

Shades of Uncle Redmond. The smirk, the preening pride. *Why do they think their flabby flesh is so attractive?* It took her back to another day, another lifetime, seventeen years old, visiting the family mansion in Richmond. Late night and the tap came at her door. She had opened it to find the favorite son of an historic dynasty standing there with a bottle of champagne in one hand and a pair of wine glasses in the other. His dressing gown was open all the way down to a horrendous spread of nudity. For an unforgettable five minutes he had chased her across the bed and around the room until she had threatened to wake the whole house if he didn't leave. It had left her with a small but pervasive aversion that shadowed every encounter, afterward.

Even when she and Phin had discovered the mysteries of sex together and found it titillating, she never quite got over the spasm of distaste. No matter how much fun it was, the conjugal act seemed somehow dirty to her, just an earthy adjunct to the more important aspects of marriage — the closeness, the holding. The love.

She went to draw the curtains across the

window by the fire escape. On the far side of the courtyard other apartments were alight. The pianist was running exercises, good old Hanon. In raucous counterpoint, from another flat a radio ad was blaring a singing commercial for cars.

"A Kaiser-Frazer yours at once,
Today at Madman Muntz'."

When she went to turn down the bed, Terra found the dress boxes there. Forcing herself, she took out the clothes and hung them up, wondering why she had bothered with new duds? Without trying to figure it out, she turned off the light.

Okay, Phin. One more day down the hatch. Three hundred and sixty to go.

OCTOBER, 1947

"No hurry, take your time, so long as you finish the job today." Ari's chuckle was diabolical. "They were supposed to go out last Monday." One thousand four hundred and seventy-five pamphlets — an entire mailing for the new psychology text — had been printed with the wrong price. The correction had to be hand-stamped on each, one by one.

"Slave driver," she said carelessly. No point in robbing him of his curious glee, but this was the kind of brainless chore she needed right now. It gave her time to think about what happened earlier that morning.

Getting up a little after five she had been making coffee on the crusted two-burner gas stove when she became aware of sounds in the hallway, a rush of feet and a mutter of voices. Not one to care about her neighbors' comings and goings, she ignored it and got dressed. But when the noises took on the sound of an invasion she finally cracked the door of her room and looked out.

A few feet away Cutter Shanahan leaned against a wall, hands in the pockets of crumpled corduroy pants, watching some medics trying to angle a gurney through the door of Three-B. He glanced at Terra. "The old lady crossed over last night."

"How — ?"

"Probably a heart attack. I noticed she hadn't put out her trash. Tried to raise her, no luck. So I let myself in, and there she was." His hard-worn face was a blank, but there was a darkness about him. The Irish, Terra knew, were deeply affected by death.

She had long since lost the sense of dread. For an old person it was a release, one that she had welcomed for her mother. Then, those years on The Hill the grim reaper had been a constant presence, especially after "The Gadget" turned out to be so hideously successful. A distinct aura of suicide had hung over the place. A number of the scientists had been cast into an ambivalence of elation and depression. Like Phin, they all shouldered a terrible guilt. If it wasn't lethal, it seemed to bring on a variety of ailments, some of them crippling.

Her father had come back from the Great

War with a case of shellshock that left him unstable. He had broken down completely with the loss of an adored wife. Terra had taken over, shedding her childhood like worn-out bobby sox, and arranging for the unresponsive man to return to the farm where he'd grown up in Iowa. Last she'd heard he was going through the movements of existing.

Rather than live for years in that kind of limbo she would welcome a quiet end to it all. The old lady in Three B had looked placid as they wheeled her past, wrinkles smoothed, jaw no longer tensed by the aches of arthritis or the deeper cares of the spirit. *Where is she now?* Terra hadn't completely banished the thought that there might be an afterlife. Not that she believed in Heaven, but she had to admit there were several kinds of Hell. The Devil was alive and kicking.

Now the existence of God, she doubted. She glanced at Cutter. He probably hailed Mary conscientiously. Seeming to catch some unspoken question he shrugged. "I'd say she'll be with the Lord. She had a Bible in her room. I'm going to miss her," he added. "She paid her rent on time. Now I've got to look for a new tenant."

That also was an Irish trait, to do a quick

half-turn and think ahead. "You care for a cup of coffee?" she asked.

He gave her a thoughtful look, as if he wasn't sure of the proprieties. "Thanks."

She was glad she had made the bed. He glanced around as if he hadn't seen the room before, then sat down at the scuffed table by the window where dawn was lightening the sky up there somewhere. The distant voice of the city was quickening. She set a cup before him and filled it from the blue enamel pot. Part of the furniture of the place, it made great coffee. Setting a sack of doughnuts between them, she sank down opposite him.

"How are you getting along?" he asked, with only a flicker of real interest.

"I'm doing fine. I got a job with Paragon Publishing."

"Afraid I never heard of them."

"They're very small. They do textbooks. But the people seem nice enough and we have a good receptionist who happens to need a room."

"Ah." His face sharpened, he sipped the coffee and nodded. "You can act as her reference?"

"Not by a long shot. I don't know what her financial condition is, or whether she'd pay on time. But I can tell you she's tough

57

enough to handle Three-A without raising a sweat. It might get him off my case."

"He bothering you?"

"Every time I take a bath he's waiting in the hall. Don't worry, I can keep him at arm's length, and I don't want to make a fuss. But it might be helpful if he had a prettier target. Gilda's a looker."

Cutter seemed to find that amusing.

"Did I say something funny?"

He popped the last of his doughnut and got up. "Send the lady around to see me."

Now Terra glanced at the clock above Ari's desk. Ten-thirty-five, and her hand was cramping. She decided to award herself a break. The editorial staff was in a closed-door meeting in Manisch's office. Strolling down the hall she found Gilda hunched over her typewriter, peering grimly from it to her visitor's log and back.

"I can't talk," she said without looking up. "I'm behind on the mailing list, caught the devil this morning. I think I may quit. Plenty of jobs where you don't get bawled out all the time."

"Don't resign now," Terra said. "When you apply for a room, it helps to have a place of employment."

"Yeah, right, don't I wish."

"There's an opening in my building.

Super's waiting for your visit."

Gilda swung around wide-eyed. "You're kidding!"

"It's only a single room, no bath, nothing fancy, third floor walkup."

"I'll take it!"

"You'll have to get interviewed. The super's name is — I forget, but everybody calls him Cutter. He requires a week in advance, in cash."

"You're a life saver. Now get out of here and let me make some headway on this, so I can cheat a little on my lunch-hour. Wait, give me the address. How do I get there?"

It had become habit, these last weeks, to walk across town after work in the lowering dusk, with the city quieting down, a drift off the harbor smelling of fish and salt and flotsam. Terra let her senses accept it all, the feel of Fall in the air, the threads of sound spiraling down from the apartments she passed, Jack Benny, Edward R. Murrow, Paul Whiteman, Benny Goodman. *Glenn Miller, where are you, how could you leave us?* Gershwin was gone, too, and George M. Cohan. What happened to all that wonderful music after they went silent? The thing that welled up in them and poured forth to touch and unite people across the world, such great talent, how could it just — die?

That was the one catch, when Terra tried to figure out what the end of her life would mean. She wanted it to be over and done. She didn't want to believe that there was a continuance of all the grief, the sorrowing, the failed dreams, following you somewhere into the Beyond. But it would be a comfort in the final moments to look back and think you'd made a difference in the world. Left one strain of music . . . one great painting. We're the product of all our yesterdays, but that would mean that gone is not really gone. In the middle of her confusion, she became aware of a brisk, self-assured harmony, the sound of a choir. She was passing the same little church — it happened to be on her way to the subway line. Not a Sunday hymn this time, now they were tackling a great chorus, projecting electricity with such a voltage Terra stopped in her tracks.

Bach. She had once tried to learn some of the Art of the Fugue, never got past the Contrapuntus. They said the old man's fingers could span twelve notes. Her own could barely stretch to make a good octave. Those blunt hands of hers had been a source of lamentation for her mother, who had wanted so badly to have a concert pianist in the family. It had given rise to a lot of misery for all concerned.

But years had cushioned all those memories. Now she could stand here in the evening quietly and enjoy the chorus. The group was marvelously trained for a Sunday choir. She looked up at the name above the open doors: Church of the Master. A small house of worship, nothing grandiose, but the sculptures across the front were beautiful.

The singing came from a lower level, some common room beneath that was reached by a long flight of stairs. As she paused to listen she felt the plea in Phin's letter: "You've got a lot of music in you. Have fun with it, forget the concert stage." It was almost exactly what Max Wolff had told her all those years ago. Unwillingly, she went down slowly to discover a meeting hall.

The choir was silent now, standing in a semi-circle around their conductor, a tall, muscular man with bleached hair, too white for his young face. He was intent upon a folio on the music stand, pondering it, while they waited — an unusually large group for a church choir. There must have been fifty of them, men, women, youthful and middle-aged, elbow-to-elbow, all hanging on the leader's next words.

61

"I'm sorry, gang. Bach is tough, I haven't studied this well enough, I see that now. Forgive me — I'm not going to waste your time tonight. Go on home and next week we'll really tie into it."

They broke up then, chattering. Terra recognized their music-speak, she'd lived through enough of it at Gloucester College.

". . . that e-flat should have been given to the sopranos. I'm never going to hit it . . ."

"Did you notice the *accelerando* on page three? That's what's got him stumped. If you start out too fast you can't afford to speed it up without sounding like a runaway revivalist."

It brought back the fellowship of the small group of musicians that Max had gathered at his ruthlessly pink stucco cottage those Saturday afternoons down in Gloucester Town. Head of the music department, a German refugee haunted by the war, his ghosts had added depth to his own compositions, which he had tried out with the students, teaching them how to be a group. Dear Max, the one man who had pushed past the barriers of her torturous music lessons and showed her the beauty beyond. Now she could feel him behind her, urging her to go on in.

The singers had wandered off by now, but

the conductor was engrossed his massive folio. "Interpretations from every choral master who ever conducted the Oratorio, and they don't agree, not by a long shot." Frowning he glanced up, then his face went blank. "Oh. I'm sorry. I thought you were one of the gang. Can I help you?"

"I was just walking past and heard the music. Your choir is so beautifully tuned, such precision. I'm not a member of the church, but I wondered if you could use an accompanist. I play the piano."

"Most of my people aren't part of the congregation upstairs. They have gravitated here for the music. Maybe you've heard of us, we call ourselves the Mastersingers, after the musical guild in the Middle Ages? You must be a musician yourself, to appreciate 'tuning' and 'precision' — it's the basis for all choral performance. To answer your question, we already have a very competent accompanist, but we could use a few more choristers. Do you sing?"

"Oh, no," she smiled and began to edge toward the stairway.

"You've studied music, though. Can you read a score? Here —" he suddenly thrust a sheet of music at her. Turning to the piano nearby he struck a chord. "Now, let's hear you sing that opening, the altos' line, I would guess from your speaking voice."

A cappella? Terra took a deep breath, and glanced down the page. Reading music was, after all these years, as easy as scanning a letter, a message from the composer that she could enjoy, if not execute very well vocally. Her voice was reedy and nervous.

" 'Christians, be joyful, and praise your salvation!' " The timing was tricky, she started an inner metronome. " 'Christians, be joyful and praise your salvation. Sing —' " the word had to be stretched over three notes — " 'for today your Redeemer is born.' " A long contrapuntal passage was trickier, but she threaded her way through it and reached the "proud morn" at the end.

He struck another chord and she stopped.

"Good, you maintained pitch," he announced. "You got the timing right, your voice is pleasant, but happily undistinguished." A quick smile revealed intensely white teeth. "The one thing a chorus doesn't need is some diva punching through, trying to override the chorus and marring the blend. What's your name, dear?"

"Terra Berensen."

"I'm Andrew Farrell. Well, Terra. if you'd like to sing with us, we could use you. Our alto section is a little thin. We'll be adding more members to the group soon. We're moving our rehearsals up to a building on 56th Street, which means we'll have to start collecting dues to pay for the hall — $5.00 a month. Can you handle that?"

Terra found herself smiling back at him. Driven by the same keen delight in himself, in life, in her, he reminded her of Max, but without the shadow of sadness. This man looked as though he'd never been haunted by demons once in his thirty-some years. He couldn't be any older than that. The tow-hair was merely an inheritance from some Scandinavian ancestor. Every expression, every movement was full of suppressed youth. She wondered what it would be like to sing under him. Max kept urging her to go on, find out. *You don't even know yet what gift you may have. Forget your training, just look for the beauty.*

Terra was a little short on beauty right now. "Thank you," she said. "I'd love to be part of your 'gang', if you really think I'm good enough."

"We'll have to see, won't we? If not —" His eyebrow cocked comically. "Well, I boot people out if they go flat on me. I've got to be tough, to polish this group to a high shine for the concert hall."

"You're giving a performance?"

"On December 21st. We'll be singing the

opening of the Oratorio" — he tapped the folio — "plus the entire Magnificat. Then a chorus from the Stabat Mater, ending with a medley of very old folk carols brought over from England to the Alleghenies in colonial days. It's a fairly ambitious concert but you have to put on a first-rate program when you play Carnegie Hall."

From the long past she remembered that hallowed name as an icon of musical success. The challenge it implied was enough to quicken her lagging spirits. It was as if a small switch had been flipped. Like seeing a picture and recognizing a place where she had once lived and almost forgotten. Not just the brush with musicians or the prospect of being briefly among them again. It was a deeper discovery, in Andrew Farrell's face, a remembrance of what it was like to be infused with excitement. She liked to find that there was still someone in the world who was not broken.

All around her, for so long she seen the cracked edges, the deep inner fissures that showed in their eyes — the team at Los Alamos. Then the days in San Diego watching the troops come home to their families, joyful, but forever scarred and haunted by the island warfare. Clinging desperately to their wives, barely holding themselves together — well, they might mend if their families were restored. It would be a while before they realized that their women too were deeply damaged by the long loneliness.

The country itself wasn't back to normal — not any normal she'd ever known. There was something fractured in the frenzy of postwar celebration, pictures of the new housing craze, miles of look-alike bungalows thrown together in haste, jerry-built, "ticky-tacky." The new cars were coming off assembly lines so fast the welding seams still showed, even as they were driven from the showroom floors. A rash of advertising had broken out, huge crude billboards — the cigarette ad that blew smoke rings over Times Square, the ten-story tall replica of a half-clad woman rising above Broadway, advertising a new movie. Singing commercials burbled cutely about underarm deodorants and cheap shoes and laxatives. It was as if everyone in the world had lost all sense of refinement. There was a feckless-ness in the air.

And an undercurrent of anger. The taxicab driver who had glared at her for not tipping enough. The girl at the desk of the YWCA who had gloated grimly at the thought of throwing out the homeless after a two-week stay. The harried, silent strangers who settled at the tables in the Automat, elbow to elbow, without a friendly word or even a glance at each other. The food was good, you kept going back. But the people were disconnected and nervous, taking refuge behind deeply barricaded faces.

Cutter, seamed and battered, old before his time, she suspected inner damage that hadn't healed. Had he been disappointed in love? Some girl dump him in the heat of war? You sensed a resignation about him, a withdrawal. Almost worse was the frenetic pace of the men at Paragon Press. They seemed driven by the rush of life coming at them now that the war was over. Ari worked with manic drive, keeping others at bay with his acid wit. Manisch was smoother on the surface, but she sensed a dislocation, almost a threat about him. At least Gilda was in fear of the man. Poor girl, she'd been so desperate for a room of her own she had rushed off at lunchtime, then phoned in to say that she was moving, so she must have taken the apartment. Maybe now she could find a rhythm for her life.

Insecurity seemed to be the curse that lingered over the world. Look at Dixie — but then you couldn't count Dixie. She had been a nervous wreck even back in high school days. If anything, she was a little more at ease now, since she had become Dixi and found her "darling Zoey." And yet there had been a thin edge of wariness the other day, when they met. Terra represented another world which had made Dix an outcast. Everyone a casualty of the times, living precariously from day to day.

Terra started up the stairs of the old brownstone, then paused, suddenly aware of someone sitting on the balustrade at the top, dangling a foot that glinted silver in the light from the street lamp. Dixie was a fool for gaudy shoes, the higher the heel the better.

"I was about to give up," she said. "Where on earth do you work — Hoboken?"

"Lower Fourth, publisher's row. I have a job at Paragon Press."

"Never heard of 'em. So, what? You walk home?"

"Yeah, part way. I like the city this time of night when the windows start to light up." Terra fumbled a key into the door. "You should have asked Cutter to let you in."

"If you're referring to that glowering super, he flat refused. Said it was against the law, or something. Which is baloney, but you don't argue with a wolf hound. That's what he reminds me of, an Irish version of

69

Heathcliff. He looks broody. I hope he doesn't sweep you off your feet some night and carry you up these stairs and ravage you. Or am I thinking of Clark Gable in Gone With the Wind?"

They went into the flat and Terra turned on the overhead light. Frowning, Dixie glanced around, ready to scathe, and then she raised her eyes and her mouth came ajar. "Will you look at that? The original ceiling complete with ornamentation."

It was the first Terra had noticed the circle of faded cupids, flying a celestial panorama of painted clouds among birds and assorted angels.

"This must have been a rich man's town-house. We're probably in the children's quarters," Dixie mused. "Can we go up to the attic? Who knows what treasures are hidden there?"

"If there is an attic I'm not about to ask Cutter for the keys. I mean we might find Mrs. Rochester batting around." She put a pan of water on the hot plate to boil, got out a tea pot. Tatty piece of crockery, she must replace it. The cups, too, were chipped and worn, not antiques, just old. Seeing the place through the eyes of another, Terra realized she had neglected to take stock of her surroundings, committed as she was to impermanence.

"Well, that ceiling makes the trip worth while. That's why I came, to make sure that address I gave you wasn't a dump."

"Whatever its faults it was a lifesaver, to get a room so fast. I'm sorry I didn't call and thank you."

"You do have a phone?"

"Pay phone on the wall, we passed it in the foyer downstairs. I don't even know the number." And she must jot it down, Manisch had reminded her that they needed it for their employment form.

Dixie shrugged out of her jacket and tossed it on the bed. Her outfit of black silk was chic, tailored, but surprisingly understated, a concession to the world of normality. Lounging on the sofa she eyed Terra. "You're looking better than when I last saw you. That suit is — very acceptable. Whose is it? I can't quite place the designer."

"Label was removed. A girl from the office took me over to Klein's. We found it on the rack."

"Klein's is good. They take the left-overs from the shows, some of it very high style. None of my work has turned up there, I don't do the shows. I count on word of mouth. My designs are custom-made for a particular client." She spoke proudly, with only a trace of the old defensiveness.

"I bet you charge them an arm and a leg."

"They wouldn't appreciate me if I didn't." Dixie accepted the steaming cup of oolong. "Good tea. You've acquired an international taste."

"I've been living with an international crowd," Terra said dryly.

"Yes. Those scientists. It's all coming out now, the whole incredible thing about a town in the mountains that nobody knew about, full of every brain-head in the world. Were their wives intellectuals, too?"

"I don't know. We didn't talk shop. Mostly we played bridge."

"But you knew what was going on?"

"I guessed, but I didn't know for sure. Not until the test at Alamogordo. After that Phin filled me in, he knew I wouldn't blab it around. And it was killing him, the need to talk about it. He kept arguing with himself, back and forth, the good and evil of the atom. I just quietly hated the whole thing, what it was doing to him."

"He was pretty high up in the chain of command?"

"They didn't call it that. They were a team. But Oppenheimer ran the show and Phin was one of his favorites. They used to sit around our kitchen talking. Never about the bomb, not around me, but scientific theory versus philosophy, religions of the world. Oppie is a brilliant scholar."

"And you were there?" It was the first time Dixie had ever shown her any real respect.

Terra was irritated. "So what? I was there."

"But that was the making of history right at your kitchen table."

"History was made in the lab," Terra said. "What was made at my table was cheese sandwiches on rye with plenty of mustard. By the way, are you hungry? I've got some cans of beans, beef stew, a little bacon and a couple of eggs. Got to go to the store tomorrow."

"No thanks, I'm meeting Zoey for dinner at eight o'clock." Dixie glanced at her watch. Then suddenly stood, staring straight into Terra's eyes, she said, "Are you ticked off about me and Zoey?"

"No," and Terra meant it. "There was a time I was jealous. But that was a long way back, when I didn't understand — a lot of things. Now, I think I do, a little."

"I'm glad. I kind of miss you." Retrieving the jacket and putting it on, she said with careful indifference, "I hoped we could sort things out. I'd love to give you a lot of unwanted advice, the way I did in the old days. You could always be counted on to shrug it off and go your own way. You've no idea how that steadied me."

"And I was practically a rag mop then, compared to now. Go on, try to boss me — you'll see that I have gotten as contrary as a kick in the pants." Terra said it lightly.

"I noticed. The uncertainty is gone, replaced by —" Dixie blinked, as if she had just discovered a secret truth.

"Fatalism, yeah," Terra said. "Don't worry about it. Come on, give me some of the old unwanted. I need a good chide."

"One chide coming up. You really should cut your hair. Braids, buns, all that's gone out of style totally." Her own black elfin locks were stylishly bobbed just below her ears, the back shingled. "Long hair is old-fashioned and hard to wear with the new hats. Anyway, thanks for the tea. Come see me."

Terra followed her downstairs, watching from the vestibule as Dixie tripped off up the street toward Broadway, spike heels clicking, chin in air, as if she were entering a show-room where her line was about to be judged.

"Do I owe you an apology?" It was Cutter, materializing at her elbow. "Next time should I let her in?"

"It's okay," Terra said. "Yes, let her in any

time, if you will. We go way back to kindergarten."

Under the yellow overhead light he looked puzzled. "There's nobody on earth I have known for that long."

"By the way, is there a good beauty shop around here? I'm going to have my hair cut."

He stiffened, she felt an Irish twist of disapproval as he said, "Now why would you be wanting to do that, ma'am?"

He seemed to want an answer, so she said, "My sister-in-law is a fashion expert. She says the new hats aren't made for long hair."

"Ah," he said, "and herself looking like young bhoyo." They began to mount the stairs together slowly as he turned it over in his mind. "Could I be telling you a foin old Irish saying?" She realized the Irish brogue was his own variety of humor. "They say a woman should never take the advice of another woman when it comes to her appearance."

Terra played along. "That sounds like it came from a foin old leprechaun."

"Actually it was me mither, rest her soul. What you need," he went on, "is a fair, impartial judge with no preconceived ideas. A fellow like me. So how long would you say your hair is then?"

They had reached the third floor, she

unlocked her door. Walking inside, she reached up carelessly and pulled the pins on the coil of braids, running her fingers to loosen them and letting them fall in a brown silken cascade almost to her waist.

"Sweet Mary," he breathed.

"Took me five hard years to get it this long. Difficult, you know, persuading hair to grow."

"And if it were short how would you fix it?"

"I actually don't know. I had a permanent once, a disaster, all kinky curls. I couldn't wait to get rid of it." She had almost forgotten those high school days. "I guess I'd better think a while before I decide to lop it off."

"Praise the Saints," he muttered as he started back down.

"Thanks, Shanahan."

Over his shoulder he said, "Any time I can be of service. I tell fortunes, predict the weather, and rescue lost children, by appointment only."

Terra opened the steno notebook and wrote the word "Blurb." A new anthropology book was almost ready for the presses, the jacket design had been okayed. Now they needed the material for the flap. Ari tipped back in his ancient oaken desk chair and considered the ceiling.

"Okay, here we go: 'Cavendish has produced a book that is slated for the bestseller list. This book is so hot we burned out three editors and a proofreader getting it to press. It has everything, sex, conflict, drama, tragedy (gotta admit it's pretty tragic when you become extinct.) The characters leap off the page, particularly *pithecanthropus erectus,* but then he always did like to monkey around.' Are you getting all this?"

Terra had stopped writing after the first sentence. By now she was used to Ari's flights of whimsy. She was supposed to chuckle, at least grin a little. Today she wasn't in the mood. It was Phin's birthday, and in spite of every effort she couldn't shed the feelings that still swamped her on certain occasions. That love had been part of her since she was knee-high. Complicated more recently by frustration and anger, it was now all welded together by a furious sorrow that was almost as acute as it had been three months ago. Was it only three months since she got that letter?

"Snap out of it, earth-girl." Ari liked to play with her name. She was Terra Mater or Terra Firma or some other nonsense. It didn't bother her, and that had become an irritation to him. "You really don't have a sense of humor, do you?"

"I suppose not." But there had been moments of high hilarity back in the old house when she and Dixie and Phin were young and innocent.

"Of course, I realize that my wit is probably over your head." Still trying to get a rise, his right eye fixed on her like a dare.

Terra had long since determined not to be goaded by him, which wasn't easy. The man had a brilliant intellect, editing advanced textbooks in half a dozen subjects, a perfectionist when it came to grammar and punctuation. He was also a fiendish psychologist, always knew what buttons to push.

"Or maybe it's something else," he went on thoughtfully. "I've got it. You're secretly a bigot. You can't kid around with the likes of us because we're Hebrews, we're beneath you. The youngest daughter of a pure-blood line of royalty, you were taught to ignore the lowly —"

She interrupted mildly. "I grew up in a Jewish community, our high school was 90% Jewish, and I married a Jew. Maybe that does make me somewhat prejudiced. There are a lot of goys I don't much like." She looked off out the window.

After a moment in which Ari presumably had to regroup he said, tentatively, "Your husband was killed in the war, I think you said?"

"Umhm." She nodded.

"What branch of service was he in?"

"None of them." Let him muddle over that, he liked mind-games.

Ari chewed on it like a bone. "Not in the service, but died in the war. Medic? No. Chaplain? No. Red Cross volunteer."

She doodled on the pad, suggesting that they get on with the work.

"What, then? Let's see . . . Wait a minute. You once said that electromagnetics was his expertise. Good God, he worked on the Manhattan project!" And when she still didn't answer he nodded. "That would explain the poker face, the way you play your cards so close to the belt. You've been taught the art of keeping quiet. About a very big secret, I grant you, but you must agree that it's no secret any more. You were at Los Alamos."

For an instant she hated him acutely for being so clever. But he was right, what did it matter now? She nodded carelessly. "Give the man a cigar."

"So your husband worked in the labs. There must have been dozens of bright young physicists taking part in that program. The boy must have had a pretty good I.Q. to get hired into that kind of company."

As far as Terra knew, Phin's I.Q. had never been tested. She was about to shuck the questions off with her usual *I'd rather not talk about it* when suddenly irritation turned to rage. Furiously she said, "Phin was on Oppenheimer's first team. He was in the bunker with Oppie at Alamagordo when they set off the first test. He was in the first group scientists to go into Hiroshima after the war. In fact he stayed on to help with the cleanup for months, finally developed radiation sickness and died. Now don't you need to dictate this blurb? The jacket material is supposed to go to the printer today."

After a long silence Ari picked up the anthropology book. "Blurb for the textbook: PRIMORDIAL HERITAGE. 'In this unusual approach to the subject of anthropology Cavendish has managed to throw new light on an age-old science . . .' No, that sounds pedestrian as Hell. Let's start over." This time his right eye was definitely looking out the window.

Drat the man. Terra never could say "damn," that was Phin's word and she didn't have the nerve to come out with it, even in her head. Later, alone in the office, she typed up her notes, checked the punctuation and spelling one more time and left the page on Ari's desk. *Maybe I just ought to go look for another job.*

Office work was making her restless. But what else could she do? She liked to cook. She wouldn't mind house work. But that would mean a whole new set of relationships, close continuous contact with some family who would probably be even more irritating. Leaving a stack of unfinished work on her desk, she wandered down the hall to look in on Gilda.

"Hi, I was just coming to get you." These days the receptionist was a lot perkier, if that was a word you could apply to a beanpole of a woman with regal upswept Bette

81

Davis hair and silver fingernails. "We're invited to join the others in a meeting." Her tone dropped to conspiratorial. "In the coffee room."

"What others?"

"The slaves who do the work around this place," she said. "Come on, it's our chance. The Triumvirate is taking a long lunch down on Mott Street, some ritzy Chinese restaurant."

"Actually, it's *The Golden Dragon*," Terra said. "I made the reservations. It's one of Mr. Dorfman's favorite spots." The Vice President of the company had breezed into the office this morning. A handsome chestnut-haired lothario ("Call me Karl") he had taken possession of her with an arm around her shoulders, in that chummy way of all chauvinists, assuming the little girl will be flattered. With a shining flash of teeth he had made some joke about the improvement to the décor of the office — meaning her. "I go away on a sales trip and come back to find the place transformed." And so forth.

His job, she learned, was to travel the college circuit introducing the new textbooks, beguiling the tenured professors into adopting them, which in the big universities meant sales of five hundred a crack. He also owned half the company, he and Manisch having started it together a few years before the war. Ari was only an editor, but his skills were what made the books tick. The three of them had left for lunch awhile ago, a policy-planning session for the spring list that would probably take all afternoon.

"So while the fat cats are away, we mice can play." Gilda locked the entrance door and hung a sign on it. "CLOSED UNTIL ONE P.M."

"If you want to think of yourself as a mouse, you go for it, girl," Terra said lightly. "But don't include me. I tried it once and I didn't like it."

"Ah-h-h. That's the ticket," Gilda grinned. "That's what we need, another good rebellious heart."

The smell of Sanka filled the coffee room where the others had already gathered. Manisch's secretary seemed to be in charge. Henrietta Moon was a short gray-haired woman, sturdy, but not fat. Vigorously efficient, she was usually aloof in her own private office, too senior to mingle with the likes of Terra, until now.

"Good," she said, in gravelly tones. "We're all here, including Miss Innocent. Well, sit down, young lady, and listen. We have an important decision to make."

Terra took a chair next to Buddy, the mail-room clerk, the only man among them. Balding, faded, he had the look of one who simply endures life without comment. Beyond him was Ruth Jones, secretary to the ebullient Mr. Dorfman, a thin little woman with blue-rinsed hair who spent most of her days reading paperback novels. Her one assignment seemed to be opening a few letters each morning and putting them on his blotter. When he would call in she'd read them to him over the phone, take down the answers and transcribe them later. It was said that she had been with him ever since the company was formed, a legacy from some earlier job.

"Well, are we ready to take a vote?" Henrietta looked around at the lot. "Or do you want more discussion?"

"I think we should tell Terra what the vote's about," Gilda drawled. "Seeing she hasn't the foggiest idea."

"You didn't talk it over with her?"

"Not me. I don't do organizing."

"You'd better learn. We all need to spread the word," Henrietta informed her. "All right, Terra, here's the situation: We have been approached to join the UOWPA. That stands for the United Office Workers Protective Association. Miners and railroaders are not the only people who need unions. We are being exploited and victimized, here in the backwaters of capitalism. We need to rally together and assert our rights."

"Which rights?" Terra wondered.

"Well, for one thing, the right to have regular increases in our salary, or an explanation of why those are not forthcoming." The woman spoke in tones that rang of resentment. "The right to certain paid holidays, plus a schedule of vacation days earned by length of employment: one week the first year, two the second, and so forth. The right to a given number of sick days without having our paycheck docked. The right to overtime if we are required to work longer than forty hours a week. Severance pay if we are fired for no good reason, like Millie."

They nodded silently.

Gilda explained to Terra. "Millie was Ari's assistant before Crider. She worked hard, in spite of all that guff he hands out. I mean he could make anybody look inefficient if he tried. So she got very nervous, she began to cry a lot. But he shouldn't have fired her."

"She should have quit," Buddy said abruptly. "That Ari is a son-of-a-gun." The outburst surprised them all.

After a moment's silence Henrietta went

on. "Anyway, those are some of the issues we need to address. To make the bosses listen to us, to realize that we are human beings, we have to stand together. That's what unions are all about. So — are you with us?"

There was an overtone of warning in the question. Terra hesitated. She preferred fighting her own battles one-on-one. But Gilda seemed to be telegraphing a silent plea: Say yes!

Terra guessed that if she wanted to work here in any kind of harmony she'd better go along with it. After all, what difference? "Sure," she said, "why not?"

"The dues are only two-fifty a month. We'll be getting instructions and materials from the main headquarters in Washington. All we have to do right now is wait. Then when our numbers increase we may be called on to act in concert with our fellow workers. Call a strike maybe. Everybody on board? Good. I'll write to the organizers and tell them they've got some new recruits. Solidarity forever, my friends." The woman stood up, came to attention and gave a little salute.

Out on the sidewalk in the brisk sunlight with a sharp breeze rattling the bare trees around Union Square, Terry and Gilda headed by common consent for the Schrafft's over on Fifth avenue. It was almost two o'clock, the worst of the lunch hour crush would be over.

". . . first time I ever felt like I was master of my fate, captain of my soul." Gilda was babbling. "If we stand up for ourselves the boss will have to treat us as equals."

"I doubt it," Terra commented dryly. "I mean there will always be bosses and employees, and they'll never be equal. Actually Manisch is pretty respectful, compared to some other men I've seen." The insurance office in San Diego had been run by a petty tyrant.

"You haven't worked here long. Ollie can be awful nasty if you come in late. And that Ari is a downright sadist. I didn't expect you to stay with him this long."

"Oh, he's just a smart-aleck intellectual. They talk like an unabridged dictionary, but they probably couldn't change the washer in a faucet."

"How can you be so cool, with him ragging on you all the time?"

"Because I know how to change the washer in a faucet." Terra took a last forkful of her lunch, the rare vegetable plate that was actually delectable.

"Then come in tonight and fix mine,"

Gilda suggested. "It drips all the time. And I don't like to go to Cutter. He scares me to death."

"Why on earth?"

"Don't you feel the underlying violence in him? That sleepy act he puts on — it's a cover-up. He's a desperate man, probably a criminal hiding from the law."

Terra was silent. Of course she had sensed something beneath the surface of the Irishman, but it was more like sorrow. She wondered if he were grieving over a loss, some woman who had jilted him maybe? She said, "It's probably his name that makes you nervous. I wonder how he got called 'Cutter.' Anyway, I'm sure he's harmless, don't worry so much."

But the conversation had left a sliver of doubt. Terra felt a bit disconcerted that evening when a knock came and she opened the door to find the super standing in the hallway, holding a large paper bag with the distinctive *"B. Altman"* signature on it.

"This came for you," he said. "I didn't want to leave it out in the lobby, so I took it in. Here you go."

She accepted it from him curiously. The delivery tag had no sender's name. "Who's it from?"

"Can't say. Maybe there's a note inside."

He fidgeted, looking past her into the room. "While I'm here I thought maybe I'd check out your radiator. Some people have complained about the steam knocking."

"I thought that's what radiators did." She stepped aside and turned away to investigate her package while he went over to the ancient heating unit under the back window.

There was a hat box inside the bag. She opened it to a crush of tissue paper, and beneath it a charming bonnet. Off-the-face in the Flemish style, it was just a velvet cap with the back cut out so that it fit around her braided hair. In the front a neat little pleated brim flared upward in a crisp frame of burgundy silk. It was a perfect complement to both her new suits, the red and another one of chocolate brown that she had found at Klein's last week. Going to the mirror she put it on and smiled. *Shades of Henry the Eighth, I look like Anne of Cleves.*

In the glass she saw Cutter watching, and it came to her that the radiator hadn't needed his attention. He was just curious to see what was in the package. Turning, she asked him, "Well, what do you think?"

His stubby lashes blinked, and he nodded diffidently. "Looks nice. You need anything else done around here?"

"No, but there's a drippy faucet in

Three-B. Gilda would be happy if she came home and found it fixed."

When he was gone she got out her address book and looked up the number of the *Galerie*. A twinge of old-times had come back when she put the bonnet on — of Dixie hauling her into Scruggs to force her to buy her first sling-back pumps. But as she started downstairs to the wall phone, she hesitated and turned back. It was long after hours, and though Dixie had given her another number, of an apartment over on the east side, she was reluctant to call. She had never met the marvelous Zoey; she didn't really want to leave any messages with her. *And if that means I'm prejudiced, maybe I am.*

It wasn't until two nights later, as she headed for choir rehearsal in the big building on 56th which everyone called The Annex, that Terra acted on an impulse and detoured over to 57th on a route that would take her past Dixie's showroom. The light was on up in the ornate window with its gold lettering. ***Galerie de la Coquette,*** indeed. All that high style, why didn't Dixie send her some flirty Breton that would make her look more like a New Yorker rather than a prim little bonnet? Terra hadn't worn anything that demure since college days. *She's trying to shame me into getting my hair cut.*

When she reached the entryway she almost ran into another woman leaving, a blond girl with a sweet face, blue eyes delicately outlined in mascara, rosebud lips and small, pretty white teeth. She was smiling politely. "Can I help you?"

"I was looking for the owner of the gallery . . ." And then it hit her. "You must be Zoey."

"And you're Theresa Berensen. I'm glad we've finally met. Come on in." The voice was warm, but the cock of the head a bit defiant.

"Sorry, I can't stay. I'm due at a rehearsal in ten minutes. I just wanted to thank Dixie for the hat."

It drew a blank stare. "I didn't know she'd given you one."

Or that Dixie had even been over to see me, Terra's mind raced. "It was probably an impulse. She doesn't like the way I wear my hair, and said so, the last time I saw her. Maybe this was her way of needling me a little."

"Oh that does sound like Dix. Well, I'll tell her you dropped by."

"Thanks." Terra juggled a complexity of feelings that weren't going to be sorted out easily. Putting them from her mind she headed for The Annex.

It was a strange phenomenon, the change that came over her when she walked into rehearsal each time. It was as if she became someone else. No more a lonely widow at odds with the world, she was part of an instrument bigger than her small personal voice, one committed to a single harmonic purpose. She couldn't say why this concept seized her in such a grip when she took her place with the others. All of them were still strangers. There was no connection between the members of the group outside the rehearsal hall. They gave up their separate identities when they gathered together here. Ranged in a circle now they became mere components, waiting for Andrew to create them again.

Lonely on the podium, his long bones clad in blue jeans and T-shirt, bleached hair tousled as if he'd been tearing at it, he rechecked his folio one last time. "Okay, people, let's sing." He gave the sign to the accompanist, a surly boy in a heavy woolen sweater of multicolored yarn. Jean-Claude by name, he was shaggy and rude, and so gifted on the keyboard his hands seemed endowed with a special genius, now some-what wasted on the warm-up round.

The chorus burst into "Row, row, row your boat . . ." repeating it each time a half-tone higher until the room was rocking with layers of "merrily, merrily, merrily, merrily."

Andrew held up a hand and the racket stopped. "That was pretty ragged, folks, we need to tune it. Link elbows please." And when the entire group had completed a human wall around him, he said, "Kick off your shoes and brace your feet against one another."

It was a new strategy to Terra, making physical contact with her fellow musicians. It produced an odd sensation, of energy flowing around the circle like an electric charge. Andrew got out a tuning fork and tapped it on his music rack. A tiny bell-tone vibrated in the silence clear enough for all to hear. "That's your note. Sing it, just the one tone, 'Ah-h-h-h,' at whatever pitch suits your voice. All together now —"

They broke forth in a great comfortable unison.

"Harder," he called out. "Bear down."

As he kept beckoning with those long white fingers: *more, more, more,* it became a challenge, to strengthen it, to project every ounce of sound in you, clear on down to the bottom of your sternum. Terra poured on full effort. The others were leaning forward with the tension, focusing . . . And miraculously they began to hear echoes. High in the ceiling of the big rehearsal hall there suddenly existed tiny chimes of sound above the range of the human voice, pure fifths, shimmering in the air like celestial light that has no origin. The force couldn't be sustained very long. After a minute they all collapsed a little, breathlessly slumping in place. Andrew smiled.

"And that, people, is the phenomenon known as high harmonics. It only happens when we are perfectly tuned to each other. Congratulations. I think we're ready to sing the Lord's music."

Christians be joyful. Terra tried to borrow the message, to regain the harmonies that had electrified the rehearsal hall. But out on the cold city street next day, there was no way she could fight off the bleakness of heart that pervaded her. She even tried humming, as she left the apartment and turned southward down Broadway, passing by the subway entrance, walking briskly to get the circulation going, maybe stir the dregs of sadness from her blood. *Praise your salvation.* Well, the choral group had been a salvation, but it was only an aspirin pitted against the massive ache of amputation.

And yet, today the city was at peace. With the gaiety of holiday in the air, the streets were deserted. The shops on Broadway all bore signs: CLOSED FOR THANKS-GIVING. The old town was daring to reveal a tender side for those who gathered around a table.

As for the unfamilied, it offered only a respite from work and a quick trip to a restaurant.

HORN AND HARDART

At Broadway and 56th Street the automat flashed its neon invitation to the lonely. Not a bad offering — the aromas were rich enough, each dish tucked into its own hot chamber behind glass windows, the change machine dominating the floor. Terra usually enjoyed punching coins and pulling out a steaming dish of baked beans and franks (25 cents) with hot apple pie (15 cents) and a glass of milk.

Today she felt a pang of remembrance of other Thanksgivings and chose to walk the cafeteria line, collecting a plate of turkey and dressing and cranberry sauce. Maybe if she tried hard, she thought, the smell of the feast would remind her of all the things she had to be thankful for. Turning away from the food line she began: *I have the chorale, I have a job, I have a room . . .*

And stopped short. Over at a table to one side was a familiar face. Cutter had actually combed his hair, for once it was free of dust. He looked reasonably presentable in a blue turtleneck sweater over dark corduroy pants. Glancing up at the same moment, he saw her, then gave a hesitant wave: *join me?*

Veering in that direction, Terra sank down opposite him. "Hi. Happy turkey-day."

"Likewise."

She glanced around at the big dining area which was half full. "I see we're not the only outcasts."

"Is that what you feel like? Outcast?" he asked munching his turkey sandwich. He had pulled his dinner piece-meal from the coin operated drawers, including a monster of a baked apple.

"Not exactly," she said, digging in with a nudge of appetite. A little company didn't hurt, even if he was nine-tenths a stranger. "That implies somebody cast me out. If any casting was done, I did it."

He nodded. "Likewise. I choose my own way, I don't blame anyone else. I'll trade you half my apple for a couple of those olives."

She picked them up. "Excuse my fingers."

And planted them on his plate. "I don't like olives, the cook just added those to be jolly."

The word amused him. His mouth did funny things when it tried to smile, it crimped, tightened, twisted and retreated rapidly into its natural straight line. Solemnly he divided his apple in half and balanced it on a spoon precariously over to her plate.

"I guess you don't have any family nearby?" he suggested obliquely.

"Nope. You?"

"I've got a father out in Montana. That's my nearest and dearest."

"Well, technically I have a father in Iowa." Suddenly she could imagine the Millers bellied up to a big oaken table stacked high with every food on earth. Farm folk, they were lusty of appetite.

"Technically?"

"Dad was shell-shocked in The First War. After my mother died, his mind collapsed. He's just hanging on, going through the motions."

"Mm." The blunt Irish face darkened. "Wars, violence, many a good man . . ." His voice faded into some remote place that was closed to the public.

"Were you in the last one?" she asked.

He roused. "Oh yes." Then added,

"Army." And further, "Pacific. Guadalca-nal."

"Jungle warfare." She had read the Tre-gaskis book. "I think I'd rather be a sailor."

"Not if you get seasick." He shook his head at some memory. "Worst part of Guadalcanal was getting there on the damned troop ship. Excuse me," changing the subject, "but I noticed a ring-mark on your finger. Were you married?"

She nodded. "He was killed in the war." *And don't let's get into that.*

"Sorry, didn't mean to pry." Not a clever delver like Ari Scheidler. Not going to pursue it at all. "Well, it's a whole new ball-game, isn't it?" He looked around, but he wasn't talking about the Automat.

"New York is more like a different planet."

"Greatest city on this side of the world. Attracts the very best and the very worst."

And which are you? The thought bounced sideways and she flashed on a thing that Gilda had said. "He scares me to death." Terra had to admit that there was a quality about the man, as if he could turn violent and be very good at it.

"What brought you here?" he asked off-hand.

"Oh, it was girlhood dream — I wanted to come years ago. But then I got married instead and it got put on the back burner. Now — well, I thought at least it wouldn't be boring. What about you?"

His shoulders twitched in a shrug. "Hunting for tiger, I guess."

She understood that. "After the battlefield Montana doesn't offer much challenge?"

"Well, some. You fight the weather. The distances. Open range, hundreds of miles, empty except for winter wheat. I guess the old-timers found it tough going. My granddad went out there in the eighties, working on the Northern Pacific, laying track. Whole crews of Irish immigrants. Time they got to Montana he was tired of driving steel and went off to work in the Washoe district digging coal. Didn't last long at that, Dad hated the mines. Ended up homesteading down in the Clark's Fork Valley."

"You come from a family of tough working men," she observed. *So what made you settle for a janitor's job, rolling out the trash cans?*

"And you — I bet you're originally from bluebloods."

"On my mother's side," she acknowledged without enthusiasm. "You know what F.F.V. stands for?"

He shook his head.

"First Families of Virginia. My great-

great-grandfather fought with Washington. Great-grandpappy was one of Jeb Stuart's cavalry. When you get drilled enough on the glories of the past, you start running from it, looking for some new direction." *And you never ever want to return to the great mansion in Richmond.*

Cutter nodded slowly, thinking it over, an alien idea. "Not all beer and skittles, being the crown Princess."

Terra laughed in spite of herself. "You hit it right on the head."

"Family expects a lot."

"Nothing less than total superiority. I was supposed to be a concert pianist. Look at my hands." She spread them out, her father's short stubby fingers, not a trace of artistry about them. "I can hardly reach an octave on the piano."

"So you took up singing."

She stared at him, suddenly cautious. "What makes you say that?"

"Oh, sometimes when I'm cleaning the stairs I hear you running scales." He stared back, the reddish eyes complicated, unreadable. *Of course you can't expect to find privacy in a city. No reason she should feel irritated.* But it left her uncomfortable, the thought that her life was so easily available. "That's just a hobby," she said. "A choral group, The Mastersingers. Ever hear of them?"

He shook his head. "I don't keep up with stuff like that. And I try not to get nosy about my roomers." He knew he had upset her. "That was a pretty good feast," he added briskly, pushing back from the table, picking up plates to carry to the disposal drop. "Think I'll take a walk over onto Fifth and look at the windows. Saks, Lord and Taylor, you ever see their Christmas displays?"

"No." He was waiting for her so she followed him out. "Is it something special?"

"People come from all over to look at them."

The Sugarplum Fairy pirouetted on tiptoe spreading a glitter of sequins over the elves below that hammered on toys to load onto the train that ran past every minute or so. Terra got on it . . .

She was rocking along a bumpy track through the hills of West Virginia, where kerosene lanterns pricked the darkness, from the windows of distant miners' shacks out there in the night. She was going home for Christmas. A war had just been declared, and in a wild celebration at Annapolis a new class of officers had thrown their caps in the air. June Week was held in December that year. A feverish Tommy had asked her to marry him before he joyfully rushed off to the cold waters of the North Atlantic. Gently she had declined.

Hours later, as she sat on her suitcase in the club car a frenetic crowd around her was singing college fight songs. "Cheer, cheer for old Notre Dame . . ." Everybody seemed hepped up about the coming war. All she could think about was her dying mother. At a junction the crossing light swung back and forth and the ding-ding-ding woke her up. Her alarm clock.

Terra lay in the six a.m. darkness and still felt the rocking of the railroad cars, saw the moonlit hills. Tomorrow she would find Phin waiting for her in the train yard in St. Louis with the snow coming down, and it would happen. They would finally and forever be promised to each other. Tears began to come, slowly, first just a watering of eye, and then flooding her face. She turned over and sobbed.

"Where I come from —" Gilda twisted the end on the leather curler — "women start baking Christmas cookies about December the third." She began a new lock, her hair startlingly golden after a trip to the beauty parlor yesterday. Cross-legged on her bed, her knees cocked, her red-nailed toes stacked on the white bed-spread like radishes, she was a vision of plucked eyebrows and cold cream.

Terra was intent on her own nails, the ones on her hands. Toes would have to wait. Applying the new shade of persimmon pink, she said, "I think you mentioned you were from Indiana?"

"Little town, about thirty miles from Indianapolis. Nobody ever left until the war came along. Then the boys shipped out and the rest of us moved to Chicago or Gary. I took a job in a defense factory, punched holes in aluminum sheeting all day. Talk about tiresome. But we were making airplanes and that kept us going. When they came out with that poster, 'Rosie, the Riveter,' I never felt prouder in my life. Kind of took the sting off being a mere female."

Everybody had responded to that one. Terra remembered. The picture of a busty, sexy girl in a defiant pose with a machine tool in her hand, it stood for the sudden discovery that women could help the war effort too. Thousands of them had taken to trousers and overalls, learning to hold down a job, make a quota, to swear like a man and smoke cigarettes and ankle up to a bar alone. It was great while the war was on. Afterward some of them reverted to homebodies and got married, out there now having babies all over the place, so they said. But then there were some like Gilda.

"You still have folks back there?" she asked.

"Yeah, and sometimes I miss 'em. But I love this city. Here you can be whatever you want to be. Or try, at least. I guess my trouble is I don't know what I want. Certainly not another job as a punch operator. I thought publishing was pretty high-tone, but maybe it's too fancy for me. I never seem to get things right. And it's lonely out there alone at the reception desk, you know?

I thought I'd meet some men, but the kind that come in our office are mostly egg-heads." She finished with the curlers and tied a scarf on over her lumpy locks.

Terra was done with one hand; she held it out to dry. They were in Gilda's room, a smaller narrower version of her own. Apartments A and B had originally been one big sitting room at the front of the townhouse. Now they were divided by a partition, thin wood, no insulation against sound. Next door 3A was playing the radio, a football game. What else on Sunday afternoon? Jack Olander of the hairy chest. An insurance salesman, he had tried to sell each of them policies, by smirk and by leer.

"Something about that one I don't like, he's too smarmy." Terra said.

"Yeah," Gilda agreed, "he sucks around. I prefer the big tough kind who don't take any guff off people, including me." She grinned a little. "The kind who believe what's in their pants is a prize package and you better worship it. That's what being a male is all about."

Terra felt herself flushing with embarrass-ment at the plain language. She got a quick flash of her mother trying to convey to her the facts of life. It had been done so ob-liquely it took some imagination to picture that aristocratic lady ever being in the marital bed. And true to the family esprit, Terra had kept her virginity until her own marriage, though barely. Now she was glad that she and Phin had learned the basics together, though she doubted that they ever were all that expert. Didn't matter. Since her sour experience with Uncle Reddy she didn't care much for the act. It secretly disgusted her.

"Were you ever married?" she asked Gilda, just an extension of her own thought, not meaning an intrusion.

"Never met the right fellow." The other girl colored up. "If you want to know, I've never been asked."

"Oh. Sorry. I didn't mean to —"

"Damn it! I don't know what they want. I'm too tall, and I'm not a beauty, but then that's true of practically half the world. I treat guys with respect. I let them be the boss, I don't mind at all. But after a while they begin to get bored. Seems like all they want is for me to put out. Maybe I should go to school some more, learn how to talk about stuff. I don't know . . ."

Such a humble revelation, Terra didn't know how to react.

"Anyway, I'm still looking for a boyfriend, and it's not happening at Paragon Press.

Maybe I should move to a bigger outfit. Receptionist in an insurance company maybe, lot of people coming and going. Maybe I'll let my hair grow. Men like that feminine look — they like a primitive woman, like you. By the way, lately you've been stalked." She giggled. "You didn't even know it, did you?"

"I don't believe it, either. Who'd stalk me?"

"Oh, there's a certain party who hangs out every evening waiting for you to come home. Saw him follow you that day, Thanksgiving, when you went off walking . . ."

"You mean when I went down to the Automat for dinner?"

"Mm-hm. The Irishman was right behind you. I was looking out my window when he took up the trail."

"Cutter?"

"And don't you wonder how he got that nickname? I bet he carries a shiv in his sock."

"Oh, I doubt he was following me." But it sounded lame. "I mean, he couldn't have. He was there first, at a table." Only, come to think: he could have come in after her, gone to the ranks of cubbyholes, got a sandwich and sat down before she cleared the cafeteria line.

"Uh-huh." Gilda's turbaned head bobbed. "You did see him then."

"I had dinner with him, in fact. We walked over and looked at the Christmas windows along Fifth. He was a perfect gentleman. He's never even seemed interested in me except so far as I pay the rent on time." *But he wanted to see you put on that hat.*

"Gentleman, my foot. The day he's a gentleman I will dance a jig and sing 'Danny Boy.' I bet his picture's on some post office wall. I tell you, the guy is hiding out. When I went down to his apartment to pay the rent last week he only opened the door an inch, but there was a strange smell came from that room. Like raw earth. Like he might have just been burying a body or something."

Terra started on the nails of her other hand. For some reason she had trouble getting the polish on smoothly. *And he does have the master key that opens all our doors.*

"Shoot, I'm sorry, I shouldn't have told you. Now I got you all jititery. I didn't think you'd spook at anything," Gilda added, "since you manage to work for Ari Scheidler without getting a nervous breakdown."

"Well, at least he is no moocher," Terra said with a laugh. "The only thing he gets emotional about is punctuation. He explained to me the other day what a unit-modifier is — you know, when you hyphenate two adjectives that describe something? And when I said, 'Why is that important? Who cares about a hyphen?' he almost got tears in his eyes." Well, not really, but his look was so aggrieved she had apologized.

"I tell you," Gilda lowered her voice as if there were spies in every shadow, "when we get going in the UOWPA we're gonna make the whole lot of those smart aleck bosses show a little respect."

Terra screwed the top back on the polish. She hadn't made up her mind about joining that outfit, even though in the meeting she had given her vocal consent. Her father had been dead set against unions of any kind, said they were a bunch of Communists. But that had been back in the thirties when a lot of people talked about Communism. Since then Russia had been one of the United States' allies during the fighting in Europe. And yet she had noticed lately were people growing fearful of them again, calling them the "Reds."

"You are coming to the meeting tomorrow night?" Gilda prodded.

"Tomorrow? I can't. I have a rehearsal. Andrew has stepped up the schedule, with the concert only three weeks away. He told us yesterday that we will be accompanied by some of the musicians from the New York Philharmonic Orchestra. Can you believe it?"

"Mmm. Nice. But as soon as Christmas is over, I hope you'll start attending our meetings. It means a lot to the others, Henny and Billy and all. You want to stay on good terms with the office folks, Terra. They can make life easier, or not."

At least somebody wanted to make her life easier, Terra thought. A single red rose in a tall cut-glass vase stood on her desk that Monday morning. She paused, staring at it with her coat still half unbuttoned. Over in his cave of papers and galleys and proofs Ari glanced across at the flower and his lip curled.

"Loverboy strikes again."

Terra frowned and took off her coat, hanging it on the rack nearby. On top of it she perched her new hat; she'd decided to go and see Dixie after work.

"Nobody has filled you in on our Veep?" Ari leered with his right eye, his jittery hands fidgeting with the flotsam on his desk. "Let me tell you what is about to happen. He'll drop by in a while, ask you to have lunch with him at some posh place, probably the Waldorf. He'll imply that your future depends on how you comply with his 'suggestions,' which will include a night on the town in the near future, and/or a trip to his apartment at the Ritz. He will tell you he is wallowing in riches, and that's true. He inherited money from his father, who was a land speculator back in the twenties, made a bundle. If you cooperate nicely, he may go so far as to promise you a new apartment, a car of your own, plus assorted other benefits. All you'll have to do is be his mistress." He grimaced. "Chance of a lifetime, girl."

"I'm afraid he'll be disappointed," Terra said flatly. "I don't have any interest at all in romantic entanglements."

"That gets into tricky territory, so I'll give you a good tip. Seriously: if he hints that your job may be at stake, you can choose to ignore that. You will work here as long as I say so. You're the first girl who's got along with me since this company began. I have a well-deserved reputation as a slave driver." Now his left eye was fixing her with a look as sharp and faceted as a piece of jet. "I have damned well earned the right to pick my own slave. So prepare for further lashings."

"Oh shoot," she said, in a phony southern

drawl, "Ah think y'all are downrat sweet, honeybun."

Ari cocked back in his chair and howled with laughter.

In a matter of seconds the subject Karl appeared in the doorway. Natty in a Navy blue double-breasted suit with four-in-hand golden silk tie, he seemed intrigued. "Are we having fun?"

"How could we not, with all these hilariously ungifted authors to nurse?" Ari subsided into snickers and turned away to focus on his work.

The Vice President was mystified, but not that interested. With his most winning smile he spoke to Terra in confidential tones that somehow implied intimacy. "I see you got my little token."

"It's pretty," she said matter-of-factly. "Thank you."

"Just a hint of things to come." He glanced at Ari's back. Still being secretive he murmured, "How about we catch some lunch later? Can you get away from that tyrant of a boss?"

"He allows me to eat," she said carelessly.

"I'm glad. I have reservations for us, and do please wear that hat." He glanced at the bonnet atop the coat rack.

Terra was glad she had decided to doll

herself up for Dixie. Wearing the chocolate-colored suit with its chic styling and a turquoise silk blouse that she'd also found lurking on Klein's racks, she was over-dressed for the office, but right on target for the elegant dining room into which Karl ushered her that afternoon.

A waiter held her chair, while in the corner a small string quartette played undistinguished baroque music. Karl faced her with a slight smile and a tilted brow, as if inviting her awe at the surroundings. She was glad her coat had been consigned to the cloakroom. Those rabbit skins were visibly tired. Next pay day she would have to go shopping.

"We don't need them." Karl waved off the waiter with his menus. "We will start with a nice Cabernet Sauvignon and then I think the roast duckling and chestnuts, fresh asparagus Hollandaise, tossed salad and bring the oil and vinegar to the table. We'll make our own dressing."

"I don't take wine," Terra said. "No alcohol of any kind."

Karl made a sophisticated little moue. "Well, I do," he said to the waiter. And to Terra, "It really does wonders to prepare the palate, you know. Have you ever had duckling? It's rather rich."

"If I had been allowed to order for myself," she said dryly, "I would have probably picked ham-on-rye with a dill pickle."

He laughed with an open row of very white teeth. "You are indeed a charming child. You are apparently demure, but that hat is as subtle as a gray hackle. Did you ever do any fly-fishing? The gray hackle is so modest the fish can't believe it's a lure and will strike every time."

"I have never fished," she said.

"I believe you. No one could fake such innocence. Let me guess: you grew up in a small town and went to church every Sunday."

"I grew up in St. Louis, Missouri, and the churches in our suburb were mostly synagogues. No, Mr. Dorfman, you are way off the mark." She didn't want him to entertain her under false pretenses. Pure curiosity to see a really great dining room had prompted her to accept his invitation, and she wasn't disappointed.

The trimmings so rich, the ceiling so high above, the linens so white it was like something out of a movie. When the duckling arrived it was protected by a great glass cover which the waiter removed with ceremony. He carved and served and poured Karl's wine as one would wait upon royalty.

"How long have you been in New York?" The Vice President was prompting, and Terra allowed him in quiz her on her impressions of the city, her luck in finding an apartment. The details she sketched over lightly. "It's a nice place, only a block from Riverside Drive. No doorman, it's not that big a building. But it's convenient to a taxi stand on 86th."

Dorfman laughed merrily. "You are living in a West Side brownstone walk-up with a fire escape and a grungy super. Don't try to kid me, my dear, I know this city. It can be very bleak and shabby. We must do something about that. You should be surrounded by luxury, the finest things that life can provide."

A memory flashed on her and she shook her head, smiling. "That's almost exactly what my uncle once said to me, the time when I was visiting the family home in Virginia. Hamilton House, it's called, near Richmond, one of the better known Colonial mansions. Uncle Redford described how great it is to be rich — I should mention that this was while he was chasing me around my bedroom with his dressing gown open. I had to threaten to wake the household if he didn't leave me alone." It was funny now. It hadn't been, then, not to a seventeen-year-old girl.

The anecdote reduced Karl to bemused silence as he attended to his meal. "I didn't know you came from a wealthy family."

"They were my mother's folks," she said. "Not mine. Never mine. I don't have any people, really."

"And therein lies a pity." He had got back in stride. "The world is hungry for love. Without it we are all adrift. To feel needed, to feel adored, it's a basic human desire, don't you think?"

"I don't think, I know." She spoke curtly.

"Really? You seem a little cool for one so young and vibrant, as if you only await the touch that turns you on."

"You know who turns me on?" Terra said, on impulse. "Harry Truman. He comes from Missouri, too. He says what he means and he means what he says and he sticks by it. He doesn't talk as if the people are all suckers and he can fool them with slick promises." She never discussed politics with strangers, but it seemed only fair to this fool to send him a firm message about the kind of person she admired, someone alien to his ilk.

"Shall we call over the dessert cart?" Karl said a bit grimly.

Back out in the lofty lobby of the hotel

Terra said, "This has been a lovely luncheon, the duck was delicious. Thank you very much."

Brightening, visibly becoming the consummate salesman again, Karl said, "My suite is even more a treat. I happen to have some excellent pieces of sculpture, including a genuine Paul Manship. You know, the fellow who did the Prometheus over at Rockefeller Center? And my living room windows overlook Central Park, it's quite spectacular. Come along, I'll show you."

He had appropriated her elbow.

With a sigh, Terra disengaged it. "You've been very kind to me, Karl, so I'm going to be frank with you. I lost my husband less than six months ago. I may not wear black, but I am still grieving for him. He was the great and only love of my life and I can't imagine any other relationship. I really need to get back to work. I'm helping Ari with that index for the Civil War history. You know, the one the author botched so badly?" She was moving away as she spoke, on out into the street where the doorman waved down a taxi.

That afternoon clouds moved in over the city. It was gloomy in the back office where Terra sat across from Ari with a sheet of paper on which the revised index was beginning to take shape.

"Chicamauga, 39, 171-174." She said.

The editor hunted through his copy of the proof. "He must have meant Chickahominy. Yeah, here it is in the chapter on the Peninsula campaign. So scratch page 39. Chicamauga didn't happen until 1863. Wait a minute. Okay, here it is, the 171-174 is correct. And you can add page 177 to that, he missed another reference. Good Lord, it would be easier to start over from scratch." He leaned back and stretched his shoulders, looked at the big round clock on the wall. It was after five. "I'm tired of being a slave-driver, time to turn into a honeybun. Go on home."

Reluctantly Terra went back to her own desk. She felt the sour aftertaste of the heavy lunch, the verbal sparring, the whole episode with Karl Dorfman. *Should have been more diplomatic.* But the truth was, his type had to be hit over the head.

"You didn't succumb to the golden boy's charms, I take it?" Ari was putting on his coat, of shabby black wool, and brimmed hat smacking of the Orthodox. It made him seem more diffident.

"I never succumb," she told him, "and I'm not very graceful about saying so. Which is too bad. I guess I just realized, I really do like working here."

"Glad to hear it. I told you, your job is not at stake."

"There are ways to get rid of people short of firing them," she said. "And I'll bet Mr. Dorfman knows them all."

"The only person you have to be concerned about," Ari had lowered his voice to a murmur, "is Manisch. And he likes you, so relax."

As she walked out onto Fourth Avenue clouds were moving in. It was misting, creating a deep chill right off the harbor. Terra pulled a scarf from her pocket and put it over her head. She had left the bonnet in the office, she wasn't in the mood for Dixie tonight. A taxi cruised by, but she ignored it. The walk to the subway would clear her head, and the tatty old coat still had a certain insulating quality, thanks to those furry little deceased rabbits.

At the Church of the Master she paused, but the basement room was quiet tonight. *Never been to church in my life. Never knew what the point was, never good at saying prayers. Atoning . . . too many errors to confess.* She had sometimes envied the Catholics, relieving their minds of guilt by talking to a priest. *Bless me, Father, for I have sinned. Forgive me, because I don't trust You.*

119

You aren't fair, to take a good woman like my mother just when I needed her most. To kill my husband so young, and do it in such a way I've come to hate the man I loved. Forgive me, because I don't want to live in Your world. It's too hard. Forgive me because I don't believe you can fix all this, no matter how many Hail Marys I might say.

She pushed the big wooden door ajar and saw the votive candles flicker wildly in the sudden draft. Slipping inside, she shut it behind her and they quieted down, humble flames that people had lit to remember their dead. Terra wandered into the nave of the church, bigger than she had thought, nice arches, an ornate window behind the cross. Dark now, but in daylight the stained-glass Christ would glow amid his saints.

The place was empty, the pews deserted. She walked slowly forward to take a closer look at the organ, a small pipe organ, but there was a triple row of stops. She had played on one once, in the chapel at Los Alamos. Tricky, working the foot pedals, like rubbing your stomach and patting your head at the same time. But the results were powerful, a sense of creating music out of the earth.

"You want to try it?" The voice startled her. She swung around to find Andrew there, watching. He was dressed in black, no reversed collar, but you sensed these were ministerial clothes.

"Do you work here?" she wondered. "I mean beside being choir master?"

"I'm the assistant pastor," he told her with a smile. "Go ahead, I know you could play it. I mean, after the job you did at rehearsal the other night — that was great."

The boy-pianist had come down with bronchitis and she had offered to play accompaniment for the group. "It's been a long time since I touched a keyboard," she said. "I'm afraid I missed quite a few notes."

"You kept up the tempo admirably. You read music very well." He sat down on the front pew, his body language inviting her to join him. "I don't want to pry, but is there anything troubling you? Something brought you in here tonight. I'd like to help if I can." It was said so simply, she found herself perched beside him like an obedient student. It brought back a fleeting remembrance of Max Wolff, the rescuer who had turned her around and shown her the truth in music.

"Look," he prodded gently, "I'm no miracle worker, but most people don't need miracles. They need someone to talk to and that's what pastors are for."

"I know. I mean, I have known a man who could do that, heal you just by listening."

"Then he's the one you should turn to now."

"Long gone. Before the war," she said with a twinge of sadness.

"You're married, aren't you?"

"Yes. I mean, no. My husband left me, he died." Awkward words that betrayed her hurt.

"And you're angry. Terra, that's common enough. You feel deserted, even though you know it couldn't be helped."

"But it could. He didn't have to do what he did." The whole story poured out of her, Los Alamos, Hiroshima, the bad days afterward when they realized how devastating the price of victory had been. "Phin felt he had to go over there and die. It was more important to him than living. It was more important than me."

Andrew listened gravely, nodding once in a while. "I know," he said. "It's hard on you, but I can sympathize with him. His deepest concern had to be for his immortal soul."

"Phin wasn't a religious person, he never went to synagogue."

"He had the belief, whether he knew it or not. To feel so compelled to atone, this is the characteristic of a man of strong morality. Religious services are just a framework." He glanced around at his church. "They help people to find a faith that is sometimes elusive. Different rituals work for some people, sacramental acts, repetition, rosaries. In our church it's music that draws us closer to the Lord. These simple hymns that everyone can sing — holy, holy, holy — the chants focus our minds toward worship. The voices raised together in praise are a kind of tuning. The way we did it the other night was special, but in church it happens all the time. We make our own force field of belief and optimism. I wish you'd come and try it. You need help to get rid of the rage. Nothing destroys you like anger. Just as love fills you up, fury drains you. It can leave a cold, brittle shell." He took her hand and gripped it hard. Looking up at the multicolored stained glass window he said, in a conversational tone, "Father God, show your daughter the way to inner peace. Help her find the path through all the bitter disappointments and disillusionments of our dangerous world, and bring her home to Your fold. Give her the grace of forgiveness and bless her with an open mind, to receive all the love that will come her way. We pray this in the name of Jesus Christ. Amen."

Stunned, Terra sat speechless. No one had

ever prayed for her personally before. She had her doubts about it now. "Love" was a trap. Forgiveness doesn't work when there's nobody left to forgive. Heartache is a disease, sometimes fatal, and she never did believe in all those New Testament miracles about healing. But that strong hand holding hers imparted some kind of temporary remedy and for that she was grateful. She felt steadier than when she'd walked into this quiet place.

Andrew smiled, relaxed his grip and stood up. "You'll be fine. I sense in you a great inner strength, Terra. And the intelligence to use it. Whether you come to church or not, please keep on with the chorale. You can't weep while you're singing joy to the Lord."

Of course, the momentary panacea got lost on the subway, somewhere between Fourteenth and 86th Street. The sense of permanent loneliness came back, that chilling inner Hell. As she climbed the stairs to the street she pulled the old coat tighter. The mist had turned to drizzle, the streets gleaming in the headlights of the dinner traffic heading down Broadway for the theaters, the pulsing heart of New York. As she turned to walk up to 88th Street she heard soft steps behind her and went alert.

From somewhere off her left elbow came

a low voice speaking words so filthy she wasn't even sure what they meant. In her pocket her fist clenched around the bunch of keys. Those months in San Diego she had taken jujitsu, a class for single women. She braced now for a touch on her arm, but suddenly the footsteps was gone and when she risked a glance back the sidewalk was empty, except for a few late rush-hour commuters scurrying for home with heads down and shoulders bunched.

Refusing to bow to the weather she turned the corner and walked briskly up 88th, trying to think whether she had any Alka Seltzer. Her stomach was queasy, probably due to the gluttonous lunch. She still felt sated. A little nauseous. And it was disconcerting to think that there were low-lifes even in this respectable neighborhood.

As she stood on the top step of the rooming house, trying to settle her key in the door lock, another pedestrian came along, turning in too, heading for the stairs down to the basement apartment. On a hunch she challenged him.

"Shanahan!" Not going to give him the satisfaction of his lethal nickname. "Were you following me?"

Cutter stopped still in his tracks, and looked up at her. His face, caught in the misty glow of the street light, was amazingly unrepentant. "Yes, I was. Thanks be. That bum needed to know that his sort's not welcome in this neighborhood."

"And you just happened to be there?"

"You were late getting home. It's not your music night, and you'd hardly go window shopping in this muck. I was concerned."

"But I'm not your — it's none of your business, to nursemaid me."

"I don't know." He cocked his head, the drizzle standing in droplets on the shock of russet hair. "Doesn't your preacher tell you we're all our brothers' keepers?"

For a panicky minute she thought he must have been following her all the way back from the Church. "What makes you — where did you get the idea that I have a —"

"You practice those religious songs. I just figured."

"Our choral group has nothing to do with church. Nothing at all." She sounded too emphatic even to herself. "And I am able to take care of myself."

"Maybe, but since the war there's no safety anywhere. Used to be a pretty nice neighborhood, but now — did you know we have a cathouse only two blocks over? Doesn't hang out a red light, but the word gets around. I'm seeing some sad types on the street, guys home from the Pacific, lost their balance out there, forgot the old values. Who knows what'll set 'em off. Maybe some nice girl walking home from the subway."

"Okay, I appreciate the thought. But I don't like to be followed — by anyone."

"Whatever you say." He shrugged. "I won't do it again."

As he was turning away she called. "Shanahan." And when he glanced back she added, "If you should just happen to be having a cup of coffee in the shop near the subway and see me come by, I'd be grateful to have you walk home with me." Slight emphasis on the word "with."

Upstairs in her room a few minutes later she scathed herself. *Why did I do that? He'll think I'm encouraging him.* And staring into the mirror at her face, so unfamiliar these days, so tight against the emotions that she was trying to control, she said aloud, "Therissa, you are a complete ninny!"

CHRISTMAS, 1947

Be sure to walk down Fourth Avenue. Why did Ari add that instruction to his directions? Needing to buy one Christmas present, Terra had asked him to advise her on a store with a name that would impress a rich woman in Virginia.

"Wanamakers," he'd said, without thinking twice. "You are full of surprises, Terra Cotta. I wouldn't expect you to care about impressing anybody."

"The Hamiltons are my mother's family, and I don't want to let her memory down, if that makes any sense. My grandmother is the kind of lady who judges you by your good taste."

"So you do come from royalty," he commented. "I've often noticed your chin. It's doing it's princess thing right now, in fact." He gave her a cock-eyed grin. "That's okay, I have nothing against the historical elite. Wouldn't hesitate to join them, if I could, but I will never have the credentials. My own family tree goes back to Poland where it is buried under the ashes of a holocaust."

"A what?"

"You aren't familiar with the word yet? Didn't you see the movies last year that finally revealed what Hitler and Company were up to? All those Jews, the death camps, the ovens. Did you think that was some sort of Hollywood concoction?" The bantering tone was well laced with acid by now.

"I did. I saw the pictures, but it seemed so far removed from all I ever knew of humanity. I guess I didn't realize that the horror might be connected to anyone I know."

"Our family lost seven people in those years. We still hope that one of my uncles is alive somewhere and hiding out, maybe in Norway. By the way, what did those aristocrats of yours think of your late husband being of the Hebrew persuasion?"

"They never met Phin," she said curtly. *And my husband is not for discussion.*

Ari nodded. "None of my business. Okay, you want to buy something wrapped in a touch of class, go down to Wanamakers. Don't take the subway. Be sure to walk lower Fourth Avenue. And don't try to do it on your lunch hour. Take the whole afternoon off."

As she strolled along the undistinguished street Terra was puzzled. It had no special appeal. A few dowdy Christmas trimmings. Along the sidewalk some venders with trays were selling old photographs, family portraits of people long gone and forgotten. Why would anyone want to buy a Daguerreotype of some bearded 19th Century patriarch or an unknown woman in Victorian costume? To create a mythical heritage of their own? It was a touching thought: little did they know that those ancestors had some shocking flaws. Snobbery was the least of it. Self-indulgence. The smugness of the effete. The reason she would never have taken Phin to meet the Hamiltons was that he was head-and-shoulders above them in intellect, in decency, in relevance.

And yet Grandmother Hamilton had been kind to her, and helpful with money in her mother's final days. She had written after Phin's death and invited Terra to come and live at the ancestral mansion in Richmond, at least for a while. An offer politely declined. Even though she was old enough now to fend off Uncle Redmond's advances, Terra would have felt it to be a retreat from reality. From pain, which was part of her personal legacy and should not be avoided.

All she wanted now was to send some small gift that would testify to the fact that she hadn't forsaken her mother's memory. Glancing up she found herself in front of a used book store. And across the street was another. Grungy repositories of the literary past, they touched her strangely, the thought of all those words, all the authors who had lived and died and left a mark on the world.

She went into the nearest and began to browse. The collection was huge and non-judgmental. The Tarzan books stood shoulder to shoulder with the complete works of Byron. In the library where she had worked back in school days, this would have been unthinkable. In fact most bookstores didn't even stock Edgar Rice Burroughs, yet some of his writing was as imaginative as the less readable Jules Verne. She wondered why Ari had directed her to these ghosts of the past. Was it remotely possible that he was a touch nostalgic himself?

Two hours and four book stores later, she rounded a corner — and saw Wanamakers. A tall and ancient building dominating one whole block of New York City, it too was of another time. The window displays of Fifth Avenue had been clever and lively. Here was Turn-of-the-Century elegance, the decorations rich and hung with dignity. Inside, the store had a quiet aura of holiday cheer, tinsel and lace and very tall ceilings populated by pale angels. An open wrought-iron cage, the elevator lifted her slowly above the panorama of the great lobby into the upper reaches where the uniformed operator called out the virtues of each floor. "Household furnishings, children's toys, ladies clothing . . ."

Terra spent an hour wandering the aisles before she gravitated back down to the cosmetics department. A certain sachet that her mother had loved — of course, they had it. They would indeed gift-wrap it and send it, and she was sure it would be done with such class that even the Hamiltons would be impressed. Mainly, she knew that the delicate scent would remind Grandmother of her departed child, and that was the only gift Terra could think of that would matter in that ancient house. She felt a little sorry for the lot. No Hamilton had ever ridden a subway.

Of course, the concert tonight, they would approve. They had always wanted a performing artist in the family. Late in the afternoon Terra frowned, as she brushed her hair, parted it down the middle and began to braid it. The whole focus of her early life had been on becoming a prominent musician. So what if now she was just one of a hundred? It was Carnegie Hall and you don't get any more high-class than that.

They had first walked onto the great stage for dress rehearsal last Saturday, awed at the ornate glory of the famous auditorium. The seats were dotted with kibitzers, musicians from other groups, places like Juillard, the New School, students, teachers from the Art Students' League, the City Center. By now The Mastersingers were becoming well known in the city, and the word had got around that this was going to be a special concert. Andrew told the group in a hushed voice as they gathered on stage that some of the pick of New York's cultural elite had come to listen in as they ran through the program for the first time with orchestral accompaniment.

"Why didn't they be decent and pay for their tickets," one of the men groused.

"Because the performance is sold out." Andrew broke forth his most beatific smile. There was a kind of glow around him, Terra thought, not visible, but you could feel it. "Which means we will break even on the concert." It had not been cheap to engage a mighty hall and all its attendants, including a great brass section, tympani, a small string section and a few glorious woodwinds from

133

the Philharmonic. Backed up by such strength, the chorus had burst out in elation, and that's when Terra felt it — the thing that Max Wolff had once tried to describe to her: When the audience is hit by that stream of energy they give it back like a powerful reflector, returning a giant "Yes!"

But that was rehearsal. Tonight, as she looked in her mirror, she searched for a glimmer of elation and saw only a worried face. *Why did I think I could sing? I'll be a sour note, I'll ruin the tuning.* The only reason she went on dressing was the thought that maybe when she saw Andrew the confidence would come back.

She had decided to wear a new green silk dress which she had bought, hoping it would give her some holiday spirit. Of course they would all be clad in long red robes to the floor, the dress wouldn't show. But it felt good on her skin. You grasp at small pleasures. But it hadn't worked. For some reason, tonight the darkness was pressing in on her extra hard. *If only Phin were going to be out there in the audience. . . .*

Almost everyone had got tickets for friends or relatives. Terra shrugged off the thought. The only kin she had was Dixie, who wasn't even vaguely interested in music. Tying a scarf over her head, she went on downstairs thinking she might walk the thirty blocks to the Hall, try to summon some imitation euphoria. As she stepped outside she saw a familiar figure waiting on the stoop, one hip hitched onto the stone banister. As if the night air weren't frigidly cold, he looked comfortable, patient.

"Evening, ma'am."

"Hello, Shanahan. Aren't you freezing half to death, sitting out here?"

"In Montana this would just be a nice night," he said, standing up and falling in beside her as she went down the flight of steps to the sidewalk. "Thought I'd walk you up to the taxi stand, if that's all right with you."

"Well, thanks. Certainly, it's okay. Only I wasn't planning to take a taxi."

"I am," he said carelessly. "You can share mine. If you want."

"Where are you off to tonight?"

"Well, there's a concert going on down at Carnegie, and I've got a ticket," he said seriously. "Never been there, so it seemed high time."

"How did you — ?" She broke off.

"Mastersingers. Right?"

Of course. She had hurled the word at him in a rush to distance herself from the con-

135

notations of "church." And there had been quite a large ad in last Sunday's paper.

"Fact is, I sort of wanted to see what all that practicing was about. I like choruses, I like Christmas music." He was explaining himself under duress. Cutter was not a person to make excuses. The fact registered on her that he was presentably dressed in a dark overcoat and even appeared to be wearing a necktie.

"Well, I hope you won't be disappointed," she said. "I'm personally not in very good voice tonight."

"It'll come when you walk out on stage," he told her matter-of-factly, as they headed up the street. "I've never been a performer, but I've known a few."

"Well, the rehearsal went okay," she said, trying to make conversation, awkward and resentful that once again he seemed to feel he had to shepherd her around. "We have a very good conductor."

"I read that on the posters outside the Hall. A minister from some church downtown?"

"That's right. Andrew Farrell, assistant pastor at Church of the Master."

"Is he inclined to be open to suggestion?"

The question rattled her. It would never

occur to her to suggest anything to Andy. "Why?"

They had reached 86th Street where a taxi was parked at the stand. Helping her in, he took a seat beside her. "Carnegie," he said to the driver and they moved off into traffic.

"Why did you — ?" She couldn't let it go, the question disturbed her.

"I'd like to make a request." Shanahan hesitated. "I hope it won't offend you, but it seems to me that — well, faith! I can only come right out with it: I wish you'd let your hair down. You look like a Quaker in those braids. But if you let it fall loose — and you'll be in one of those long robes, right? Let it down and you could pass for a heavenly herald, singing joy to the world. It's just more artistic."

Terra fought an impulse to laugh — and laugh and laugh. Shutting down the panicky urge, she tried to think of a polite way to answer him. He didn't seem to need it, settling back in the taxi, looking out the window. Said his say, and that was all.

"Uh — I appreciate your advice. I'll — uh — take it up with Andrew."

"I know you think I'm daft," he said agreeably. "Now go ahead and forget it. I don't want you to be distracted with your big event coming up."

In front of the Hall they went separate ways, she scurrying for the stage entrance while he paid off the taxi. In the dressing room she found others already gathering, Andrew distributing the long scarlet robes. Amid the nervous chatter she put hers on. Fingered her braids.

"You know what somebody told me," she said offhand to the group at large. "That we should take our hair down, let it fall over our shoulders. So we look like angel choristers from on high." Laughter.

Andrew didn't even smile. He looked ajar with discovery. "Good Lord, what a great idea!" It eased the self-conscious tension that had gripped them. In a flurry of fingers and hairpins, the girls unwound their chignons, Terra used her fingers to comb out her braids. Some of the girls had bobs, and no one's hair was as long as hers. But a good number of them were flowing now with blond and brunette locks around their shoulders.

"Has anybody got a comb?"

"I have."

"Here's mine." The men all seemed to have one.

With sudden gaiety they lined up to file on stage where the musicians were tuning instruments, tootling little flurries on horns, the mellow tones of oboe and French horn dissonant in the way of all orchestras before a concert. Out in the great Hall the massed audience was murmurous with talk, muted laughter. A sense of expectation rippled the air. And Terra felt an eddy of spirit herself, thinking how edifying it would be for Shanahan to see all these long locks he had provoked.

Magically, the crowd went quiet as the choralists moved onstage, two crimson rows. Andrew raised his expressive hands and the kettle drums beat a solemn opening.

"Christians be joyful . . ."

After the show, backstage the anti-room was filled with friends, families, babbling about the music, hugging each other. And there among them, looking perfectly at ease as part of the theater crowd, was Cutter Shanahan. It was the first time Terra had got a good look at him in his concert mode: overcoat across one arm, practically natty in his dark blue suit, his hair gleaming like brushed copper. When he saw her, long tresses still rippling over her shoulders, his face struggled with a smile that finally won out — she got a glimpse of white teeth.

"Hello," he said. "It was a wonderful

concert. The Mastersingers are worthy of the name." No doubt that he meant it, his eyes were the color of straight whiskey held against an inner light.

"Thank you." For a minute Terra almost wished she were the girl, whoever she might be, that he once loved. *(Who was she, how did he lose her forever?)* She half expected him to sweep her up in a great hug, aware that this was a moment to be shared. It was a temptation to imagine that this was Phin, just to feel it again, the old joy.

Gone, girl! And don't look back. She went into reverse fast, defense mechanism. Trying to distance herself, she grew chilly and remote, plunged into an unreasonable gloom.

So of course the evening went sour. All the way home in the taxi together, she and the Irishman sat apart by common consent. A proper Celt, he picked up on her gloom and turned moody too. At the door of the apartment building they separated like a couple of strangers.

On the final arrival of the eve of the holiday Terra was in a lonely place; the office itself felt alien. *Why must everybody celebrate?* She ached with sadness, in an absolute fever for Christmas to be over.

"It's an unfortunate custom which seems to have perpetuated itself for reasons that pass all understanding," Ari said with his usual sardonic grimace, "but it seems on this most un-Jewish of all eves I must ask you out to lunch and you must accept. I hope Chock Full O' Nuts is okay, because their coffee gives me a reason to go on living."

"Thanks, but I'd just as soon stay and finish this index."

"Oh, we'll get it done if we have to spend all next week on it. But as I said, tradition must be observed, and this is the only present you'll get from me, so put on your silly little hat."

For some reason his sour demeanor suited Terra's spirits, as she donned the Flemish bonnet that she had left on the rack ever since the ill-conceived luncheon with Karl. It was hardly a day to dress up. A gray sky was shedding a slight mist. The tarnished garlands that hung from the light poles on Fourth Avenue were beginning to droop. The street was slick and the traffic impatient, honking at the crowds of late shoppers who looked harassed. It was almost two o'clock so the eating places were half empty. They had no trouble finding a seat at the counter in the coffee house.

"Nutty cheese sandwich and a bowl of pea soup," Terra said, and Ari gave her a grin.

"You've been here before."

"My favorite place after the Automat."

"Selection's good there. Coffee's better here."

The food was set before them by a weary waitress in a very crisp uniform. It was said that the management of the franchise was rabid about cleanliness.

"So here's to the old holiday spirit." Grimly Ari raised his cup. "My own favorite memory of the season goes back to the third grade when I beat the crap out of a snotty little goy who told me a 'kike' had no business attending the Christmas party."

Terra tried to bring up a memory she could bear to share. But there had been little to recall from the strange episodic celebrations at Los Alamos, festivities sandwiched in between work sessions, mistletoe and holly and talk about isotopes and triggering devices, and Phin scribbling equations on the tablecloth. Much less did she want to remember the one last year a few weeks after she'd received the news that he wasn't coming back from Hiroshima with the rest of the team of scientists? Trying to understand why atonement was more important than his marriage, or his brilliant

142

future, or the needs of a new world? The only words of that letter which stayed with her was the one sentence, "I look at this ruined city and I feel heartsick." Resentment swelled inside her like a lump. She couldn't eat the sandwich.

"O-kay, you've lost your appetite, I'm sorry." Ari said. "Let's change the subject. I hear you've been doing some singing."

"Yeah." It must have been Gilda who passed that along. "The concert was last Sunday. We were sold out."

"I'm impressed." With a smirk that meant he wasn't.

"Me, too," she said carelessly. "Carnegie Hall is pretty impressive, especially when you've got half the New York Philharmonic backing you up."

"Wait a minute. Carnegie? I read about that concert in the Times, and their critic is a hard nut to crack. He said they were — what was the name? The Mastersingers — he said they were outstanding. Don't tell me you're in that bunch?"

Fine, I won't tell you.

"You really are a puzzle wrapped in an enigma," Ari marveled, with momentary sincerity. "So old-fashioned in that pilgrim bonnet, and yet so secretly modern. Terra Incognito, did you ever think of going back to college and getting a degree?"

She shook her head. "Not unless they give a doctorate in Who Cares?"

It shocked him. In the homely face with its usual black stubble and sardonic mouth, the right eye was fixed and appalled, while the left wandered like a lost soul. For once Ari was speechless. At last he said, "Who the hell did this to you?"

The man I adored. She said, "I think I was born under a black star."

"There's no such thing. There are novas and supernovas, which lead to black holes, but —"

"There you go. A black hole." She liked the analogy.

"You know, you could attend CCNY for free. You're a resident of Manhattan. They give a good education — I'm a graduate of their hallowed halls. You know the buildings, down there off Washington Square? Easy to get in, hard to stay there. One student in three flunks out the first semester, but then you seem to like a challenge."

"Once, a long time ago, I'd have been interested. But I bet you have to have some great goal, some idea at least what you want to major in. I haven't a clue." She shook her head. "Never did, really. My mother wanted a musical career for me, but I never felt that drive you need to make it happen. Now, I don't feel much of anything, except sore."

"Toward whom?"

He would be grammatically correct, she thought irritably. "Whom," she said, "is the United States government, mostly."

"Apart from our Harry, I suppose? Karl tells me you admire Mr. Truman."

Why would they be talking about me and the President? "Yes," she said. "He's okay. I'm thinking of the nameless crowd that runs the store. Like taking our income taxes and giving the money to Germany and Japan to get back on their feet and undersell us on making steel and clothes. And the people who say big industries are better than little businesses, so pretty soon there won't be any mom-and-pop grocery stores. Or the folks who make junky cars and junky houses and are turning the cities into second-rate rubbish." Terra wasn't sure where all that had come from.

It must have been building up since San Diego. The returning veterans who wanted to start small shops couldn't begin to compete with the new giant corporations that had taken over during the war. Kroger had opened their supermarkets and the great A&P had grown to dominate whole neighborhoods . . . Remotely she realized that Ari was saying something.

". . . channel all that fury to good purpose. But you have to know where to direct it. Have you ever thought of the New School?"

"I've heard of it."

"The New School for Social Research — it's a lively unconventional place with courses that can orient you politically. In fact I'm going to be teaching there after the first of the year. Night school, a course in sociology."

"Good for you," she said carelessly.

"Well, it is and it isn't. Teaching is going to take up two evenings of my week until ten o'clock at night. To make the Long Island train out to Katonah I'll have to leave early and run like hell, and even then I'd only get about two hours' sleep before I'd have to get up and head back into the city."

Terra was mildly fascinated, to hear Ari talk straight for once, about a subject which mattered to him.

"The bottom line is, I need a room in town. Nothing fancy, it wouldn't do me any good to spend my New School salary on an expensive apartment, defeat the purpose of the night job. So I wondered if there were any openings in your building?"

"Huh?" Then she realized he meant it. "No. I don't think — I mean I know there aren't any right now. Of course," she added flippantly, "you could always start an affair with Gilda. Maybe she would let you share her bed." It was funny, to picture the receptionist, who was terrified of Ari, ushering him in . . .

"I'd rather share yours," he said, so mildly, it took a minute to register.

That's Ari. Back to his outrageous self. "I doubt if your wife would like that."

"My wife," he said soberly, "is a wonderful woman. She's highly intelligent, in fact, she's a perfectionist. That's why I married her. She's a great mother, but —"

"I didn't know you had a child."

"Two of them. Son, Daoud. Daughter, Miriam. He's five, very nice, like my wife. The girl is three years old, and can read already. Nothing difficult, right now it's the Wizard of Oz. Fantasy is fine for small children. Stimulates their imagination. Time enough for her to start tackling the New Republic in the first grade. Point is, they will both need to go to college, which is why I'm moonlighting. To get back to your question," he went on, "my wife never monitors what I do when I'm not home. Wouldn't occur to her. But she does like it when I'm not deprived of sleep. I can be a bear around the house when I'm tired. So I'd say she wouldn't mind if I found a bed in town even if it included a roommate. What's the trouble, you look shocked? Of course, you would be. You're the child from the boonies with a golden ruler up her back. But old-fashioned morals are gone now, the war did that. All that matters is logic and reason, common for-God's-sake sense."

She couldn't grasp it. Ari really didn't see anything wrong with being unfaithful to his wife? Didn't his wedding vows say something about *keeping only unto you?* Did he think fidelity was obsolete?

"You can't be worrying about sex?" he snorted. "You're much too worldly for that. Not sophisticated, of course, but you've been through all sorts of misery. You've been married, you must realize by now that the simple pleasures of the bedroom don't matter a damn in the big scheme of things. Sex is just one part of life, like eating, we all need it. I know that you and I would have fun together, so think about it."

"What I think," she said slowly, "is that I'll go home now and go to sleep in my own bed alone and not get up for a hundred years. Thanks for the lunch. Tell them at work that I'm taking the afternoon off, I don't feel too well."

"Uh-uh," he said. "Can't do that. We're

expected at Manisch's office in about twenty minutes for the usual fatherly blessing and our bonuses. Joy to the world, washed down with a glass of champagne. Did I mention we all have to make a toast. Our boss is a consummate sadist."

"Now I *know* I'm going home."

"Woman, please don't do that to me. If you fail to join us strange things will happen. You will be found wanting and probably have to do penance. Manisch never fires you, he just makes your life miserable. Never mind my inappropriate offer, but the fact is at the office I need you. Half my kingdom if you'll come back and go through the motions of merriment." He was kidding now, but beneath his banter was the earnest ring of truth.

"All right. For a little while." Terra stood up and got out a quarter to lay beside her plate. "No, I insist. The tip is on me. It's all the gift you're going to get from me, so make the most of it."

The party had already begun when they got there. Everyone had gathered in Manisch's office. Karl Dorfman was pouring from a huge bottle of champagne. Terra thought the chatter seemed a little forced. Ruth Jones looked nervous as she drifted in Dorfman's wake like an adoring acolyte, hair vibrant with fresh blue rinse. Henrietta Moon seemed anchored to a spot by the big globe on a stand in the corner, as if to lay claim to the world, one way or another. Her fist was clenched defiantly around her glass of bubbly. Buddy and Gilda made an odd couple by the bookcase. He held his champagne glass in a fierce grip, as if it were a water glass. She had already downed half of hers.

Center stage, Manisch stood dapper in a pinstriped gray suit that matched his eyebrows. "Here they are." The expansive smile was a trifle impatient with the late comers. "Now we're a family. Pour these folks a drink, Karl."

The smell of liquor in the room added to the growing unease in Terra's stomach, but she took the glass politely.

"Our custom," the boss was explaining, "is for each of us to hail the season in his own way. Buddy, start us off."

"Here's to Santa Claus," he held up his drink.

"To Santa Claus," they all echoed solemnly until Gilda giggled and they all smiled. Buddy wasn't sure exactly why. Terra had eased around the room to the President's private restroom. Stepping inside she poured out the champagne and filled her glass at the basin, while the others were kidding the mail clerk, asking what he wanted in his stocking.

When she rejoined the circle she stood next to Henrietta, who hadn't missed a thing. In a sotto voce she said, "It's bad luck to toast with water."

"I'll take the risk," Terra muttered back.

"All right, all right. Who's next?" Manisch glanced around. "Ari, do the honors."

"Here's to finishing the index on Smith's Civil War Book and may he spend his days in Hell alphabetizing an unabridged dictionary." They toasted that with common sympathy.

"Gilda, the golden." Manisch raised his glass in the girl's direction and she went into a flutter.

"Okay-y-y. Let me think. Here's to me getting a boyfriend next year."

Cheers all around.

Dorfman leered at her and raised his glass. "I'll give you my number after work, Gorgeous."

Ruth Jones almost gagged on her champagne. With all of them looking at her, she choked, hastily, "Here's to love."

"Can't say anything against that," Manisch chuckled. "Henrietta, my dear, let's hear from you."

Ready and waiting, she raised her glass. "Here's to the little people who have been forgotten over the years, but will be heard from soon."

They glanced around at each other, suddenly nervous, all except Manisch. "Good sentiment, my dear lady. And before you all get the jitters, let me say that I am quite aware of your decision to join the UOWPA and I applaud it. For too long the office workers have fallen into a crack between labor and management, their lives unshielded by any kind of protection. One tip: make sure you demand retirement benefits. Then, whenever you are ready I will negotiate with you and I can tell you that whatever requests you make, within reason, will be respected." His clever face was so reassuring it spread its own kind of holiday spirit. Picking up a stack of envelopes from the desk, he went on. "In fact your Christmas bonuses will be somewhat fatter this year, because I'm proud to be your boss, and I hope you'll be happy here in the future. Satisfied employees make for good profits." He began to hand them around.

Henrietta looked bemused, his speech having punctured her rhetorical balloon. Glancing inside the envelope, she shut the flap quickly and put it in the pocket of her sedate blue tunic dress. Gilda was staring at her check with open joy.

"Oh wow, thank you sir!"

Terra had hesitated to open her own; she'd only been with the company four months, after all. But the others were all inspecting theirs, so she slipped a finger under the flap and peeked inside. The bonus amounted to an extra month's pay. It floored her with its generosity. She raised her head to find Manisch watching her, smiling a little at her reaction.

"Thank you, sir," she managed. "Thanks a lot."

Dorfman seemed a little miffed to be shunted to the background. Raising his glass, he said loudly, snidely, "Well, I've got a toast. Here's to the gentle Jew of Jerusalem who made this hullabaloo possible."

His tone jolted them all unpleasantly.

Manisch frowned. "I have an idea that Terra can make a better one. What's your toast my dear."

Without hesitation she raised her glass. Articulating as delicately as a rabbi, she said, "To Hanukkah."

In the awkward silence that followed, they heard a rapping on the door of the front office.

Ten minutes later in the cab Terra said to

Dixie, "Your timing was perfect. Lord, you do know how to make an entrance!"

Dressed in a tuxedo of green velvet topped by a red bow tie, looking like one of her own fashion sketches, Dixie had ankled in on four-inch green satin heels to join the group looking like a caricature of the spirit of Christmas. Her pixie face she had made uglier by the deliberately outrageous makeup, very black mascara, greenish eye shadow, red mouth like a wound. "Hate to break up your fun, sister dearest, but we're all waiting for you at our tea-dance uptown."

Leaving an astounded office family behind, Terra had grabbed her coat, hastily pinned on the Flemish bonnet, and followed green velvet down to where a taxi was waiting. To be out of that clogged atmosphere of false conviviality was such a relief she didn't question what new frying pan she might be jumping into.

"I had an idea you'd be trapped in an office party," Dixie was going on, "and it seemed too selfish of me to be having fun while you suffered." The cabbie was threading his way through Fifth Avenue traffic, honking wildly at pedestrians, windshield wipers flailing at the rain which was turning to snow. Late shoppers scurried before it and the street was shining with headlight glare. "Those people back there looked lethal."

"I've been to a few office parties before," Terra said, "but never one where the Christmas spirit was held in such contempt."

"That's New York. It's a great place, but I hate it at holiday time. That's why I always try to help the less fortunate by throwing my own bash, where people can be themselves." They had pulled up in front of an apartment hotel, the doorman stepping forward with an umbrella. Elderly, black, elegant in a white uniform with gold buttons, he helped them out of the taxi adeptly and through a polished brass door into a lobby deep in luxury.

"Thank you, Chuckles. Merry Christmas."

Soberly he folded the umbrella. "May I wish you the same, Miss Dixie."

As they moved on toward the elevator, she bent closer to whisper, "No one has ever seen the man smile."

"You don't actually live here?" The floor looked like genuine Italian marble.

"Yeah, isn't it swanky? Like I told you, Zoey is richer than plum pudding. After those early years when we slaved and sweated together in the marketplace, all at once the aunt dies and leaves her whole estate to her beloved niece, Zolinda. I can tell you this, it's more fun being rich than poor." She pushed a button and the elevator rose almost unnoticeably.

In a narrow foyer on the fifth, Dixie bent to insert a key in the only door on that floor. Over her shoulder she said, "My beloved guests are already pretty well snockered. Don't mind their antics. Just wander around and have some snacks. I'll get Herbie to make you a non-alcoholic beverage, with some orange juice in it. You look malnourished."

"Herbie?"

"It sort of adds flavor to life, to have a male maid." Dixie's mouth twisted in an impish sneer. "He's cute, he actually blushes." As she opened the door, noise gushed out at them, a chatter of feminine voices, trilling of laughter. There must have been thirty women in the big ornate room. "Here, I'll take that," Dixie appropriated the bedraggled fur coat. "Geez, girl, you really need a new garment, something in a nice seal —"

"I will never again wear fur," Terra said irritably. The coat looked unusually shabby hanging in that rack of sables and minks. "Animals are human, too." Phin had taught her that, among so many other things.

"If you say so, but get *something* that has

at least some touch of New York about it. And the hat. For *God's* sake take off the hat."

"Oh, yes, the hat. I was going to thank you for it, even though I know it was a joke. But I like it, I really do."

"Thank me for — ?"

"Giving me the hat."

"Me? I wouldn't even go into a store that showed a hat like that."

"You wouldn't go into Altman's?"

"You're kidding? Dear God, I hope that isn't some preview of the spring styles. What made you think I — ? Oh, here's Zoey."

"Welcome." The pretty little thing came up to join them. Such shining candor in her wide blue eyes, it was a relief after the aura of false cheer that Terra had left back at the office. "I'm so glad you would come."

"Nice of you to have me." Terra fought a small tickle in her chest, trying not to cough. "I can just stay long enough to say 'Holiday Greetings' and so forth. I'm really not feeling too well." I think I'm coming down with a cold."

"Well, orange juice for sure, then." Dixie beckoned and a young man came over. So thin he looked malnourished, his face was blank as a mannequin's. "Herbie, fix my sister a screw-driver without the screw, please."

"Dix, if you didn't send me that hat, who did?"

"You must have a secret admirer. With very bad taste. Get rid of him at once. Oh, excuse me a minute, there's one of my best customers, I have to go genuflect."

Herbie was back with the glass of juice, ornamented by a sprig of mint. She thanked him, and the boy's stolid face came alive for an instant. They looked at each other. In a low voice, she said, "Is there a back way out of here?"

"Yes, madam," with perfect comprehension. "I'll just get your coat."

He surpassed himself, he also brought a dark waterproof hood that protected the hat. "It's raining harder out there," he explained. "The freight elevator will let you out in an alley. Go around front and get the doorman to flag you a taxi."

It was turning to snow as, a few minutes later, she stepped out into the alley and followed it to Fifth Avenue where the urbane "Chuckles" was helping a newly arriving pair of women whose furs and high heels gave no hint as to who was which, and who did what to whom in the merrier hours of the night. Terra didn't want to think about it. Her stomach was truly queasy; she breathed in the cold air gratefully.

Walking up toward the nearest stop light she looked for a cab stand. Then remembered, this was Fifth and there were no subway entrances. At the corner she paused and glanced around to get her bearings. Eighty-sixth Street — she was directly opposite her own neighborhood on the West Side only the width of Central Park away. She hardly gave it a thought. Running across with the light she followed the street into the darkness of the Park.

The far-flung lamps hung dimly in the thickening snowfall, but the cross-town traffic was brisk enough to light her way. And the sense of isolation was welcome. Flakes on her lips, crystals crunching underfoot, it took her back to a time — so long ago — five years? She and Phin had run together down a cobbled street in Gloucester Town, with the hoot of the train in the distance and snow flowing in their eyes. A time when everything was ahead, when maybe she could have reversed the course of fate. But she wouldn't have. It was too inevitable, a sequence of events that had to be played out.

As she walked other memories drifted in, the path through the woods to Max Wolff's house, that horrible cottage he had inherited from the French teacher who was on sabbatical. The place was dripping with ruffles and flourishes, but the piano was stark and honest and powerful under his hands. One snowy afternoon they had played a duet together, side by side on the bench . . .

And they were together in another snowstorm. They had gone to Washington, D.C. for a concert. That was the night Max had deserted her abruptly to return to Switzerland on the eve of war. *What is there about me that draws these men who can't stay?* That night, instead of taking the train she had climbed into an unfamiliar car and tried to drive it back to Gloucester. Wrapped it around the piling of a bridge at Fredricksburg. Awful memories, but she had been young, she had survived. Now she was old and it was all over.

Out of the woods, crossing Central Park West, Terra had lost track of time. Just aware that her feet were totally numb and she suspected the pumps were ruined forever, didn't matter. *Thank heaven for the rain hood, the hat's been saved the worst of it. Drat Dixie, I love this hat.* Still two long blocks to go to Broadway. She was getting awfully tired, a little dazed. *Shanahan, did you buy me a hat?*

But the thought flitted away. She forgot where she was for a moment, had to think hard — wanted to make it home. Concentrating, she focused on the streetlight ahead, putting one step after another. Breathed a hoarse sigh of relief when she saw the snow-rusted sign: 86th Street.

A tremor shook her. *I'm not going to make it.* Panic . . . knees starting to buckle. *I really am sick.*

Urgently an arm came around her and bolstered her warping body. He was muttering ". . . . had a hunch. I knew you were probably at some party, but — good God, you're soaking wet." Cutter had picked up speed, walking her along, faster than she wanted to go, half carrying her. "Why weren't you on the subway?

"Walked over from the East Side . . . through the park."

"Angels and ministers of grace!" He was opening the rooming-house door now, dragging her inside.

She blinked at the sight of that long flight of stairs. *Never make it.*

"I can't carry you properly," he was explaining, "because I've got a tricky right shoulder. It dislocates when I put strain on it. So it's got to be — this way." Bending, he took her over his left shoulder and ran up the stairs as easily as if she were a child. *Now I know how a sack of potatoes feels.* She thought that was very witty and snickered and coughed and they were in her room. He sat her down on the bed.

"Take those clothes off right now, fast." He tossed the terrycloth robe at her. "I'm going to run you a hot bath."

Afterward Terra was not quite sure what happened. The next days were scrambled in her feverish mind, just a muddle of impressions, snatches of conversation.

". . . ought to be in a hospital."

"Gilda, if you can figure how to get her to a hospital . . . There isn't a vehicle moving in this city, including the subways. Broadway looks like a graveyard of abandoned cars. It's going to take a week to untangle the mess."

"But she's dying, I think."

"We're all dying. It's just a question of when. Bunny, look at me."

Bunny? When did Phin start calling me Bunny?

"You listening, girl? Don't you dare go and die on me. It's bad for my reputation as an innkeeper."

Phin has red hair, I never knew that . . .

Later another fragment reached her. "How many aspirin left?"

162

"Not many, about six. They're not doing any good anyway."

"They're all we've got. Maybe a little brandy would help —"

"No alcohol!" she managed to get the words out. *"Not ever!"*

"Got it," he said. "So brew up some tea, Gilda. Could you quit with the gloom and get useful?"

"What use is tea?"

"It'll make her sweat. That's the only thing that helps, sweat the fever out of her."

"How do you know?"

"Where I grew up in Montana there wasn't a doctor for fifty miles. We made do. Tea is one of the best cures there is. If you won't make it, then sit and hang onto her hand, and I will."

"Hang onto her? You think that's going to — ?"

"Damn it, just do it."

Hands, yes, it works. Need something to hold to keep from falling down the long skid. Forget tea, I hate tea, I had enough tea for all my life.

And later, something out of a spoon. *Don't want something in a spoon, what is it?*

"Well, I don't want to give it to her either, but we've got to get her to sleep. She needs to replenish her strength to fight the fever, and laudanum will do that, if it doesn't send her too far under. What would you do, just sit there?"

"There's worse things than doing nothing."

"Not after this long."

How long? Long long time, so long . . . whatever was in the spoon, everything faded out into a deeper blackness.

It seemed strange, to wake up with a clear head, to hear the little sounds like icicles dripping, the radiator knocking as it always did when the heat rose. To crack an eyelid and see sunlight driving in the back window, must be afternoon. *I slept the clock around.* Terra turned over and tried to sit up but the blankets were piled too deep. *They must be made of lead.*

Out in the hallway voices . . . she recognized Gilda's bronze contralto. "Well, if the deli wasn't open how'd you get the soup?"

"The lady owns the place is a friend, she likes to make soup. Now if we can get the patient to eat a little — I think she's thrown off the fever, but she's going to be almighty weak."

They came in together and stopped when they saw Terra hitched up on her elbows, awake and aware. "You two look like consp . . . con . . . you're plotting things."

"Plotting to get you back in shape," Shanahan said readily. "Get some pillows, Gil. How you feel, Bunny?"

"What's — why — who's Bunny?"

"Sorry," he said sheepishly. "I didn't mean to take liberties, but you looked just like a little wet cottontail the other night when you came out of the park and collapsed in my arms."

"Did not. Did not collapse."

"That's it, good. Fight back. You feed her the soup, Gil. I've got to go down and kick the oil burner again. It's cold in here."

"Don't make an enemy of the thing," Gilda called after him. Then with a wry grin, she said to Terra, "He's not so bad after all."

"Listen — mm, good soup — listen, was Andrew here? Or did I dream that?"

"Who's Andrew?"

"The Pastor down at my church."

"No, nobody's been here but the two of us. The blizzard smacked down this city like Joe Louis flattening Max Baer. Eighteen inches in twenty-four hours, and they don't know what to do with the snow. Been wrestling with it for four days, hauling some of it over to the river, but mostly they're shoveling it down the manhole covers. Talk about panic, I swear you'd think people were going to die of starvation, the way they rushed out to the shops and cleaned the shelves. Landsakes, back in Indiana we had one or two sidewinders every winter, didn't even close the schools."

The chatter of the girl's voice brought a profound comfort over Terra. She pushed the soup spoon away and delved back into the pillows, asleep before she knew it.

When she roused again it was morning, the sun was slanting across the rooftops to light the houses across the courtyard. Cheerful damned sun, downright smug, shining on all that snow. The blanket load seemed lighter, she managed to push them aside and get up. Knees buckled a fraction, stayed in bed too long. *Did somebody mention four days! Must be wrong about that.*

Over by the radiator a makeshift clothesline was hung with nightgowns, her nightgowns. She looked down to find herself decked in a man's blue flannel shirt, felt good, felt warm. She moved slowly over to the wash basin, toilet in the corner behind a curtain. She seemed to remember Gilda helping her over to it a couple of times in the midst of the dizziness. *But it can't be four days?*

She had just managed to make it back to bed when Shanahan walked in. "How d'you

166

feel?" He eyed her with an air of satisfaction.

"I'll live."

"Damned right, b'gorra! How about some coffee? We're all out of tea."

"Shan, did you buy me a hat?"

"Now why would the man do a thing like that? What he did do was whittle a bit while sitting around being useless this week. Here." He set down on the bedside table a chunk of wood the size of a baseball. The color was strange, an orange flame of sap wood against darker red hardwood. The grain subtly dictated the contours of — a rabbit.

Terra looked at the carving, beguiled. "You made this?"

"Yep."

"It's — good. I mean really good, it's beautiful."

"Glad you like it. I had that piece of co-cabola hanging around for a while, felt like whittling on it. Happy New Year, Bunny."

January, 1948

Bundled in her new coat, Terra sat on the bench soaking up the sun's heat and staring out across the Hudson River. Something nagged at her, a thought, a recollection . . . during those lost days of Christmas she was sure that she had seen Andrew.

Not exactly. She hadn't seen him, but he had been beside her. As she floated with the currents of fever and sorrow in a kind of daze, too weary to fight the drift, knowing it would take her eventually to a place of limbo where she wouldn't have to think any more, she felt him come. He took her hand, strength flowing into her almost against her will. Words, not spoken but resonating in her brain . . . "Hang on, I am with you."

And yet both Shanahan and Gilda had said it was impossible, with the snow paralyzing the city. Even the subways had been closed down when torrents of snow-melt had flowed into the tunnels. A hundred-year blizzard, they were calling it. There were still piles of soot-blackened snow in humps around Riverside Park. Melting fast now under the sun.

Terra luxuriated in it, as if she could feel her skin drinking in the essence of the bright sky. One o'clock on a working day, she felt guilty just to sit here, but she wasn't ready yet to face the irritations of the office. Anyway, it didn't matter. She had no future to worry over. Impatiently, she wondered: *Why didn't I just go on floating? Get it over with? So easy, no need to make plans how to do it or when or where. Just let it happen. Now I have to think about it.*

But not today. It felt good to just sit here in the sun. Enjoy this new coat. Something about cashmere bestows instant *noblesse*. One of the Hamiltons' favorite words, they were loaded with inherent nobility. They would have loved the coat. Of course they would despise Dixie. She had arrived at the rooming house two days ago carrying the oversized garment box and chattering, which she did when suffering from insecurity.

"I swear it was like a miracle. I happened to be walking through Lord and Taylor's and my mind flashed back to something mom taught me years ago, namely, that right after Christmas you can find great bargains in the will-call. People can't get up the money to make the payments, store doesn't want to return the stuff to inventory. I was drawn by a magical force right straight back to the stock room, and there was this coat, with your name written all over it. Doesn't contain a scrap of dead-animal fur, though there is now a small herd of goats running around the Himalayas in their skivvies."

Speechless, Terra had buried her face in the soft folds. A light brown color, the natural hue of the shearing, it conveyed an elegance so muted she knew she would be comfortable with it, and still feel like a secret princess. "You're right — this is the work of a magician."

Dixie relaxed then, her cheekiness took over. "Yep, I really am good at my profession. How many times does anyone ever know for sure what they were meant to do and be? Ter, I am so dead-happy it's indecent."

Terra envied her. But then, she always had. The only time in her life she had felt a touch of that kind of joy was in the first year of her marriage to Phin, and even then they were shadowed by the knowledge of what was to come.

"Listen," she said, "I'm sorry I ducked out so fast on the party last week, but I could tell I was coming down with something. No point spreading it around like a Christmas present."

Dixie nodded. "I started to get hurt, but then I realized you really had looked fragile, and Herbie bore witness to the fact that you were feverish, though how he knew that — ?" She frowned at the thought.

"I think I was staggering a little. I barely made it home. Anyhow, I'm sorry I couldn't stay longer. I like your Zoey, she has a lovely smile."

"And the rest of the crowd you hated. I know, they can be awfully overt. It's sort of shocking until you get used to it. Before the war," she went on, "we'd have had to hide out, pretend to be normal, whatever that is. It's a great new world we live in, Ter. Individuality is actually respected. Women can be whatever they want."

"So I am hearing. Our office workers have voted to join something called the UOWPA. I've forgotten what that stands for, but —"

"United Office Workers Protective Association, and you be careful, sister-girl. That's a pinko bunch, what they call 'fellow-travelers.' "

Terra had heard talk of the "Commies."

Half the scientists at Los Alamos had dabbled in the movement in the thirties. With the Depression in full swing people had floundered around, looking for a better form of government that would keep financial disaster at bay. But the hard times were over now. The country was so prosperous manufacturers couldn't produce goods fast enough for the war-starved populace to buy them.

"Why would anybody want to be a member of a Russian political party?"

"No idea, but the unions are organizing cells. They say they want to run a Red candidate in the election next fall. Oh, don't mind me, I don't know a thing about politics. But just think before you sign anything, if they ask you to join."

"I'll have to go along, or quit working there."

"Shoot, that bunch didn't look very special to me. You could get another job easy."

Not if I needed a reference from Manisch. The flicker of doubt was unfair. The man had never been anything but warm and appreciative. And yet, as she sat there in the sun that afternoon Terra knew, with native certainty, that even a small lapse of loyalty might bring retribution. *I bet he would squash you like a bug if you crossed him and never lose that pleasant smile.*

A bit sadly she reflected on her own cynicism. But the fact was she didn't trust anybody. She didn't think anyone believed in morals any more. In these hectic months since the war, it was as if the world had reversed itself. There was no generosity — everyone was conniving to get ahead, at all costs. There were no new standards of ethics to take the place of the old ones that had become skewed. Married men — two of them — had propositioned her, without a flicker of embarrassment. And that scene of the women in Dixie's apartment had been a glimpse into perdition itself.

She had never understood the overriding power of sex, but now it obviously had nothing to do with wedlock. And whatever happened to the other aspects of marriage? She and Phin had been welded in a union based on love, yes, but also need and fear and mutual concern in a world that had just blown up. He was more than a sex partner; he had been the one constant in her life, so powerful a presence that to lose it was to perish. The other night when she had come out of the Park, stumbling with exhaustion, and that strong arm had come around her she had thought, *Phin, what took you so long?*

The memory made her uncomfortable. It kept happening, Shanahan rescuing her. That whole long week which she had lost, he and Gilda had boosted her along and forced her to throw off the ailment whatever it was. Gil said the flu, Shan held out for pneumonia, and she thought he probably was right. Didn't matter, she was sitting here now in the sun thanks to the both of them. *And please, for God's sake, let me go next time.*

For an instant she thought she heard Andrew's voice somewhere off her left shoulder: "God was the one who wouldn't let you go." It was so strong an impression, she glanced around, but there was no one on the sidewalk up here in Riverside on a work day.

When she did go back to work that next Monday morning, she found the city changed. Or maybe it was a new perspective she found in the wake of Christmas euphoria, the cataclysmic effect of the storm. New York seemed to have grown harsher, uglier. Terra noticed the unswept lobby of the building, grime tracked in from the street, gum wrappers on the floor of the elevator.

Gilda was not at her desk yet, her tardiness legendary by now. Manisch would not be pleased. The offices seemed dampened by a bleak silence except for Ari's cubicle, which gave off impatient stirrings. He glanced up as she came in.

"Good morning," he said, "you look like death on a cracker."

"That good?" She took off her coat.

"If your so-called illness was a gimmick to get out of work, you fake it well. I'm tempted to recommend a good undertaker."

"Don't bother. I requested them to shovel me down a storm drain with the snow, but I'm afraid I lived."

"And here I was, counting on applying for your room. I still haven't found one." He eyed the cashmere coat. "You must have inherited wealth to afford that."

"Christmas present."

"Oh Gawd. You've got an admirer."

"No. Just a sister-in-law who's a fashion designer."

"Ah. The green velvet tuxedo, I'll bet. Got to admire her pizzazz, the way she marched in here Christmas eve and saved you from that wretched office party. You looked pretty grim even then, probably coming down with the plague and didn't know it. Anyway, I'm glad you're better. I need you to get busy on that pile of manuscripts. Every inept author in the country mailed us his precious creation over the holidays. See if you can clear your desk by this afternoon. I have a new challenge for you —"

"Which will have to be reassigned." Manisch spoke from the doorway, having materialized from the shadowy corridor. "Why are all the lights off? Gilda's supposed to get them on by nine o'clock."

"I'll —" Terra turned to the door.

"No, you won't. We will leave that for our receptionist, who is about to become our late receptionist. Meanwhile I've got something else for you." One wiry brow cocked and his smile was mysterious.

Ari groaned. "Oliver, I need the girl myself. I'm about to start on the Buschmiller manuscript. I thought I'd use the opportunity to teach her some of the fine points of copyediting."

"I sympathize, but there are better uses for this young lady. If you need help, Ari, I'll send over Henrietta." He beckoned to Terra. "Bring your coat. By the way, that's a very nice cashmere. Gift?"

"Yes." But she was nervous now, following him back to his own office, through it and beyond to another room where a large oaken table was piled with manuscript pages, photo paste-ups, galleys, bristling with red pencil marks. Over by a window at the back stood a large drafting table with a T-square and scattered drawing implements, protractors, pens, bottles of ink in various colors. Beside it was a desk, empty except for a row of books: "The Art of Direct Mail Advertising," "Basics of Ad Art," "Selling by Mail" "Use of Graphics." On a separate typing table was an old Royal Standard machine, with paper on a shelf beneath it.

"Well, my dear, how do you like your new office."

"My — ?"

"When we took this suite I had expected to hire two editors. Ari, for the science and history books, someone else for liberal arts. But I've been handling those myself." He motioned toward the scattered papers on the work bench. "I may still impose myself on you at times, but this is your bailiwick. You'll need elbow room to tackle my project: a direct-mail advertising campaign to every college in the country. We've been compiling lists of key personnel at each institution. We already send them catalogs. Now we're going to back that up with brochures. You'll be in charge of those. Find a printer who will help you. I'm not happy with our present outfit. They tend to be careless about deadlines, and they're too expensive. If you shop around you'll find some hungry little jobber who'll be glad for the work and do it on schedule."

"O-kay," she said, slowly, trying to take in the fact that she was being promoted. "And maybe in my spare time I can still help Ari."

Manisch was amused. "I doubt you'll have much spare time. You will be creating the mailers, yourself. For each title you'll design a pamphlet, write a description using quotes, decorative graphics — we want the product to be eye-catching. You'll choose colorful paper, pick out type fonts, do the layouts, the proofreading, and make sure the mailings go out on time. We have fifteen texts coming along this spring and each will get its own brochure, directed to a targeted clientele. Your budget will be $25,000. It's a big job, Terra. Are you up to it?"

Twenty-five thousand . . . Knees playing tag with each other, she took a surreptitious grip on the corner of the desk and said, "Yes sir."

"Right now," he added kindly, "all I want you to do is read those books and familiarize yourself with the tips you'll find there. Did you know that some color combinations are almost irresistible? Like white on red. And certain others are so hard to read you never want to use them — green on blue, for example. I browsed the literature myself, it's not bad. So take your time. We'll get started on the real work tomorrow."

Later, as she delved through pages of material, examples of good and bad commercial art, tips on graphics, new methods of printing, Terra glanced up to find Ari, watching. He had come in the back way avoiding Manisch's office.

"So this is where you are."

"I guess so. I'm sorry."

"Don't be. You didn't desert me on purpose." He looked over her shoulder at the reference book. "I wonder what the hell he's really up to?" And slanted off through the rear door into the corridor before she could focus on the question.

The same thought was in Henrietta's eyes as she came in that afternoon with a batch of letters in her hand. "I've got Ari's manuscripts packaged up, ready to send back. Haven't done *that* in a while. Does he like to sign the letters himself?"

"No. He always told me to do it." Terra looked up at her helplessly. "Henny, what's all this about?" She waved a hand at the easel, the desk, the reference books. "I don't have any credentials to be an ad person."

"Don't ask me." The older woman plucked at her girdle to ease a wrinkle. "I've been

Manisch's secretary ever since he started this place back in '39. The war years were very lean. We couldn't buy paper even for textbooks, or if we found some it was poor quality, not fit for a library or a classroom. Ink was hard to come by. Publishers cut their lists. Sales were nil. To stay alive we finagled a job printing Army pamphlets. That helped us scrape by, Karl and Oliver and me and Ruth. But I still can't read his mind, and I wouldn't be surprised if he suddenly walked in and fired me with no notice. I don't move fast enough to suit him, and even though we go back a long way he doesn't let sentimentality stand in the way of business. That's why I want the security of a negotiated contract. We need it, Terra, so you'd know you couldn't be shucked off on somebody's whim, just because he's had a bad day. I hope you're coming to the union meeting tonight after work."

"I — Henny, I really don't feel up to it. I've only been here a couple of hours and already I want to lie down."

"That's another thing we're going to discuss: putting a cot in the ladies' room. Plenty of times I would've liked to put my head down for a few minutes. Okay, I'll explain to them that you're still weak and not just disinterested."

"Thanks." *But I am disinterested. I don't care about contracts. They can be written with loopholes that get around any rule. All you can do is trust an employer to treat you right, and if he doesn't you can leave. Plenty of other work to be had.*

Of course there once was a time when jobs were so scarce men stood in breadlines or jumped off buildings. Terra wondered, could it happen again? If it did, would the union make things better? When businesses go broke, there is no work. Period. But it wasn't anything to worry about in the next few months. After that, if a new Depression came, she wasn't going to be around to see it.

Right then, as she walked out onto the street that evening, she didn't feel she'd even make it to next summer. The fever had left her listless and unable to ward off the old depression which had been stronger than usual lately. For the first time in a month she walked along the cross street to the Church of the Master. Not that she expected to see Andrew around on a Monday night, but there was something restorative about the remote hush of the church itself, a refuge from the world. And it provided a place to sit down on the long trek home.

181

Walking into the shadowy chamber with its high-vaulted ceiling, she felt a welcome peace close over her. Like the sensation she had always associated with death. A state of grace. Taking a seat in one of the front rows she leaned back wearily, her eyes closed. She wouldn't mind it if up some heavenly emanation would speak up and dispel all the bitter questions. But that wasn't going to happen, there were no answers.

After awhile she was aware that someone had come to sit with her and looked around to find Andrew at her side, his grave face sympathetic.

"Did you make a connection?" he asked, with a glance upward.

"With — ? Oh, no, the Lord's got better things to do."

"No, He doesn't. His time is infinite and you are part of His concern whether you ask for it or not. But it helps to put your troubles into words. Helps you, I mean. He already knows."

It was a disturbing thought that someone, Anyone, could read her mind. "Andrew — or maybe I should call you 'Father' in church — ?"

"No, our Father is up there." He jerked a thumb toward the arched ceiling with a small grin. "Andy will do."

"I don't suppose — The fact is, I haven't been well."

"I noticed you looked drawn. And you weren't at rehearsal last Tuesday."

"There was a rehearsal? I thought, with the performance over —"

"And wasn't that great? You guys outdid yourselves. But we've got an even bigger challenge coming up. We're going to tackle Mozart's *Requiem Mass* and perform it at Carnegie on Good Friday next spring."

Terra was floored. She and Phin had heard a great choir perform the Mass that year they were at Oak Ridge, when life was relatively normal. The monumental piece of music had rocked the rafters of the opera house in Knoxville, so overpowering it even distracted Phin from his awful focus. "Can't afford to do this," he had said afterward. "Music complicates my head."

"So we need you at rehearsals as soon as you're up to it," Andrew was going on. "There's no time to lose."

"Sure. I'll be there."

"I have another question for you. It's about the organ — do you think you could pick up the knack of those foot pedals? You have a very solid background in piano music, and the organ is not so different. I need someone to play for our choir on

Sundays, plus we rehearse on Friday evenings for a couple of hours. It's a lot to ask for a small amount of pay, only ten dollars a month."

It struck Terra like a bright ball bounced in her direction. "I'd like that! Only I'd need to come in ahead of time and practice the instrument, learn the stops and all. Is there anyone to show me the ropes?"

"Our present organist, Mary Cordelia, will be glad to get you started. She's had to give up the job because of an ailing mother who can't be left alone, some dreadful mental condition with a strange name, I forget. But Mary can make arrangements for someone to stay with her once in a while. What day shall I ask her to come in?"

"I have a job, but I'm free on Saturdays."

"That's good — next Saturday then? Try it out and see how it feels to you. Now let's get back to that muddle you're in."

"Oh, that's not important. I've got to be getting home. I kind of got my energy back sitting here."

"Church can do that, if you give it a chance. Whether or not you decide to play the organ for us, I hope you'll join us Sunday mornings." His warmth was irresistible. It was the only pure source of relief she had felt in a long time.

"I'll do that," she said impulsively. "Andy, when I was ill I got the most curious dream — or maybe it was delirium or something. I thought you were there, beside me. Hanging onto my hand. You didn't somehow happen to — ?"

He was smiling. "Terra, dear, I don't even know where you live."

"Oh. Sure, of course you don't." She felt herself blushing. "It was a silly notion."

"No, it wasn't," he said still with that look of delight. "I think you just met Someone who is very good at dispensing comfort and courage. I'm so glad for you." As he had done before, he seized her fingers in that strong grip and tipped back his head. "Thank you, Lord, for helping this little one when she needed You most. Watch over her, please, for she is still in some distress which only You know. Make your presence known to her, and give her your abiding strength. In the name of Jesus, amen."

Bemused, puzzled and trying to be skeptical, Terra considered what he had implied, as she walked out of the church. She doubted it was possible — just the natural assumption of a man who had strong beliefs. Sure, if somebody is comforted it has to be God who did it. And yet, she wondered, *who else?*

■ ■ ■ ■

The subway was a manifestation of New York, so unique to Terra she didn't know whether to love it or hate it. The morning commuters crowded the platform, cramming themselves furiously through the doors as if it were their only hope of heaven. And all the time there was another train waiting just down the track, ready to pull in within minutes of the last. Sometimes she waited through three or four, until one came that was not so full. Even then, it was standing room only. The jostling lot of strangers would sway and claw at the hangers with one hand while reading The Daily Mirror with the other. The trick was to fold the tabloid in quarters, long narrow strips of news columns which if unfolded judiciously and turned and refolded would maintain that meager width all the way down to the station at 14th. The wild seventy-block rush through the tunnels only took ten minutes.

At 14th Street, as she untangled herself from the crowd that pushed greedily out onto the platform Terra saw a familiar face. Gilda had got off one of the cars at the far end of the train. They managed to reach the turnstile together.

"I saw you ahead of me, when I came out of our building." The receptionist shoved back a long lock of fiercely golden hair that dangled in her eyes. "You were already turning onto Broadway. I couldn't catch up. You must have let some trains go by. When I got there you were still waiting, but you were way up-front . . ."

"I like the first car." Hurtling through the dark with the little red lights turning green ahead of you — "It's better than a carnival ride."

"Yeah, I used to do that too when I first came here. By the way, you look better this morning."

"I feel okay, thanks to you and Shan. I appreciate all you did."

"He turned out to be a trump, didn't he? I mean, he took the snow shovel and dug a path all the way to the Deli. The old lady down there is a friend of his. I never figured Cutter as the friendly type, but he sure was determined you weren't going to die and ruin his reputation as a super." She had a hee-haw laugh that burst out at unguarded moments, her large white teeth gleaming.

"So how was the union meeting last night?"

Gilda beamed. "Swell. I like being part of a movement. This country could use a few crusades. Like they were saying, the soldiers got medals for fighting in the war, but the rest of us got zilch. I worked every day for three years and eight months without missing a lick, and all I got was a letter of commendation. Why didn't they make a 'Workers Bronze Star?' Wouldn't have hurt 'em, for the lovamike."

"Was that what you discussed at the meeting?" Walking together across Fourteenth, they had to raise their voices above the honk of taxis, the heavy roar of the delivery trucks that swarmed the broad street. "I thought it was going to be about contracts and so forth."

"That, too. But mainly we had a speaker, some guy from the New School, talking politics. Afterward they had a discussion and I told the guy I didn't give much of a hoot about Republicans or Democrats, and he said that was great, I'd make a good Communist. He was kidding, I think. It doesn't matter, it's just nice to be part of a group, you know? You gotta come next week."

"I'm afraid I can't." After what Dixie had said Terra wished she hadn't agreed to be part of this union, especially if they were going to talk about Communism. She'd had enough of that down at Los Alamos, where everybody took sides on politics and philosophies and quoted Kant and Marx and Winston Churchill to prove their points. "When I went by the church last evening the Pastor offered me a job playing the organ on Sundays. It's a way to make a little money. But it means I have to accompany the choir at their practice, and study up on the instrument, and so forth. It's going to take a lot of my spare time."

"Well, shoot. Of course, if they're going to pay you for it, I can appreciate that. But there must be better ways to make an extra buck. Like prostitution." She gave another long equine whinny. "I'd rather get round heels than a flat brain."

Terra didn't get the connection.

Gilda sobered. "I'm sorry, it's none of my business, but — Well, just don't get taken in by all that God talk. I went to church for years, I really believed that junk. Then the war comes along and both my brothers got killed — both of them. And me praying my head off, not to mention my mother. She was on her knees most of the time, and still we hung the black flag in the window. No sir, no more of that nonsense for me. Religion is a flim-flam they use to keep the stupid people in line: 'Be good or you'll go to Hell.' Like there's this bonfire where you'll stand around and burn forever. I'd tell 'em: if you want to talk about Hell, talk about the islands over in the Pacific where the men almost hoped a bullet would get them before the jungle rot did. That's what my brothers wrote us. Cutter Shanahan was there too, by the way. He was at Guadalcanal. That boy's got scars you can't see. There's plenty of good old Hell right here on earth. Come down to it, living itself is mostly Hell. And saying a few prayers isn't going to fix it."

Terra silently agreed, but for reasons she wasn't about to reveal. As they came through the doors of their building they broke into a trot for the elevator whose doors were just closing, as always.

Back in her new office, she found Manisch working at his table, a small pair of wire-rimmed glasses perched far down his nose, so that he could see through them or over them. One gray eyebrow cocked when he saw her, reminded her of some movie star — she tried to think.

"Good morning, you're in early," he observed. There was a very large clock on the wall, its hands clicking like the one she remembered from grade school: 8:47, 8:48, 8:49 . . . "I'm glad, because I want to get right to this book. It will be the top of our new line." He had thrown down his red pencil and come to join her at her desk where a manuscript lay, its title page in large bold-faced type:

WORK
PROVIDED
ACCORDING TO NEED

"It's a study of the Works Progress Administration," Manisch was going on, "which saved our culture from extinction during the Depression."

Terra could remember that time. She'd only been ten or so when the avalanche of letters hit, NRA, TVA, SEC, REA, CCC, programs launched so hard and fast by President Roosevelt after he came to office in 1933 that the whole country roused up, shook itself and began to live again.

"The WPA funded our arts and letters," Manisch went on. "Creative people in this country would have starved or drifted off into other pursuits without the assistance of the government. Roosevelt ran very close to the edge of socialism. He drew a lot of criticism, but he knew that capitalism wasn't working, so he overrode the conservatives. A courageous man."

And the only President that Terra had ever

known until his death threw the country into a massive upheaval, three years ago. Truman was plain-spoken and pragmatic. She liked his flat Missouri speech, his blunt answers to pointed questions. But he didn't have the towering presence of Roosevelt, the charisma to inspire the country in these days of aftermath. All he could do was clamp controls on prices and wages and rents and hang on, hoping the world would settle down. So far, it hadn't. People were still running off in all directions, greedy to buy things in a frenzy of self indulgence . . .

Manisch was silent, watching her with a small smile. *Claude Rains, that's who he looks like.* "I'm sorry," she said, "I guess I got lost for a minute. It took me back to my childhood, Roosevelt's fireside chats."

"That's quite all right. If you recall the 'good old days' you can more easily appreciate the mess we're in right now. The Depression was a time of mixed emotions. There was the despair of being penniless, but it invoked a marvelous strength. It brought us together, we helped each other and were assisted by a benevolent dictator. It was a time when our limiting system of checks and balances was over-ridden by a strong hand. Much as I admire Mr. Truman, he doesn't have the personal power to rule an unruly country. Usually one man can't. Right now, with our values careening all over the place, we need a new kind of government."

It was so much what Terra had been thinking, herself — the problem of lost morality — though she would never have looked to Washington, D.C. to solve it, she found herself interested, nodding in agreement.

Manisch read her expression and smiled back. "Good. You're not afraid of the idea. Sit down, my dear, and let's get busy. This book is multi-faceted. It can go out to several mailing lists — political science, of course, and the history departments, some of the philosophy courses may find it of use. And the art studies, they are of top concern. The W.P.A. was a cultural awakening. First thing to decide: shall we do a large double page spread with one good four-color illustration, or a smaller four-page brochure with several black-and-white prints and a lot of descriptive material?"

Terra was thumbing through the manuscript. "Pictures are worth a thousand words, or so it says in that book over there."

"And we have some excellent illustrations. They're in that other pile. The Thirties were a great time for murals, huge ones, done by some very impressive painters. The book contains a whole chapter on the Coit Tower alone. So read up on the times and circumstances and see if you can draft a few paragraphs to describe the scope of the text. Then we'll get to captions for the illustrations."

As she delved into the manuscript Terra began to sense an undercurrent of purpose in the author's message. She couldn't put her finger on it, but it intrigued her so that she forgot to look at the clock. Suddenly she realized that she was hungry. Since her bout of fever she had no appetite, but all at once she felt that she could eat.

Before she could act on the thought, the door opened and Manisch appeared bearing a wicker basket. "Devil of a time getting waited on," he explained. "Seems as though everyone had the same idea at once — to have an indoor picnic." Beginning to unload a variety of sandwiches, fruit and appetizers, he set out a bottle of wine. "I trust sauterne is satisfactory?"

"I don't take any alcoholic beverage, thank you anyway, sir."

"Oh dear, don't tell me I have to drink alone." Then fixing her with a cocked brow, he said, "Let me guess: you're an alcoholic."

"Uh — yes sir, that's it. I'm an alcoholic." It was the quickest way to divert him from pressing her to join him in the nauseating stuff. It would have been painful to explain the truth: that her mother had been addicted to brandy and the smell alone was enough to make Terra sick.

"A shame, really. Ah well, I hope the rest of the viands are to your liking." He relished words like "viands."

And they were great. How could you not like a perfectly seasoned pastrami on rye, with just a touch of mustard? For himself Hamisch chose a Swiss cheese on pumpernickel.

"I understand that alcoholism was the ailment of choice at Los Alamos," he remarked, offhand. "Terrible pressures in a place like that."

"There never was another place like that," she said mildly.

"No, I suppose not," he marveled as if she had revealed some great truth. "Must have been interesting, though. To know that you're in a deadly race, with the fate of the country in your hands."

She wouldn't have put it that way, exactly.

"Well, I'm sure you were aware — or at least your husband would have been — that the Germans had a head start on the A-bomb."

"We were never told much about what the project was. It was called 'The Gadget.' The men had instructions not to talk about the work. Of course, they did — I knew they were making some kind of explosive device. Most of the wives didn't even know that much. Everybody tried not to discuss it outside the Tech Area."

"Hardly seems fair," Manisch said thoughtfully. "You women were enduring a lot of discomfort to be there for your husbands."

"Not as much as the girls all over the country who didn't even know where their husbands were. Writing letters to an APO box, getting back v-mail with half the lines blacked out. Driving old cars and trying to get along on an A-sticker, gas rationed, sugar rationed, meat rationed — they are the real home front heroes."

"You weren't much more than a box number yourself," Manisch persisted. "Just a little office in Santa Fe, fronting for one of the biggest secrets in history. No one but Oppenheimer could have pulled it off."

"And General Groves," she added, determined not to let him lecture her on a subject about which she knew more he did. "The General was the pragmatic one. He made the project work." And dealt with all those complaining women doggedly, even sometimes with inspiration.

196

"Did you actually meet Oppenheimer?" Manisch sounded impressed.

"Of course. Everybody knew Oppie. He visited our kitchens all the time." *But Phin was his fair-haired boy, and he loved my sugar cookies.* "He was the one who started calling me 'Terra.' I'd had so many other nicknames, Terry, Tris, Therissa. But Oppie claimed I was a daughter of the earth and should have a graver designation."

Manisch shook his head in wonder. "One of the greatest minds of our time, to be so approachable — amazing."

"Oh yes, he likes people, he likes to talk."

"You don't still correspond with him, do you?"

"Good heavens, no! I haven't had anything to do with that crowd for over a year. They didn't like it when my husband stayed in Japan for the clean-up. Teller wanted him back to work on the new project."

"The H-bomb. Oppenheimer doesn't approve of it, I understand."

"I wouldn't know about that." She began to be suspicious of the trend in the conversation. Even though the acute secrecy had been lifted, it was best not to gossip. That had always been the rule on The Hill. "Thank you for a great lunch. I'm ready to get back to work."

"Oh, not quite yet." Manisch put on his mysterious smile and went to a cabinet in the corner that, she had noticed earlier, was secured by a small padlock. Taking out a key, he opened it and hunkered down to peer inside. "Let's see, what can we enjoy without spiraling off into total euphoria?" He took out a box and brought it over to her. "Have you ever tried happy dust?"

"Cocaine? No!" She said it so emphatically he looked flustered.

"My dear, it's not a scandalous substance, not at all. It clears the mind and quickens the circulation. And does wonders to rid you of weariness."

"I've seen people use it. I don't want to." Some of the women on The Hill snorted it in a desperate effort to stave off the sheer boredom of being locked up in a polite prison. A sniff of the stuff and their faces would be transfused with a dreamy joy that was so obviously unreal it made Terra uncomfortable. She knew some of the scientists partook of it from time to time, but they had an excuse. They were under such pressure it required some sort of artificial respite. "I really don't need a thing, sir," she added apologetically. "I'm fine as is."

Manisch sighed. "Terra, you disappoint

me. I thought you would be more adventuresome. Our new culture is so full of possibilities that our parents would have never imagined."

"My husband," she said, "was the experimenter in our family. He couldn't forego a new experience. But even he wouldn't have risked a drug that would alter his mind. He used to say it was the greatest gift God ever gave the world — the human brain. So thanks, but no thanks." And her tone made it final.

FEBRUARY, 1948

The organ had a mysterious power to rally the emotions. When Terra carefully toed the bass pedals, the powerful sounds which came from the pipes overhead were like a release of spiritual energy. The old church shuddered with the massive music, too rich to be borne for more than a few bars. She broke off the Great Fugue and closed the page.

It was one of several pieces she had found in the bench, mostly Bach. Now she began "Sheep May Safely Graze," a message of incredible peace. Played quietly, it produced a fulfillment she'd seldom felt when on the piano. Of course the organ wasn't a concert instrument; her mother would have dismissed it. And yet the possibilities were endless. She hadn't even begun to learn the stops yet. When a hand reached around her and flipped one, lifting the melody to a new level of ethereal delicacy, she shivered. Smiling up at Andrew, she said. "Thank you."

His blue eyes glinted with delight, as he sat down beside her on the bench. "You are a remarkable musician, Terra. Mary tells me you can already play better than she does."

Her tutor had been a cute girl with short auburn curls. After the two of them spent one Saturday afternoon together, she had said, "You're a natural at this. I just learned it because Andrew needed somebody." That last statement had overtones of adoration. *Lord, she's in love with him.* Terra had felt a pang of envy. Great to be so innocent.

All she said now was, "I wish I'd tried the organ before, but the truth is, I never have been comfortable in a church. I feel like a hypocrite. I can't pray the way you're supposed to, I just feel silly. And I'm sorry to say that the sermons don't uplift me."

Andrew smiled a fraction. The previous Sunday the primary pastor, a very old man, had given a long-winded reading from the Bible, the Book of Job. "It wasn't the most cheerful of messages," he agreed. "Sometimes the Holy Word helps us sort out our personal problems. But communication with God comes in many forms and right now it's the music that connects you. One of these days you'll learn to pray. We can help. The community of the church is a great support group. Give us a chance and faith will come."

Maybe, if I were going to be around that long. "Thanks," she said. "Right now I need to get home."

She wasn't sure why she had been growing uneasy. All afternoon she'd had a sense of something wrong. Trouble brewing back at the rooming house? Gilda, maybe, struggling with a problem? Or was it Dixie waiting for her there? Whatever, the feeling escalated as she rode the subway uptown.

When she came out onto 86th Street it was full dark. She had spent longer at the church than she realized. Glancing around for Shanahan she couldn't spot him, so maybe he had taken her admonishment to heart. With choir practice making her late now, as well as the rehearsals for next spring's concert, she had urged him not to waste time hanging out at the subway.

"Honest, Shan. I can take care of myself. Last year, living alone in San Diego, I did just fine." The course in self-defense had done wonders for her confidence. Usually the poor damned lonely sailors got the message with her first rebuff. Only a few times did she have to face off, with a grim posture that made them back down. And these streets were so respectable that, except for the one encounter early on, she hadn't been approached. And yet tonight there seemed to be trouble in the air.

As she mounted the stairs to the rooming house she saw the front door ajar. That alerted her. Cutter was a stickler for locked doors. Going on up to the third floor she found more evidence of trouble. The waste-basket that she had left outside her room had not been emptied. Nearby stood the cardboard box into which the super collected the trash to take it down to the barrel. It was half full, but deserted near the open door of Three-A. Glancing in, she could see that the front apartment was in disarray, the bed unmade, dresser drawers pulled out and empty. It looked as though the tenant had made a hasty exit.

But where's Shanahan?

Going back downstairs and out the front, she descended the steps to the basement apartment and rang the bell. Imagined that she heard a noise inside, and rapped on the door. "Shan! Are you there?"

Distantly came a couple of words. "It's open."

She hesitated to turn the knob. He had been so unwilling to let anyone see inside the place. Every Saturday he would collect the rent at each door upstairs. If you came down here to pay it ahead of time he would retrieve it through a narrow crack, close the door, return with a receipt and poke it out, then close again quickly. As Gil had once noted, his apartment always gave off a dank odor which evoked visions of graveyards.

Now, as she looked in, the muddy aroma wafted forth. Dark inside — *why doesn't he turn on a light?* She felt around by the entry and found a switch. It produced a pale glow from an overhead bulb in the vestibule, beyond which a spacious room was dimly visible.

"Are you okay?" she called.

"Come on in, Bunny." His voice seemed to originate from the far end of the room near the large glass door that led to the patio. As she advanced she felt the brush of a light-pull from overhead and yanked it to flood the place with a burst of 200-watt brilliance.

"Hi." The super was halfway lying on the sofa, propped against a pillow, the rusty shock of hair shadowing his eyes, his mouth in a tight press.

"Uh — hello." She was aware of a broad table stacked with white pieces of something, looked like broken plaster. Chunks of it lay around a small figurine, an inept model of a boy sitting cross-legged. Buckets and rags were strewn about, sacks of powdery materials stood open under the bench. The place was all work shop, except for a tall brass bed in the corner and the threadbare old divan where Cutter sat motionless. His clothes were torn, one knee of the blue jeans ripped, the flesh beneath scraped raw, and his hands were scuffed.

"You been in a fight?" she wondered.

"Uh-huh. Had a . . . little trouble . . . Three-A." He was speaking between short breaths.

He's in pain. "What happened?"

"I was picking up trash . . . heard him in there, so I knocked . . . guy owes me four weeks' back rent. Don't usually . . . let it go that long. Knew he'd give me hard time . . . which he did. Opened the door and came at me . . . suitcase. He swung it, caught me in the knees. Followed him on downstairs. I was sore, got careless. Outside, he turned . . . slung the suitcase again, knocked me sideways over the railing. I reached out to catch myself . . . wrong arm. Right shoulder dislocates if I put any weight on it. Went over the rail and came down hard, knocked the wind out. And there went the rent money."

Shucking off her coat, Terra located the sink. She had to remove a bucket full of some odorous substance — wet clay. Finding a clean glass on the shelf, she filled it with water, cold right out of the tap down here in the underground apartment. Carrying it over she gave it to Cutter. He took it with his left hand, awkwardly . . .

With a wet rag she tried to clean the bloody knee that showed through the torn jeans. "What else did he damage?"

The odd sound that came from the super sounded almost like laughter. "He personally couldn't damage a paper bag. It was the fall that did it. Probably cracked a couple of ribs." Finishing the water, Shanahan spoke more evenly. "I keep forgetting that I can't count on my shoulder. Put any stress on the joint, it pops out." With enormous understatement he added, "Damned nuisance."

Terra had seen this before. One of the men at Los Alamos had a shoulder that dislocated at the drop of a hat. It caused him agonizing pain. "Well, let's get you to an emergency room. I'll go call a taxi — can you walk?"

"No hospitals."

"Shan, you've got to do something about this."

"Last time, the intern in the ER wouldn't listen to me. I tried to tell him to go ahead and slip it back in, but no. The bhoyo was squeamish, insisted on an anesthetic. I can't take ether, my lungs are not too great. I spent three days in a ward. No, no hospitals."

"But you have to do something."

"Yeah," he hesitated. Then blurted it out. "I thought maybe you'd give it a try. It's not all that hard to put it back in."

"Me?" Everything in her rebelled. She never had been great with pain, especially in others. Some women were born to be nurses, but she wasn't one. And yet she owed the man, after the way he had stood by her in that long week of illness. "Do you really think I'm strong enough? Because if I try and fail it would put you through a lot of misery for nothing."

"I know . . . believe me." He waved the glass at her and she went to fill it again. "Find a bottle of aspirin over there somewhere."

She brought it, and he downed four of them in one toss, wincing as the movement disturbed the loose shoulder. "Give those a few minutes."

"You have any whiskey here?"

"No, ma'am. Not any, not a drop." His face twisted in that unwilling smile. "But it's nice of you to offer, seeing how you feel about the creature. It's all right, the aspirin will take hold in a minute." He tried to stand up.

She helped and they got him on his feet. "You'll have to coach me," she said. "How do we go about this?"

He backed up against the wall nearby, leaned on it and braced himself. His breath was coming easier now that he was standing. "Okay, the trick is not to falter. Don't start unless you are ready to go all the way through with it. Come here beside me, grab hold of my arm above the wrist with both hands. That's it. Now you're going to pull steadily down and forward, without hesitating. Keep going, no matter what happens."

"Like what? What might happen?"

"Like I might scream bloody murder."

"Oh. Well, that I can handle."

He started to laugh. And quickly Terra began to draw the arm forward and down, steadily, as hard as she could. *Do it, do it . . .* He made a strangled noise and she felt the bone seat itself in the socket. Sagging, gasping for breath, he held onto her as he stumbled back to the divan. "B'gorrah, you're a tough little rabbit. I thank you sincerely. Now go home. I'll be okay."

"But don't you need to tie that arm to your side for a few days?"

"I can manage that."

"No, you can't. And your knee is swelling. This is my emergency room and I'm running it right. You're going to bed."

"Look. I need to take a shower." The sweat shirt was soaked through. "Then I have some strips of sheeting already cut. I can loop one around and yank it tight. I'll be fine."

"Yes, a warm shower, not too hot. Soak in it. Want some help to get those clothes off?"

"Sweet Saints!" He shrank back with such alarm she had to laugh.

"Okay, I'll leave. But I'll be back in ten minutes. You don't make a move with the arm until I get here. I can't go through that again."

Upstairs, Terra hung up her coat. Her stomach was in a knot, but it was no time to give in to the willies. Back out in the hallway she finished emptying the wastebaskets into the trash box, took it down and dumped it into the oil drum that served as a trash can. Rolling it on its rim, the way she had seen Cutter do, she got it out to the curb and left it there to wait for the collection truck.

When she went back into the super's apartment he was sitting on the rococo old bed clad in a red flannel nightshirt that came down to his bare shanks. It was damp, he hadn't been able to dry off much after the shower. She said, "Where's the thermostat? It's cold in here."

"Over by the door to the furnace room. Don't turn it higher than seventy, you'll spoil the tenants."

She pushed it up to seventy-five, then went to the stove. A respectable GE range, it was newer than the gas burners in the rooms upstairs. She turned the fire on under the coffee pot. "You could use something hot to drink. Now where are those strips?"

"Under the work bench in a box." Then he added, "I'm glad it was you that came along. You're the only person —"

She had found the rags, lengths of torn sheeting five inches wide, neatly rolled. "What on earth do you keep these for?"

"Making molds. Strengthens the plaster. Just tie some of them together and wrap them around the whole chest area. If I do have a couple of cracked ribs they'll mend along with the arm. There, that's got it. Thanks." He was talking more easily, but the perspiration stood out on his forehead. No need to ask whether he was still in pain.

Terra brought a steaming cup and set it on the bedside table. Taking one herself, she sat down on the nearest chair. The hot drink steadied her. "So tell me about molds. How did you get into that kind of work?"

He sipped cautiously, then took a grateful gulp. "Came to New York back in the thirties, bound that I'd make a name as a sculptor, going to be hot stuff. I learned the hard way: this is a city of failed dreams. Actors, writers, artists. I was luckier than most. I got a job with Paul Manship. Biggest name in sculpture that this town ever has known. He was creating the decorations for the '39 Worlds Fair. Huge panels, but the original models were done in his studio in the basement of his home over on the East Side. He had imported a crew of European craftsmen, experts in woodcarving, stone, plaster work. Hired me as an apprentice. It was better than any school, working under them. I learned the skills. But it was plain enough I was never going to make a living at sculpture. You have to be a socialite to get those commissions. Anyway, about then the war came along . . ." He was rambling, probably, she thought, to hold the pain at bay. "When I got out of the service, I needed some kind of work. I'd learned the craft of mold making, I decided to free-lance."

"Is that how you got your discharge — the shoulder thing?"

"Oh no, accidents like that were run-of-the-mill in the Pacific. You go to move some heavy piece of machinery, muddy in the jungle, you slip and grab for a hold and there goes the shoulder. I'm not supposed to haul around hundred-pound bags of plaster, but the work pays pretty well. Amateur sculptors don't know how to translate their stuff from clay into bronze. Not the foggiest idea about casting. Of course it's illegal to do it here, not zoned as a professional studio, so I kind of keep it low-key . . ." His voice had begun to fade.

"I won't tell anybody. But I'm concerned about your knee." It was visibly swelling. "I think we should put some ice on it." Foraging, she found a refrigerator in the furnace room. "Pretty nice," she commented. "Your own private ice cubes." Wrapping some in a towel she made a cold pack and brought it to lay on the swollen joint. "Hold that there for a while, but take it off before you lie down or it'll melt all over the bed."

"Okay, thanks."

Terra could sense that now he wanted to get rid of her, so he could stop trying to camouflage the suffering. "I guess you're all set. But I'll be back tomorrow morning, so don't lock the door. If you shut me out I'll bang on it until —"

"I won't lock it," he said, between gritted teeth.

Terra drew another glass of water, put that and the aspirin within his reach, and left. Reluctantly. What she really wanted to do was fuss over him, make comforting conversation, mop the shine off his brow. The odd maternal impulse made her snicker in self-disgust. *If ever a man didn't want coddling . . .*

Next day she said something of the sort to Dixie. "I must be going soft. I hardly know the man."

"Yeah, but consider the situation. Here's Heathcliff, the mysterious peasant with the face of a ruffian and the heart of gold, now wounded and vulnerable, in need of the touch of a good woman . . ."

"Yeah, except Heathcliff's heart wasn't gold. It was hard and broody. And this isn't the setting for a Gothic novel. In those you have to have a moor to walk across under a lowering sky."

"You're right, darn it. They forgot moors when they built Central Park. But there's a dandy monastery uptown. Called The Cloisters. It might come in handy if you want to become a nun after he spurns you. He's bound to spurn you good now. It's part of

213

their ethic — men really hate to be caught in a moment of weakness." Dixie always managed to put in that sliver of contempt for the opposite sex.

"They only spurn if they're discovered by their secret love," Terra said. "Which lets me out. To Shanahan I'm just a bothersome female who has to be protected from the big bad City. Or possibly I remind him of his little sister."

"Oh, I'd say his feelings aren't all that fraternal." Dixie spoke cautiously. "He sounded pretty worried about you last month when you got the bug."

"How do you — ?"

"I called to find out how you were, after you left the party. You really were pretty pale that day. And the damned snowstorm throttled the city, I couldn't get over there. Anyway he answered the phone, and we had quite a talk. Didn't he tell you?"

"No. It probably slipped his mind." Terra wanted to change the subject. She was still embarrassed whenever she thought of those missing days. She wished she could remember the details. "Thanks for being concerned. And especially for buying me this great coat. I've had more complements on it." She hadn't relinquished the cashmere to the mercies of the cloak room at the classy restaurant where Dixie had taken her for lunch. Pretended to be chilly, but the truth was, it gave her a sense of luxury that none of her other clothes ever achieved.

"Just don't wear it to union meetings," Dixie advised. "They'd lynch you as an *aristo*. The minute people organize they revel in poverty, even when they're being pretty well paid. I hope that evil master gave you a raise along with your promotion."

"He did. I now pull down $55.00 a week and that, as they say, ain't hay."

"Good, then you can afford some decent shoes."

"If you mean spike heels, I've tried them. They ruin my feet."

"You've got to make a few sacrifices if you want —" She broke off. "Sorry, didn't mean to criticize. I just hope to see you attract some nice guy — what am I saying? New York is no place to find a 'nice guy.' "

"Let me clear one thing up," Terra said soberly. "I am never going to get married again. Once was more than enough."

"You're still sore at Phin, for dying."

"I am."

Dixie tasted her vegetable platter critically. "They put onions in the dressing." After a minute she said, "How's your soup?"

"Excellent. How's *La Coquette* doing?"

"The action is very slow. After New Year's everybody goes on a thrift kick. They humbly wear last year's duds and genuflect when they pass the Salvation Army. So I've decided to close shop temporarily, take a cruise around the Caribbean. We'll probably be gone a month or so. That's why I wanted to do this lunch today, so you'll know I won't be here to give you fashion advice for a while. Or rescue you from the enemy."

"What enemy? If you mean Manisch, don't worry. He's harmless — I can walk out of there any time."

"Famous last words. Actually, I'm worried about that union thing. The pinkos are getting restless, and the good old boys who like to lynch people are gearing up to go after them. I can't tell you how I know, but we have a sixth sense about such things, we people of the shadows. When you are one of the hunted, you recognize the scent of the hunters, and I swear to you, they are abroad. So watch out."

Terra was baffled. "For who? Who do I watch out for?"

"Let's just call them the Furtive Bosses of Intolerance. If a man in a blue pinstripe suit starts dogging your footsteps, walk a very straight line and don't throw out any incriminating trash, like the secret codes or the rendezvous spots."

Furtive Bosses of . . . "Good grief, are you talking about the FBI.? I thought they were the good guys."

"Not if you're a Jew, a homosexual or a Democrat. Actually they're not as bad as certain others, like the HUAC."

"What's — ?"

"A little-known bunch of snoopers called the House UnAmerican Activities Committee. Kicked a lot of shins back in the Thirties. Then they got sidetracked when we shook hands with the Russians during the war. Now they have regrouped, I understand, and are out hunting Reds. Outfits like the UOWPA make them drool. So steer clear of the solidarity gang, sis. I mean it."

It was after six when Terra left her desk that afternoon and the light was still on in Ari's office. All day he had been over at the printers' — not the little jobber she had found to do the direct-mail ads, but the big press that put out their texts. He had taken her over there with him once so that she could experience the making of a book.

In a huge warehouse of noise, great machinery slammed down the uncut sheets of pages, while on another floor ranks of linotype machines rattled, conveyor belts bore away the galleys. The air shook with the mad cacophony, until there would come a moment of juddering unison when the presses were all in sync and for a beat the whole building rocked to a common rhythm. An instant of mechanized "tuning," it stole the breath from your lungs. The printers' was one of Ari's favorite places.

But today he had been on a grim mission: to try to stop the process long enough to make a correction. The new book on astronomy had suddenly become obsolete because of the discovery of a nebula or some such. The report had been in the late edition of the New York Times. Now in the waning daylight he sat in his office, tilted back in his chair, scowling out the window at the sky as if it had betrayed him.

"No, I did not get there in time. The book will be out of date before we see bound copies. Don't send flowers. I hate pity. Get out of here, unless you've found me an apartment."

"Would one small room do?"

The legs of the chair came down hard on the floor. "I'll take it!"

"You didn't even ask — ?"

"It doesn't matter. That room is mine! Do you know what I did last night? I dismissed the class fifteen minutes early so I could make the Long Island train, got into Katonah at 12:45 in the morning, drove home, went to bed, got up, cut myself shaving, drove like a madman to reach the station at 4:49 just twenty seconds before the commuter train stopped, no time to buy a paper, got here ten minutes late. Just tell me: where do I go to nail down this room, den, closet, whatever?"

"You can do it right here, with me. I am acting for the super, who is laid up with a bad knee. When I told him this morning that I had a prospective tenant all he said was, 'Get the first month in cash.' Four weeks at ten dollars —" The smaller front room was bargain-priced.

Ari already had his wallet out. "And how much for the agent who closed the deal?"

"Me? I don't want a thing. But if you should care to slip the super a little it would be appreciated. The last tenant stiffed him on the rent."

Ari counted out three twenties. "That cover everything?"

"Very generous of you. He wouldn't ask it, but —"

"But you need to keep on the good side of a super. What's his name?"

"Nehemiah Shanahan."

Ari let out a hoot of laughter. "That's almost as ethnically subtle as Aaron Scheidler."

"He's also red-headed, if you want to compound the cliché," she said. "Anyway, he's a good man. Call him Cutter."

"Call me grateful. When can I move in?"

"I've got choir rehearsal tonight. How about Monday after work? Here's the key to the front door — address is 226 West 88th. I'll give you your room key when you get there." And hope the repairs get finished over the weekend.

In cleaning up the vacated apartment Terra had noticed a watermark on the ceiling. She had flagged down One-B, who looked like a burly carpenter sort, and asked him to climb up and check out the attic, where he had found a leak in the roof. It turned out that he knew all there was about fixing leaks, but had no tools. Two-A took care of that problem. Lively little old elf of a man, retired, but he still had his belt. Came back bristling with hammers, screwdrivers and pliers, and a great piece of plywood. Who knows where it came from?

It was in the nature of a miracle the way the tenants had rallied around to help out, since they learned Shanahan was down, and why. It had started that first morning when she'd been running the vacuum on the stairway. Gilda had taken it from her.

"Let me help. I can do that much. It'll make me feel homesick."

Now, on Saturday afternoon there was an air of festivity about the repairs as Two-A scrambled right on up the ladder to help One-B while Shanahan fretted.

"If they fall I don't know whether the insurance covers it. This place is my responsibility!"

"Which you have officially assigned to me and I delegated it to them. Just let them be, Shan. They never even talked to each other before, and now they're all friends. Miss Pulver in One-A made coffee for them and Mrs. Aldershott, in Two-C, is doing the laundry so you can rent the room again."

"Which I need to do," he groaned. "Every day that room stands vacant I'm out some more cash."

"How come?"

"That's the nature of my contract with management. I lease the whole building at a rent-controlled rate, which I send in monthly. The rest is up to me — to collect on the rooms enough to make expenses plus a little. If there's a shortfall it comes out of my pocket. And don't you go around taking up a collection. I'll never speak to you again." But surrounded by solicitous tenants his image as a hard-nosed landlord was permanently dented.

Now, to Ari she said, "By Monday he'll be back at work. Just don't mention anything about the extra money. He doesn't like to take bribes. Especially don't tell him I suggested it."

"Ah, a man of conscience. Dying breed. Tell him it's a security deposit. That's the in-thing these days, security. A fragile commodity." He glanced darkly down the hall where Manisch was bent in conversation with Henrietta about something. "How do you like working for the impresario?"

Terra had to smile, the word fit. "He's a good teacher. Did you see the proofs for the first brochure? It's going to be a knock-out."

"Well, how could you go wrong with those four-color reproductions of the Coit Tower murals? I'll bet this one mailing has eaten up your entire advertising budget."

"No, not really. There's a new process called photo-electric engraving that cuts down the cost."

"I've heard of that." Ari chewed on his pipe thoughtfully. "But how do you know?"

"My printer." She spoke with slight pride. "I found a jobber who's just getting started, a young man who worked on photography in the Army. He used his GI Bill to get take advanced courses up at Columbia. He doesn't have a big staff, does most of the jobs himself, and he wants a spread that will showcase the quality of his work. So he offered to do our brochure at cost if we allow him to use it in his sales room."

"Brilliant. Manisch strikes again."

Terra frowned. "I swung that deal myself."

Ari switched from right to left eye, the sinister one. "And what hidden price did you have to pay?"

"I didn't pay anybody anything." Terra was starting to get irritated.

"Not yet at least. But you will, one way or the other." He turned to his desk and she stalked off back to her own office, fuming. *What's made Ari so bitter? Just being pug-ugly and Jewish? He should have been at Los Alamos. Nobody cared about such trivia, the mind was all that counted.*

It was late. The wintry stars looked pale, frozen in an icy sky, as Terra came up out of the subway that night, suddenly feeling the full weight of weariness. A cold wind was blowing off the Hudson River, right in her face, as if the city were giving her the razz. She drew the wonder coat closer around her. Those goats knew how to keep warm.

Walking slowly, head tucked against the cold blast, Terra realized, to her disgust, that she missed Shanahan. She'd got used to finding him here, waiting. Not that he could do much good if somebody jumped her now. His right arm was still a long way from functional. She was glad he was taking care of it, she told herself. She certainly didn't want him to feel that she was one of his "responsibilities." *Never going to need anybody that much again.*

Then, as she passed the coffee shop he came through the door and fell in beside her, silently. It seemed the most natural thing in the world to hook a hand through the crook of his elbow.

"You shouldn't be out in this cold," she scolded. "It's hard on the joints, and that shoulder hasn't healed yet."

"Don't rub it in. I know I wouldn't be much help if somebody really wanted to mug you. But just seeing a man on hand might discourage them."

When they turned down 88th the wind gusted in their faces. He braced her with his left arm around her shoulders. *Never did that before.* At the brownstone he let her go, darkness hiding his face, but he sounded grumpy.

"Good night, rabbit."

"Wait. Shan, I've got some money for you. That fellow I told you about, the new tenant? He paid in advance." She followed him down the few steps and into his apartment.

He had cleaned up the floor, got rid of the pieces of plaster, put a lid on the bucket of clay. "My customer came by and picked up her dinky little creation," he remarked. "I had to refer her to somebody else to finish the job. Still needs to be put into wax and taken to the foundry, but it will be awhile before I can do that. I don't think I'll accept any more commissions until next spring when I can work out in the courtyard. I need some time for on my own project."

"Is that it?" With the clutter gone, Terra realized there was a shrouded figure wrapped in wet rags now taking center spot on the work table.

"Yeah. What was it you mentioned about money?"

"Hey, I'd really like to see what kind of sculpture you do." She started toward it, but a small motion from him made her stop.

"It's not ready for unveiling. Tell me more about the new tenant."

"His name is Aaron Scheidler. He's an editor in that place where I work. He needs a room for the nights when he teaches a class down at the New School, so he can

225

stay over. It doesn't matter that it's small or that there isn't a bathroom. I asked for a month in advance and he gave me the cash, plus a security deposit."

Cutter took the envelope and glanced inside. He had tossed his wind breaker aside and she could see he was no longer using the strips of sheeting. "I don't ask for a deposit."

"He said it's the usual thing — to protect the landlord from being cheated. Sounded like a good idea to me." Carelessly she started back outside.

"You did this. You told him I needed a bribe to give him the room."

"Actually, I told him you didn't," she snapped. "Anyway, he'll be moving in Monday. If you have a big case of Irish guilt about being over-paid you can always give it back to him." And walked on out.

MARCH, 1948

As Henrietta mused over the new brochure her severe face softened into a rare smile. "The Coit Tower. That brings back memories."

"You've seen it?" Terra asked. Early morning, they were alone in the office. The secretary had wandered in, carrying two cups of coffee, which in itself was amazing.

"Seen it?" Henny said. "Girl, I lived it."

"Lived — how?"

"I bet you haven't even read the book yet. If you do you'll find mention of the Pacific Maritime Strike. Back in '34, that was a big one. My husband was a longshoreman, one of the organizers. We shut down the entire west coast. Even Roosevelt couldn't stop us. The papers called us 'Reds' and 'Commies,' traitors to our country. The Coit Tower became our symbol. It was government-funded and employed twenty-some starving artists to do its murals. That was called socialistic and un-American, especially when some of the paintings featured the crowds of jobless men reading newspapers like The Daily Worker and The New Masses. One of the artists named Zakheim, I think it was, even sneaked into his mural a copy of Das Kapital. The press played it up and everybody got scandalized. It was a great time to be alive, even if we were all living off catsup and crackers."

"Did you win the strike?"

"You don't 'win' these things. You make a statement," she said. "We were protesting the lack of jobs. Actually, there weren't any, there wasn't any money in the piggy bank. FDR was paying for his artists on the cuff, running up the national debt to millions of dollars with his programs. He'd have made a good socialist if he hadn't been such a Democrat. You can't be a reformer half-way, you've got to go full steam. He needed to reorganize our whole form of government, but he was too much a traditionalist. Rich men usually are. They're terrible economists. He was bankrupting the treasury. Of course the war in Europe bailed him out — the defense industries began to employ all those jobless hordes. Then we were in the thing neck-deep and all at once the Russians were our Allies. HUAC shut down."

"I've heard of that. House — ?"

"House UnAmerican Activities Committee. Rabid anti-Communists. Now it's starting up again. The right wing is talking about the Red menace, casting new shadows of suspicion, getting this country all worked up. They like to scare people to death: 'Oooh, the Russians might learn to make atom bombs!' Well, I should hope so. If somebody doesn't, America is going to be the new empire-builder. We'll make Hitler look like a sissy. Wave that bomb over the rest of the world and we can bully everybody in sight."

Terra listened silently. There had been endless arguments at Los Alamos about sharing the secrets of the bomb with the Communists. In fact, half the scientists there wanted some world-wide organization to take central control of The Gadget just so it would never be used again. Phin had been one of them.

She said, "On the other hand, if Russia did find how to build their own bombs, wouldn't it start a competition? Already the Soviet Union has begun to get unfriendly. Churchill says they've dropped an 'iron curtain' between us, that there's going to be an arms war."

"Well, we won't win that one," Henrietta

said, almost with satisfaction. "They don't have a Congress to argue over how much they should spend. Their government could order an arsenal and we'd have to follow suit. You know what happens when you try to keep up with the Joneses? You go bankrupt. So deep in debt your money isn't worth spit."

Debt was a foreign concept to Terra. Her father had been rigid on the subject of buying everything for cash. She'd always followed the same principle, to stay within your paycheck. "Why wouldn't the Russians go equally bankrupt?"

"Because," said Manisch strolling in, "they don't indulge in sentimental nonsense like the Marshall Plan, sending their hard-earned taxes to prop up all the tattered economies of Europe. Sorry, ladies, it's an interesting discussion, but we're not going to solve this country's philosophical anomalies this morning. Terra, we've got a new brochure to plan."

Henrietta had already moved off toward her own office.

"This one's very exciting," he was going on, setting a stack of pages on her desk. "I'm still editing it, but I believe we can peddle it to both the Literature and Political departments on our mailing list. The author has excerpted passages from some very great writers, from Plato on down to Thoreau, fifty-eight of them, covering every aspect of independent political thought. The book will be titled — with a bow to Tom Paine — 'Common Sense For a Post-war World.' "

Grasping at the thread of a connection she hadn't quite got hold of yet, Terra said, "Does it include Karl Marx?"

"Oh yes. Very much so. And Mao and Robespierre and Jesus Christ. Well, you'll see. Let's go over some of it . . ."

The day went fast. The material in the manuscript was so new to her, so full of overtones, she had to read carefully to confirm what she suspected, namely that the book was a tribute to rebellion against authority. Put that together with the "W.P.A." text and a theme began to emerge, a sly nod to the revolutionary. It struck a note in Terra. She had always been inclined to resent authority herself.

But in this day, the stakes were high. One of the new films, called "The Beginning or the End," was supposed to be about Los Alamos. She had gone to a matinee, just to see if they had got it right. Didn't come close, but they weren't trying to be realistic. They just wanted people to think about the terrible power that the United States now held, with the bomb in hand.

Glancing at the clock Terra saw that time had got away from her. It was quarter to seven in the evening. Putting the manuscript in her desk, quickly she went to get her coat to find Manisch in the hallway.

"Ready to go out for a bite of dinner? We'll bring something back here and get to work —"

"Not tonight, I'm afraid. I'm on my way to choir practice, and I'm going to be late. It starts at seven."

"Oh, I'm sure they can do without one small voice." He was still smiling, but with a firmness she had come to recognize. This was the boss giving orders.

"I'm sorry," she said, "but I am their accompanist. They really need me."

The abrupt silence was like a pit between them. Then he decided to indulge her. "Go on then, we'll talk about this later. We all have to make tough choices, my dear. It's a matter of priorities."

The word hung ominously in her mind as she walked fast along the cross-street toward the glow of light that marked the church entrance. If she had to choose between the job and the choir, which would it be? The votive lights seemed to share her agitation, fluttering nervously as she hurried past.

Tonight was a dress rehearsal for a Lenten service to be performed Ash Wednesday. She wasn't sure what the ashes signified, but then she still hadn't joined the church. Terra tossed her coat aside and hurried to take her place at the organ. Vocal warm-ups were over, Andrew was waiting in front of the choir loft. He smiled at her, nodded. As he saw she was set, he raised his hands. Magnetic, the way they seemed to draw the choristers into a focus, bodies braced, faces intent.

"Oh, soul, are you weary and troubled?

No light in the darkness you see . . .

Terra hadn't practiced this one, she read the upper keyboard at sight, but it took a few minutes to get positioned on the foot pedals. Then the big pipes gave purchase to the voices.

"Turn your eyes upon Jesus

Look full in His wonderful face.

And the things of earth will grow strangely dim

In the light of His glory and grace!"

An hour later, after the choir had drifted off into the night and Terra was putting away the sheet music, Andrew paused beside the organ. "Want a cup of coffee for the road?"

"This late? It would keep me awake," she said.

"Hot chocolate then?"

"Thanks, I'd like that." The church had seemed drafty tonight. There must be wind coming off the harbor.

"Good, let's go back to my digs." He ushered her through a door at the rear of the nave into a corridor that led to a small suite of rooms. She glimpsed a bed and chest of drawers in one, a desk and bookcases in another, and the third was a kitchen. It was vibrantly yellow. Reminded Terra of her mother's kitchen in days gone by, ruffled curtains, checkered oil cloth on the table. And above the sink a clock — not the yellow china chicken of distant memory, but an equally awful sunburst whose hands showed ten minutes short of nine o'clock.

Poor Shanahan will be waterlogged with coffee by now.

"You seemed very distracted tonight," Andrew was putting the tea kettle on to boil. "I sensed that you're upset about something. Terra, I wish you'd talk to me. That's what pastors are for." He got the cocoa off the shelf and took down some cups.

"This is a new problem. Today my boss told me that if I couldn't work until all hours whenever he asked I might lose my job. He said I was going to have to set my priorities. So I was a little confused when I got here, but somehow the hymns always put me straight. I decided: If the man is trying to run my life, I'd be better off to quit. What I do in the evenings is important."

Andrew's angular face broadened into a smile. "Ah ha. A small epiphany."

"Employers should respect our privacy," she went on, sipping the hot drink, warmth returning now. "And yet I don't think we can make rules to force them. The other women in the office are keen on having a contract that will set down the do's and don'ts. But wouldn't a pressure group create a bad atmosphere? I'd rather just go look for a new job." *With only five more months to go, why fight over the mundane things?*

"If you're meant to make a change you'll find it's easy," Andrew was assuring her. "Remember the words: 'Thy will be done.' If you listen to Him, keep an open heart, and He will guide you to the place that's right for you. And don't be surprised if you're surprised." His smile was so warm, it always prompted her to return it. When the pastor conducted the group, he was all business. The quiet face with its long features and strong jaw was firm as carved marble.

But off the podium it softened, the blue eyes folded her in a look so kind that Terra felt as if her troubles had been wrapped in spiritual cashmere. "My dear little one, you've heard me pray. It's easy. Just have a conversation with the Lord."

How can I? I'd have to confess that I am going to stop living soon. If there is a God he's not going to approve of that. I don't even condone it myself, in principle. It's cowardly to run away from the rest of your life.

"Do people ever tell you they want to commit suicide?" she asked, trying to sound offhand. His face came to full-alert.

"They do. More often than you'd think. New York is a tough place to survive. Sometimes you feel you are scratching an existence out of a huge chunk of granite, just using your fingernails. Do you know someone in such deep trouble?"

Slowly she said, "As a matter of fact, I do. I've been wondering what to say to her, to make her feel there's some point in living."

Andrew nodded. "That depends on the person, of course. But if she is reasonably intelligent you can appeal to her common sense. We've all been given the gift of life, it has to be for some purpose. Until that's realized it is downright ungrateful to quit. It's as if you don't trust God to know what He's doing. That He's asked too much of you. If your friend has any basic faith, she must know that there's more to be explored. Cop out, and she'd be cheating herself of the full measure of her heritage. Until the Lord takes her Himself she has no right to throw the gift back in His face. Try to help her to realize that there's Someone always near to give her a boost. All she has to do is ask. Terra, are you feeling depressed yourself?"

"Me? No, not at all. I'm doing fine! I enjoy being on my own, making my own decisions. It's what I've always wanted." She thought that came out well.

But Andrew smiled a little sadly. Reaching across, he took her hand in both of his. Glancing upward, he added, "Lord, give your daughter peace of mind and strengthen her in the choices she must make, these difficult days. Help her find faith in You, let her feel that she is not alone."

Actually, she realized, the prayers worked as long as his fingers were gripping hers, as if he were leading her by sheer will power. But later, after she'd said "Good-night" and gone on out into the darkness, reality set in. That inspired man had never in his life felt the emptiness that was her constant companion these days. It was nice to imagine some powerful protector, but she didn't feel the hand on her shoulder as he did. Didn't want it. When you concede that you need help, you are diminished. Whatever personal strength she might have had once got lost in that total dependency on Phin. Now, she just didn't have the muscle to start from scratch.

Furthermore, she didn't believe that she was born to do great things, to leave a mark on the world. The truth was that if she died tomorrow, it would be as if she had never happened. The thought gave her a twinge of regret. But it didn't change the fact that she had no glimmer of inspiration as to what she was meant to do. Praying to Andy's God for help wasn't going to change that. *I don't really deserve His gift of life.*

As she stepped onto the platform at 86th Street, far down the way she saw Ari get off another car. They headed toward each other and went up the steps together, out onto Broadway.

"Not a bad commute," he was saying. "Beats the railroad. Ordinarily I would just be crossing Grand Central Terminal about now. Instead, I'm practically in bed."

"So the room is okay?" she asked.

"Absolutely elegant. I owe you a big one."

"No, not really. Cutter needed a tenant." She looked around, trying to spot him, but he was nowhere in sight and the coffee shop was closed. The only people she saw on the street were a couple of cabbies over by the hack stand, bundled in windbreakers and stocking caps. She was just as glad to have Ari's company. "It's good that I ran into you," she went on. "It gives me a chance to explain what's about to happen. I think I'm going to be fired."

"Congratulations."

"Seriously —"

"I am being perfectly serious. You can do better than Paragon Press."

"Well, I don't know about that. I'm interested in the direct-mail campaign now. I'd like to go on with it. But Mr. Manisch — Oliver, he wants me to call him — he's pretty put-out. I couldn't work late tonight. Twice a week I accompany the choir at the church. And of course on Thursdays I've got rehearsals for our next concert. So I just can't drop everything and stay late whenever he asks me to."

"Don't worry about it," Ari told her, matter-of-factly. "He won't fire you. He's got something planned, I know the symptoms. He wants to use you for some personal project. In fact, if I were you I'd quit."

"But you work there, and you aren't going to quit."

"Don't be too sure of that," he said. "Anyway, I'm not the point. I know Ollie pretty well by now, I know where he's coming from and he knows I won't let him take advantage of me. We need each other in equal parts, for the time being. You, however, are young and tender and he's a predator. So polish up your resumé, start looking for a better job. You've got some skills that you didn't have — indexing, production work. If he won't give you a letter of recommendation I will. Because that's the way Ollie is, if you leave him he'll try to get even. Don't even put his name down when you apply for a new job. Say you've been freelancing as an editorial assistant, and I'll back you up."

"You mean he'd really undercut me?" Terra shivered. "Is the world so different now? I grew up in a neighborhood where we all worked together in peace. We helped each other through the Depression. We lived skimpy, but we didn't prey on each other."

"Words to engrave on a tombstone," he said in his mocking way. "This country has lived in a state of hatred for the last eight years. That changes a society. Not just the men who came home from the jungles, or the women who learned to be tough in the factories. It's a whole new culture that's rises from a different philosophy: to acquire all we can as fast as we can pay for it. Which means big enterprise, big businesses to turn out the goods and never mind the quality of the product. The end result of that is there'll be no more pride of work, no more initiative or creativity. Mass production will lower our values. Hail to noise and speed and money. Let crime rage in the streets. Just go inside and close your doors, hate your neighbor, fear all strangers. Our whole society is heading for chaos, my little fragile Terra cotta. So don't worry about the loss of a job. If you want to be concerned, worry about what kind of world your kids will inherit."

But I'm never going to have children.

During the long restless night that followed their discussion Terra found a certain miserable satisfaction that they had long ago made the decision, she and Phin, that they would not start a family. It was settled before they'd ever married, when he first knew about the bomb. It had been a classified secret, but he had told her some of it, trusting that she would never reveal a word. He had wanted her to understand.

"It means," he'd said, "that if we can make the atom explode, the war will be over. But the world will never again be at peace. Other countries will learn the technology, the threat of nuclear destruction will be hanging over us forever. I couldn't even think of bringing children into a situation so ugly, it would be cruel. And it's going to get worse before it gets better."

In other words, Ari's words: chaos.

So it was good now not to have a young life dependent on her. To have to try to manufacture words to encourage a child when you don't believe in the future yourself? *I'm glad I'm alone.* Only, the truth was, when the rationalizing was over, an empty bed gets cold. *I wouldn't want it for a whole long life.*

Next morning Terra reached the office an hour early. Traffic was just beginning to fill the streets as she let herself in. *Got to remember to give them back the key.* Turning on the light over her work table, she settled down to write on a yellow tablet, her best script, the old Palmer Method she had learned in third grade. She was still at it when Manisch came in bringing with him a handful of mail that he dumped on his own table across the room.

"Morning, my dear. You're early to work."

"Yes," she said, without looking up. "I wanted to be sure to get this done first thing. I've made a list of all the brochures in progress — four of them now. I've put down a schedule for each one, showing where they are in the process. 'WPA' is finished, due to be mailed next Monday. The little book of names and their origins needs a title, the ad copy is ready to go in to the printer. The 'Common Sense' spread needs proofing. I've done the layout, but it will have to be pasted up . . ."

"Hold on, little ball of fire, what's this inventory for?"

"Oh." She looked up brightly. "It's so that you won't be in the dark about where everything is on my desk after I'm gone."

His foxy face grew still and wary. "You're planning to leave us?"

"Well, I am assuming you'll have to fire me. It's okay, I'm not blaming you at all, sir. I realize you have to run your business as you see fit. But I can't be on call, the way you want me to be. My life outside the office is important. You said I had to make choices, and I have. My priorities are all in a row. I can give full attention to my work here during the day, and even some evenings. But three nights a week I am going to be busy, with two choir practices and one rehearsal for the concert that's coming up in April. Can't let that go, I'm sorry." She had gained confidence as she spoke, the little speech came out pretty much as she had rehearsed it.

Manisch seemed amused. "*Brava!*. Dear child, I'm afraid I'm the one who should be apologizing. I must have given the wrong impression last night. I have no desire on earth to force you into a kind of slavery. I think it's admirable, that you've filled your life with outside interests. I'll just be glad if you include us in the picture. In fact, I will soon have a very special assignment for you. A matter of such delicacy" — he lowered his voice, glancing around the silent office — "I can't discuss it yet. But I think you'll find it interesting."

Oh, Ari, how right you were. A shiver ran down her back. *I don't want to be part of Mr. Manisch's delicate plans. Maybe I really should quit, while I can.*

APRIL, 1948

Good Friday. A moment of incredible glory, the singers were all shaken by the intensity of Mozart's dying message. *"LUX ETER-NAE!"* It seized them and transfigured them and frightened them. After the performance they shucked off their robes and fled out into the night.

As they trouped down 57th Street in procession Andy kept saying, "You were great, guys, really beyond great. I felt as if I was touching my fingers to a red-hot stove." As if he himself couldn't believe the power of the music that had been created on the stage of the old concert hall.

Or, as Gilda put it, "You-all kicked down the barn."

Terra laughed, a little giddy with sheer reaction to the glimpse of death that she had felt in the Lacrimosa. It had fallen across her heart like a shadow.

"Everybody, come on to the Automat. I'll

treat." Andy led the way, one arm draped across the shoulders of Mary Cordelia, who had sung the soprano solos in a voice as sweet as a drift off the Elysian Fields.

"I think I'll head for home," Gilda said.

"I'm going with you." For some reason Terra needed to get away from the group, She needed to think — about the tragedy of death in a life not yet fulfilled. The Requiem Mass had been Mozart's last composition.

"I'm real glad Cutter gave me his ticket," she was going on. "I never heard that kind of music before. It wasn't exactly church — it was more like Paul Whiteman or somebody."

"You never did say how come Shanahan had to cancel." As they had left for the Hall, Gilda had explained — something about Cutter having a cold? Seemed like a flimsy excuse.

"He's got this bad cough. He was afraid he'd disturb the audience. Anyway, it was a great show, but I have to get up early tomorrow. My boyfriend and I are going up to Storm King on the Hudson Day Line. It's really great, a boat ride up the river. The Hudson's gorgeous this time of year, all the fruit trees starting to bloom. Get off at the state park on Storm King Mountain, have a picnic and catch the next boat back down."

"Boyfriend? Gil, you've got a boyfriend!"

"Yeah. He's a merchant seaman, so he's only in port once in a while, but he really likes me, Terra."

"Why, that's great."

"Well, if you think so will you kindly tell Shanahan? He's such a kill-joy."

"Come again?"

"The man doesn't trust anybody. He says I don't know enough about Woody — that's his name, Woodrow Wilson Beste. Cutter keeps talking about 'a girl in every port,' but Woody's not like that. I don't have to have a whole family history of a guy to know he's good and true. And he's crazy about me." Her voice thrilled to the words.

"I'm glad for you," Terra said honestly. "Don't mind Shan, I think he's getting over a broken heart. At least there's something wrong with him. It's not like him to give in to a mere cold."

"Well, I guess, with his lungs he has to worry about it getting worse. He was going to inhale some vapor medicine."

"What's with his lungs?" Terra recalled that he had mentioned them before.

"Don't you know? He had T.B. That's why he was discharged from the Army. Yeah, he spent a year at Fitzsimons Hospital in Denver getting treated. They wouldn't give him a discharge until he was totally cured. But it left his lungs kind of tricky, I guess."

"How do you know all this?" They had reached the subway entrance. A dank smell rose from the depths, as if from Hell itself. . . . *Confutatis . . . maledictis . . .* the sonorous basses' voices echoed in her head.

"Oh Cutter kind of opened up one night last Christmas when we were sitting up there in your room. You were awfully sick, he was worried half to death."

"I don't think I ever told you how grateful I am, to both of you. I still don't understand why anybody would do so much for me."

"Well, you were nice enough to get me a room. And as for Cutter, that's easy. He's crazy in love with you."

The train came blasting in on them out of the dark tunnel, its rush and roar cutting off the conversation, leaving Gil's words to blaze in her mind like a neon sign. By the time they got off at 86th Street, Terra was still simmering with confusion.

"Gil, what did you mean, that Shan's crazy about me?"

"Well, it's pretty obvious. Why else would he go trekking off down here every night to see you home?" They walked fast along the dark street, the lamps making little pools of light between which the shadows were black. "It's a good thing, too. I mean, this town's getting to be downright dangerous. There was a murder over in Riverside Park last week, didn't you see it in the paper? Some GI Joe went round the bend when he came home and found his girl had got engaged to somebody else. I guess after you killed a bunch of people on Okinawa, it comes easy to cut some poor woman's throat."

When they reached the rooming house, Terra paused, looking down the steps toward Cutter's apartment. "Maybe I should drop in on him."

"Na-a-h, he's probably asleep. Don't wake him up. He'll be okay. That is one very tough man. Proud man. Doesn't like to admit an illness could get him down." Gilda had opened the door above. "You coming?"

Tuberculosis. Terra wondered why she should feel a twinge of irritation — that Gilda knew more about the super than she did. *I guess I have come to take him for granted. Should have asked more questions. He mustn't get a crush on me, I don't want that!*

The thought bothered her through a long, aimless Saturday. Trash didn't get picked up over the weekend. She had tapped once at the door to the basement apartment and got no answer. It was a relief to wake up Sunday and hear church bells pealing across the rooftops of the city. Then she remembered, she wasn't needed at the Church of the Master. They were joining in the Easter celebration with a larger congregation farther downtown, and the other choir had its own organist. So much for that.

I can go get the Times and the Trib, take me all day to read them. Maybe go down to the Automat for ham and sweet potatoes. Shanahan, how are you doing this morning?

The old house was quiet around her. Gil hadn't come home from her holiday excursion. Ari was spending the weekend with his family upstate. Streets unnaturally deserted, it was a good morning to sleep late. Terra pulled the covers over her head.

Later as she walked down to the Automat, the distant church bells only emphasized her loneliness. The heights of the tall buildings so full of private lives playing out, the knowledge of the multitudes around her, so near and yet so isolated — sometimes it was stimulating. Today she just felt depressed.

She had to admit, she could have used Shanahan. When she got back to the rooming house she knocked again on his door. Still no answer. Now in a growing haze of resignation she climbed the stairs. *Why am I loitering around?* Only a couple of months short of D-day. August 21st, the anniversary of Phin's letter, it was time to start planning.

In her room, she fingered the knobs on the gas hot plate. Just go to sleep, quick and painless. But what if some spark set off an explosion? Might blow up the whole darned place. Forget it. There were other ways to do the thing. All along she'd had a vague notion of a tall building, a long jump. But the thought of creating a mess made her draw back.

And now, thanks to Andrew, the question kept rising — afterward, what then? Certainly no *lux perpetua*. Maybe a lot of *maledictus.* That's what the ministers preach: to take your own life was such a sin you'd be cut off forever from the joys of the life everlasting. Trouble was, Terra didn't believe in an afterworld. If she did, she'd have to imagine Phin being there, and the rage would start to rise in her, cutting off that train of thought.

Monday morning she arrived early at her desk, coming at it the long way around past the mail room and down the back hall rather than go through Manisch's office. She didn't feel like sparring with him yet.

He was in there. The door was ajar. She could hear him talking to Henrietta, no mistaking her gruff voice.

"Do you really think that's a good idea, Ollie?"

"Call it an experiment. Go on, get me that fellow over at Holt, what's his name — ?"

"I've got it in my card file."

Terra sat down at her desk without turning on the light. She hadn't intended to eavesdrop, but it occurred to her she might need all the edge she could get, in dealing with her intricate employer. He was on the phone now, and listen to the different tone of voice, the slippery words of a plotter.

"Hello, John. How are you these days? Yes, it has been a while. We should get together for drinks after work. Reason I called you was to ask a favor. Do you know of any hungry editors who might be interested in joining our little enterprise here? Yes, I'm looking for someone to handle the science and math manuscripts. I guess I should add, I would like to find the type of man I can trust . . . Yes, well, I'd rather not talk about Ari if you don't mind. Let's just say I'm looking for new talent, who won't sell us out or divulge our plans and so forth. . . . Oh, I understand, you can't just pull a name out of a hat. But if you think of anyone . . ."

When he had put the receiver down Henny said, "It won't work."

"Why not?"

"Because John Withers and Ari go back a long way."

"I know that, dear lady. But just because they know each other doesn't guarantee perfect trust. If Ari is planning to make the jump to Henry Holt I have to try to plant the small seed of doubt. He's the best editor we've ever had and his politics are flexible. I can't let him go without a fight."

How can politics be — ? As footsteps approached, she quickly snapped on her light and began to fuss with the desk top as if she had just arrived. When Manisch walked in she looked up brightly.

"Good morning, my dear." He strolled over. "When did you get here?"

"Just now. Why?"

"You didn't come through my office."

"No, I stopped down at the mail desk to see whether we'd had any returns on that first brochure." They had enclosed cards for mail ordering. "Nothing yet," she added. It seemed to satisfy him.

"I'm glad we have a chance to talk," he said. "Now that your concert has been accomplished — and with excellent reviews in the Sunday papers, I read them all — I hope we'll have a bit more of your attention."

"There's still choir practice," she reminded him. "Tuesdays and Fridays."

"They must be an excellently trained group." A touch of acid in the words. "I applaud your dedication, but I hear that it has also interfered with your activities in connection with the UOWPA."

"I never had any activities with them," she confessed. "I don't think I'm a joiner."

"Pity. I believe the office is well served by a sense of fellowship. None of my business, actually, but I do hear that the others are a little miffed that you haven't shown any interest in the movement. They are planning to participate in the big parade on May Day, you know. They would love it if you would join them."

"Who's miffed?" she asked curiously. "Gil never mentioned it to me. She and I live in the same rooming house — you didn't know that? Yes, we're together quite a bit, and she's never let on that it bothered her. In fact, I understood that she was about to quit the union herself. They're asking the members to hand out fliers and stuff. She said the language sounded kind of — pinko?"

Manisch bestowed his tight little smile. "I'm afraid our Gilda is fairly naïve, politically. But then, the wattage that shines from her beautiful eyes is not overwhelming. And the girl is late again!" He glanced at his watch. "Confound it, I have just about had enough of her tardiness."

After he had strode off toward the reception room Terra reached for the phone. But there would be no one at the boarding house to pick it up, unless Shanahan happened to be handy. The faithful One-A had gone off to visit his son over the weekend, and One-B would already have left for work. One-C was deaf, never heard the thing ring. Terra resorted to mental telepathy: *Gilda, for gosh sakes hurry up!*

It was hard to put her attention on the new brochure, a philosophy text that was still in editing. One of Ari's list, though he admitted it was not his favorite field. She went down to his office — the door was closed. After a minute's hesitation she knocked.

"I'll talk to you later . . ." She heard him put the phone down. "Come on in."

"Did you see Gil this morning as you left?"

"No, I spent the weekend with my family for a change. Why? Oh, no, she's late again." He shook his head.

"She was probably up 'til all hours last night with that new boyfriend."

"Poor Gil, such a needy sort of woman. A little slow on the uptake, I'm afraid, as well as leisurely of foot. Well, we can't help her. Oliver is getting restless, and he's never happier than when he's wielding a big stick. What's up with you?"

"I'm trying to write copy for the mailing on 'Philosophers at Work.' "

"Ah yes. 'Beyond the bounds our staring rounds, across the pressing dark.' "

"Uh — what exactly does that mean?"

"Darned if I know. Ask Kipling. He loved to create poetic apothegms. Look it up, it'll be good for you. Okay, philosophy. It's just a fancy name for somebody's personal opinion on how we rationalize our lives."

"What about morality?" Terra had gently closed the door. "I'm more puzzled by ethics. Like is it unethical to reveal a secret if it's a bad one?"

"You harking back to Los Alamos? With world peace at stake, I'd say it would have been wrong to pass along any secrets, and never mind whether the aftermath is completely good or bad."

"Oh, yes. That I agree. No, I was thinking on a much smaller scale. I just overheard something . . . didn't meant to, but . . ." She was watching him closely, trying to gauge his reaction. It was hard to do with his left eye wandering toward the window. She focused on the other which was aimed at her like an icepick. "Okay, I've got to do it," she said. "You should know that Oliver was on the phone to Henry Holt this morning, asking them to recommend an editor, in case you should leave." She broke off, aware that he was already nodding.

"And I'm sure he managed to hint that I was an unreliable employee?" He began to grin, a look so full of anger it was frightening. "Terra, forget you ever heard that. I mean it, wipe your mind clean. Don't ever whisper about it again. I don't want Ollie to target you. For your ears only, I have been in touch with a friend at Holt and I may be going over there. In the light of current events, I will damned well be going somewhere! Now, let's get back to the philosophy."

They were aware of voices beyond the closed door, Manisch and Gilda. Her brassy tones were leaden this morning, the words came loud and flat.

"You can't fire me, I quit!"

At five-oh-one in the afternoon Terra put on her coat just as Henny wandered in, fists wedged onto her sturdy hips. "Going somewhere?"

"Yes," she snapped.

"Ollie said we'd be working on the catalog tonight." It was a new project, to issue one large promotional piece that covered the entire spring list. "It's already a little late to start a sales campaign. I told him we'd do better to wait until next August. Fall's a better time to try for adoptions."

"He's planning to combine pieces of all six brochures. He says it won't take long to produce it." Terra got out her purse. "But it's not going to happen tonight."

"You do like to live dangerously," the older woman said with a lift of lip.

"Well, shoot, Henny. He didn't even ask me if I was free. Isn't your union all about setting hours and paying overtime?"

"Except you haven't come down to the meetings. You aren't signed up." The lift of her chin was smug. A hairy mole seemed to accentuate her positive. "So we can't help you if Manisch takes advantage of you."

"No. You can't. Only I can. And tonight I'm visiting a sick friend." She reached over and turned out the light. Making her way across to the front office, where Manisch was still at work, she gave him a rapid "Good night, sir." She could feel unspoken comments hanging behind her like battle-smoke.

Sick friend — maybe Gil wasn't sick.

Maybe she was relieved to be rid of the job. But it can't make you happy to get the boot. You like to go out under your own steam. It's important to choose, to decide how to depart — from a job or a city or your entire life.

The streets were still bright with lingering sundown glow, days getting longer. Walking across Union Square she had a sudden notion and ran for the Broadway bus that had pulled up at the stop. To ride the long slanting avenue that split the island like a cake knife — she'd never done that before. And time was running out for the accomplishment of last-minute deeds. ". . . Go to New York, learn the city, give it a try."

Dutifully, Terra paid attention to the sights like a tourist. Dingy warehouses, small wholesale shops. A window showcasing a loom, with spools of yarn stacked around it — Swedish import house. A street where vans blocked traffic as vendors sold wholesale flowers. The sidewalk was a garden of jonquils, tulips, sprays of gladiolas way ahead of their season, hothouse roses. Then it was past and the Flatiron Building loomed on the right, a tall tribute to history. Madison Square Garden, with tonight's card posted. Undistinguished boxers, but they had made it to the greatest ring on earth.

Times Square. Towering billboards flashing, the news streaming overhead, the wail of a siren scarring across the honk of taxis — this was the heart that was driving the lifeblood through Manhattan and all its arteries. Terra let her mind come ajar and absorb the totality of it. For a few seconds she almost understood the key to the city, that it had once been very great, very central to the nature of the country. The history was there, under the cheap veneer that had taken over. The windows of the second-hand stores were plastered with placards: "Final, Final, Final Closeout Prices, Everything Must Go." Reeling across her vision as the bus proceeded: "Your Fortune Told Here, Walk In," "XXX See Nudes, Sex Slaves, Matinee Half Price," "Spaghetti: 25 Cents a Plate." Sleaziness, penury, ugliness.

And yet a hundred feet beyond, the street was blazing with the marquees of the great theaters. At the Barrymore, Marlon Brando was starring in "A Streetcar Named Desire." Across the street, "Brigadoon", and farther on "Annie Get Your Gun." If Times Square was its heart-beat, this was the soul of the metropolis, concentrated in these few blocks.

The bus carried her on and around Columbus Circle, then past the old Dakota, most historic of apartment houses, and into the middle-class neighborhoods. It dawned on Terra how much of the real essence of the city she had missed, how narrow her focus had been all these months. If she lived here another year or two or ten, she'd never exhaust the sights to see or the doors to open. Seen from the bus, even 86th Street looked different.

With twilight thickening she headed for home, glancing back once, half expecting to glimpse a familiar figure following. *No, no, don't get in that habit. You convinced him to let you be, so give thanks.* Pausing in the foyer of the rooming house, she scanned the mail on the table — a card from Dixie. That stiff backward handwriting she had concocted in the third grade as a protest against the Palmer push-pulls.

"Cancun is a fantasy. You want to tear off your shoes and run barefoot through the lovely dark-skinned beauties who populate the beaches here. The breeze is suitably balmy, the ocean is clear as good tonic water. Long way from St. Louis, kid. Be back next month. Dixi."

At the top of the stairs Terra paused and listened. Muted sounds came from Gilda's room. She walked down and tapped on the door.

"Go away."

"Not a chance," she called back. "I need to see you." *Need to make sure you're all right, not letting this set-back throw you for a loop.*

After a minute the door came ajar, she was left to walk in if she chose. Gil had already gone back to her packing. Dressed in a suede robe that had faded from gold to a wan yellow, she was folding clothes into a suitcase open on the bed.

"I heard what happened at the office," Terra said. "And I have an awful hunch it was at least partly my fault."

"Yours? How could that be?" The words sounded thick and unnatural.

"Well, Manisch was put out with me. He said the office personnel was getting impatient with me for not joining the union. I told him I hadn't noticed anybody acting unhappy about it, and I was pretty sure you would have told me if there were any real hard feelings. Then I mentioned to him that we lived in the same rooming house, and he got all tight, the way his mouth thins out, you know? I mean, what business is it where we live, for crying out loud?" She was moving up on Gil as cautiously as if she approached a wounded cat.

"That's stupid. I mean the whole union

thing. We never talked about anything important, just politics, and government, the masses taking over their own destiny and crap like that." The tone was dull, the words came out clumsily as if — Terra got a good look at the girl's face now and quailed. Gil's lip was split, she had a black eye and a cut on her left jaw.

"Who did this to you?" she demanded in a rush, not choosing her words, not caring to be diplomatic. "Was it this boyfriend?"

"We sort of had a fight. That's why I was late coming in this morning, I didn't feel too great." Aggressively she slammed a stack of underwear into the suitcase. The bras were padded; who'd have guessed her remarkable frontage was the result of enhancement? Then a couple of nighties, a box of Kotex, a pair of green satin shoes with very high heels. Tossing things in helter-skelter.

"You don't want to do this. Please Gil, don't run away," Terra pleaded. "There are so many better jobs out there."

"I'll just blow the next one, same as always. Like Woody says, I'm what they call in the Army a natural f— foul-up."

"Oh he says that, does he?" Terra felt a familiar stirring, though the anger this time was on behalf of someone else. "Any man who would beat up on a woman hasn't got the credentials of a river rat. Who's he, to pass judgment? What makes him a hero?"

"He was in the first wave onto the beaches of Normandy. He's got guts, he's — he's —"

"That doesn't mean he's a man. The way he treats other people is what counts in real life. Gil, you can't be blaming yourself for this!"

"Well, it's my fault. I know he hates women smoking, so what do I do? I light up a ciggie, I wasn't thinking. So naturally he yanked it away, and gave me a smack. I had it coming, Terra."

"No, you did not. Nobody has the right to knock you around like that."

"And then Manisch chewed me out, told me what a miserable excuse for a person I am. He's right, too."

"*Gil!* He is not! He's a bully and a sadist, and you mustn't let him do this to you!"

The wounded mouth twisted in a sad smile. "I'm not like you, Terra. I don't have a lot of gumption. I'm not a great office worker. I never did like that receptionist job. What I loved was the assembly line at the ammunition plant in Gary. I was good at that, and it didn't matter whether I was attractive." It was an admission that cost her.

"I'm too tall. I don't dare wear heels —"
She picked up the green pumps. "You want these? I loved them when I saw them in the window. I bought them without thinking. Never have worn them. They make me look like a basketball player."

Terra put them carefully back on the bed. "Okay, listen: You are going through some problems, but you needn't give up this room. If you can't make the rent, Shanahan will carry you for a while."

"It's not that. I've got to go somewhere I belong. I'm going back to Indiana. I just hope everybody didn't move away. Some of them probably got hitched by now, but I've got to try it. Terra, I need to be with old friends, you know?"

And that can't include me, because I am the person she isn't and never can be.

As they stalled, staring at each other, a tap on the door dented the silence in the room. Shanahan's voice came softly, "Gilda, you in there?"

"Come on in, Cutter." This time she didn't face away, her chin came up and she stared back at him as he swiftly took inventory without commenting. The super was sloppy of shirt, frowsy of hair, and surrounded by a faint aroma of Vicks Vaporub.

"Fellow downstairs is asking to see you. I

didn't want to let him in unless you tell me it's okay. Name's Woody."

"Wood-e-e-e . . ." she bleated and ran past him, bathrobe fluttering, fuzzy slippers pounding down the stairs.

Shanahan looked a question and Terra hunched her shoulders. "He's the one who beat her up."

"B'gorrah!" He choked, coughed, then was racked by a hard paroxysm that left him gasping for breath. *"Damn!"* he muttered in a kind of generic all-purpose curse.

"Come on," Terra said, "we can't help Gilda. But I can do a thing for you, m'boy." She led the way to her room. Dark and chilly — she turned on the light and went straight to plug in the floor heater she had bought. Offering him a wooden chair in front of it she said, "The straighter you sit, the better."

"You've had bronchitis?"

"The dust in the high desert around Los Alamos produces a variety of respiratory ailments. Especially if you've had T.B. — Gilda told me about that." Rattling along, she got out two lemons and the squeezer. "This won't cure your cough, but it will help your throat." She put a pan of water on the stove, added the lemon juice and some gobs of honey from the jar on her shelf. "That's the worst part, the way it rakes your throat raw." She dumped in a tea bag.

"I don't get it," he said and he wasn't talking about cough remedies.

"That guy at the door looked like a roughneck. This is the fellow she's been mooning about lately?"

"It beats me," she agreed. "Some people can't handle loneliness. Any kind of attention is better than none, I guess."

"God," he murmured. Then, "Was she packing up to leave?"

"Said she was going back to Gary, Indiana, where she worked during the war. Everybody like a family in those days, pulling together."

"Doesn't she know that by now those girls on the assembly lines have moved on? Plant's probably closed down."

Terra brought him a cup that steamed aromatically. Shanahan took a gingerly sip, then drank it down in slow steady gulps. "Man, that's good. You have a great maternal instinct. Got any kids?"

She started a new pan of water. "No. No children, not now, not ever."

"Sorry. I didn't mean to pry. It's just that you'd be a good mother."

"I couldn't protect my young from the

place this world is going to become. In fact, it's already starting. Everybody beginning to be afraid, need unions to protect them from their bosses. Countries all suspecting each other, secretly working on bigger and better bombs. The steamroller of big business is flattening all the little family stores, no room for the craftsmen, the thinkers, the odd-balls. My late husband was an odd-ball. He used to dream crazy visions of using atoms to light up the world. But they took him over, they used him and bent him and . . . here. Drink this one more slowly. The point is, now the old values are gone. Everybody's on a strut, because we won the war. They're all so full of . . ." The word escaped her.

"Hubris," he said.

"Is that what I mean?"

"Arrogant disregard of moral laws."

"That's it!" She sank down on the sofa. "That is what Phin grew to despise, the loss of ethics, the loss of kindness and generosity. He was a man of great integrity, which is why he —" *He ran away. He ran away and left me to cope with this mess all alone.*

In the silence, they heard a mumble of voices out in the hallway, Gilda's, almost chirpy, appealing, anxious, and a man's tones raspy and bluff. It made Terra sick.

Down the corridor and the door closed, the sounds cut off.

"Shan," she said, "where did you go to college?" *I mean, a word like "hubris"?*

"Kansas City Art Institute. They had good teachers — Thomas Hart Benton, some others. Learned a lot about technique, but that doesn't make you a successful sculptor. You have to know how to entertain the people who give out the commissions, got to spend a lot of money impressing them. You need to be a showman. That's more important than learning to handle a plaster knife."

"So you gave it up."

"I gave up any notion of making a living off it. Nobody supports themselves on art alone. You need a wealthy patron to pay the bills. Or to become part of a group, get funded, lose your identity." He sat staring into the space heater, its red coils glowing enthusiastically. "I did sell one piece."

"Where?"

"Gallery on Madison Avenue. They cater to architects, and one of the clients liked my work. Just a thing I did from memory of an Indian boy, friend of mine in Montana. They paid me five-hundred bucks for it, but by the time the gallery took out their commission and the architect's cut and so forth, I wished I hadn't sold it."

"A real — an American Indian?"

"Full-blooded Crow. They're a great nation. I grew up around them. Our spread was right next to the Reservation. His name was Bad Horse. Nice, happy kid, not a bad bone in his body. He's the one who called me 'Cutter,' because I was always whittling." Shanahan glanced over at the table where she had placed the little rabbit carving on a doily.

"What became of him?" she asked.

Hoarsely he said, "He died. Like a lot of kids in those days, he got polio."

"Phin had polio when he was about ten. It's what kept him out of the Army." Along with the demands of Arthur Compton and the Chicago physicists who had seen his work on electromagnetic separation. Better he should have gone off to battle. Then maybe he'd just have been wounded a little. He'd have felt as if he'd done his job, there wouldn't have been the damned guilt.

Shanahan stood. "That's a good little heater," he said. "But you shouldn't need it. I'll turn up the furnace."

"Since that spell I went through I can't seem to get warm," she admitted. "I know electricity is pretty high —"

"Higher than fuel oil. But that's not the point. I'm probably being too tough on my tenants." He twisted off a grin. "Don't know why you're all so good to me. Thanks for the drink."

"Oh wait — here's the bottle of honey. Keep after the thing, you'll wear it out. I know you're too old to take advice from a mere slip of a girl, but you'd be better off in bed, resting."

Cutter glanced back at her, the battered lined face inscrutable. "How old do you think I am?"

The question caught her by surprise. Without thinking she said, "I don't know — about forty?"

He coughed and laughed and choked all at once. Another of those paroxysms shook him. When he could breath again he said, "I don't know whether to be flattered or flattened. No, ma'am. I am twenty-nine years old. You don't really know all there is about T.B." And went off down the stairs.

As she stood listening to his loose jogging steps, the click of the front door, Terra became aware of another murmur of sound. It came from Gilda's room, hushed mutterings, mumblings, a muted giggle, a gasp. She recognized it well enough. That first year in Oak Ridge when she and Phin were newly married there had episodes of fun. But the sex had been sporadic and too intense and too quickly over. Something sad about a desperate coupling so brief and so meaningless, just a flash of physical gratification. Then a kind of let-down.

What she remembered best was the love, the belonging, the sensation of two bodies holding each other close — that was what she missed. And abruptly the pang of loss gripped her so fiercely it hurt.

MAY, 1948

How do you dress to walk in a political parade? Terra had put on a slightly dowdy skirt, brown wool, and a shirtwaist, what else for a union of office workers? Flat shoes, of course. Hat? No, a head scarf tied under her chin, women of the fields, arise.

When she went downstairs she found Cutter sitting on the front steps in his shirt sleeves. First day of May, the sky was overcast, the air almost muggy. He seemed lost in thought, but as she came past him he gave her a quick assessment.

"Hi," she said. "I'm off to march for liberty, equality and fraternity, or something like that."

He almost smiled. "Here — you'll need these. Going to be pretty bright out there." From his shirt pocket he took a pair of sunglasses and handed them to her, men's glasses, large and dark. Terra glanced at the sullen sky. The Irishman just sat there looking enigmatic.

Gravely, she said, "Thank you." And put them in her pocket. "How did you know I was going to be in a parade?"

"Gil mentioned it," he said carelessly. "She went out about a half hour ago."

"I didn't know she was marching with us."

"She's not. She's on her way to meet bully-boy downtown. He's going to show her his boat or something."

"Oh, Lord. I guess I can't blame her for wanting to be somebody's girl, but she could do so much better."

"Not if she thinks she can't." He had on his Irish look, fatalistic as an ancient Celtic scroll.

As she got to the corner of Broadway Terra saw a bus coming. No need to rush — it was only eight-fifteen. She climbed on and settled back in a seat. *This is a crazy thing to be wasting my Saturday on. Probably going to rain. Why did Shanahan think I needed sunglasses?* Shrugging off the question, she tried to sort out her own reasons for deciding to march in a parade celebrating nothing, at least nothing she believed in.

And the answer to that was: Henny. The old girl had been very decent, getting Gilda a new job in a place that would make her happy. She would be in a pool of office workers at a small publishing house, everybody in one big room, working together to put out a cheap magazine each week. Just a grocery-store throwaway, but Gil said they all had a lot of fun. Terra was glad and surprised at Henrietta, for going out of her way to be helpful.

"Kid got a rough deal," she remarked, carelessly. "And I told Ollie so, too. He shouldn't have canned her, but he was in a bad mood. It happens." So when Henny had reminded her, yesterday, "Tomorrow's the big day when we make womankind proud of us," Terra didn't have the heart to refuse.

"I haven't really joined the union," she protested weakly.

"Doesn't matter. Everybody's welcome to march. We're all going to meet up at the corner of 54th and Eighth Avenue. We'll walk down Eighth to Union Square where there'll be a big rally. We'd be glad to have you under our banner."

"Okay, I'll come," she'd said. But wished she hadn't, after she'd talked to Ari.

Eating deli sandwiches behind his closed office door that Friday Terra had asked him, "What's does it mean, the May Day thing? We always celebrated it in school by dancing around a pole. This is a political parade, isn't it?"

"Not much difference. Just a new pole to dance around." He put on his mockery like a garment. "You and the ladies will be celebrating Lenin and Stalin and all their communistic brethren, including the numerous socialists in this country who are plotting the overthrow of our government, that's all. Have fun."

"Come on, be serious," she urged. "I'd like to know what I'm protesting for or against."

"I'm perfectly serious. This is a national holiday over in Russia when the proletarians march and the red flags with the hammer and cycle wave. Workers of the world, unite, including the wage slaves of New York City in the year 1948. You'll be showing your sympathy for the planet's exploited masses. Do you feel exploited? You are, you know. Anyone who works for anybody else is being exploited. So have a good time protesting it. Doesn't cost a cent and may make you feel better."

"I feel perfectly fine. And I'd really rather not overthrow the government, but —"

"Well, maybe the better word is 'oust.' It's possible that we might end up with a third political party. Organized labor might help Wallace get his Progressives out of neutral."

"The Vice President?"

"He hasn't been our Vice President since 1944. Even back then he was a maverick. Now he's got the bit in his teeth, going to unite the nations of the world in a great brotherhood that will take control and keep the peace forever. Especially you must be kind to the Russians. If we tell them how we made the bomb, they'll be so grateful they'll stop working on it themselves. Don't ring them around with military bases, they'll get nervous and start building their military bigger than it already is. We should all disarm and love each other. God bless our country, and so forth. That's Wallace."

"Okay, maybe some day you'll explain it all to me, when you're not pranking around."

Ari had set down his can of Pepsi and leaned forward earnestly. "My dear girl, everything I just said was the Lord's own truth."

Remembering the acrid words, Terra stared out the window of the bus, unseeing. Phin had been in favor of sharing the A-bomb technology with the Russians. He said they would do the arithmetic themselves one of these days; maybe if we showed the hand of friendship they would join us in establishing a world-wide control over the atom. His fellow workers had called him naïve. Only Oppie was inclined to listen to his arguments, agreeing in principle. But after The Gadget worked with such deadly efficiency, even he decided we couldn't trust anybody else to handle the technology benevolently. He had backed off from any notion of confiding in the Communists.

At Columbus Circle Terra stepped off into the Saturday morning crowds, shoppers, picnickers heading for Central Park. First day of May, the vernal equinox was beginning to show results, trees flowering, ducks showing off their new broods on the lake. Walking down Eighth Street, she looked for familiar faces in the groups that were heading for the kick-off point. There seemed to be quite a gathering ahead. The C.I.O. was setting up a big placard. And then she sighted Henny, stoutly dressed in green coveralls and a red bandana tied around her neck. The woman's stolid face lit up as she saw Terra and waved.

"Let me guess," Terra said, as they met. "You're Rosie the Riveter."

"And you're Sister Carrie, just arrived in the big city, got a job in the garment district. The headscarf is perfect."

"Where's everybody else?"

"Buddy's dressed up in a Sunday-go-to-meeting suit that's right out of the 1920's. He's great, but he doesn't know it. Ruth hasn't ever been in a parade before, she's wearing high heels. They're down at the start-off point on 54th." She was leading the way at a quickened pace.

The intersection was blocked off, cops on horseback sidling nervously, other cops on foot trying to keep a space cleared for the parade to form. Several groups had their banners up and were already moving down the route. The UOWPA was having trouble with its unfurling. Several women Terra had never seen before were struggling to get the long piece of canvas open.

Meanwhile the CIO had got organized and was heading out, three men carrying their lofty sign overhead.

WHOLESALE WAREHOUSE WORKERS UNION
LOCAL 65 — CIO

Out of the milling crowds Buddy made his way to them, with Ruth tagging along, thin and colorless in a gray gabardine suit. She was already limping. "I don't think I can walk all the way down to 14th," she said bleakly.

Terra was watching a man down the

street. Suit, snap-brim hat, he didn't look like a newsman, but he had a 35 mm. camera. He was snapping a picture of Local 65 as they moved off. Then turned to point his lens at the Office Workers, who had got their message spread out now.

EQUAL WAGES FOR EQUAL WORK

"Here we go." Henny gathered her contingent to fall in line behind the other assorted members of the union. On the far side of the street another man with a camera focused on them. Terra felt in her pocket, got out the sunglasses and put them on. When Henrietta looked at her, puzzled, she shrugged.

"Having trouble with my eyes."

Later in the day after it was all over she returned the shades to Cutter when he stopped at her door to collect the trash.

"These came in handy," she told him. "How did you guess?"

"There was word on the street that the parade would be carried on television. I just figured maybe you might not want your face broadcast in all the saloons around town." Television, the new-fangled entertainment device with the square screen — the bar owners put them up to offer their clientele the prize fights.

"So that's what those news crews were doing down on Union Square? They didn't bother me, the crowds were pretty thick by then. It was the men along Eighth Street with the little candid cameras snapping away at each of the groups as they came past — they didn't look like television people."

"Probably weren't." He went to get Gilda's wastebasket, dumped it.

"Then who?"

"I don't know, but I'd guess it was the F.B.I. or the O.S.S. or some other bureaucratic posse."

"Why? I mean, we weren't doing anything wrong."

He hitched a hip on the banister railing. "Back at the turn of the century, this country got into a twist over the Commies. Coal miners went on strike, stayed out all winter. Town people got pretty chilly. They blamed it on the Communists. There was a group called the W.W.W., preached the overthrow of the capitalist system. They wore red neckerchiefs. That's so when the shooting started you didn't gun down the wrong people. There were some pretty bloody skirmishes in the coal fields and with the smelter workers and such. Of course conditions in the mills and mines were bad, no doubt about it. But city folk got spooked and the 'Red Scare' was on. The power structure — Rockefeller and Guggenheim and other moguls — ran some of the union organizers out of the country, men like Big Bill Haywood. There was fear in the air and hatred on the streets. It took a war to make that go away, First War. My dad was in it."

"So was mine. The 'war to end all wars,' " she said with a touch of bitterness. "But that's ancient history."

Shanahan shrugged. "It set the stage. That and the Russians with their revolution. When they went Communist, they sided with Germany in the thirties." Cutter shook his head. "Never did understand why Hitler invaded them. Seemed like a stupid move. With them on his side he might have actually won the war in Europe. So we took them on as allies. We fought together in mutual defense, but the hatred never went away. The old fears are coming back strong now that we've got the bomb to wave at them. Going to get worse, too, I expect."

Phin knew, he expected this. How could he have left me alone in this treacherous world? Subconsciously Terra had directed the question to some unseen Know-it-all on high, and was startled to have an answer pop into mind: *He figured you were strong enough to handle it.* Where did that come from? Curious she prodded a step farther. *If that were so, I would have some plan. And I haven't. I mean how could I face the whole long future?* But of course there was no response to that. Hearing things in her head, not enough sleep last night.

Those days she moved about her life automatically, refusing to confront problems. Decisions were a pain in the neck. Why worry? The past was done with, she didn't even nurse her anger any more. What difference? As for the future, who cares? There was nobody who mattered to her, she thought — until she got the invitation from Dixie.

At sight of the cross-sticks writing on the envelope Terra realized that she had missed her loony sister-in-law. Actually had missed her all through the war years. They had been so close in early days, almost inseparable, until Dix had left to pursue a dream and Terra had been stuck at home. Stuck in school. Now all that mattered really was an old and comforting friendship with the one person on earth who really knows you.

In a quickening of anticipation, Terra opened the envelope.

You are cordially invited
To
A Very Private Showing
At the
Galerie de la Coquette
May 9th
4:00 P.M.

On the back, Dixie had written, "This is just for you, sis. Let me know if you can't make it, but please make it."

They hadn't seen each other since the cruise, but Terra was sure the change of scene had prompted some new sketches. She had always been in awe of that amazing talent, the way the slightly skewed brain sent the stream of creation down the skinny arms to the awkward fingers, and through a piece of charcoal onto huge sheets of paper. In the old days it had been butchers' wrap, but even then the drawings were extraordinary — sharp, inventive, irresistibly exciting.

She had always known that Dixie was earmarked for a great future. Knew it, because her own efforts to rise to a calling fell so short. You can master a skill, more or less, but you can't summon inspiration where there isn't any. It even took considerable effort for Terra to imagine what kind of outfit she should wear to the "showing."

She settled on a white silk party dress that she had bought at Klein's. She really hadn't needed anything so dressy, but the price was low and the soft clinging lines were marvelous. The mid-length skirt made her look taller and the ruffled front softened her chin, which she knew was too hard-set these days. As she stood before the mirror, putting on her lipstick, she made her mouth a little fuller for Gilda's sake. The girl was hovering, her long fingers twitching to help with the make-up.

"You really should use eye shadow with that dress. I mean, it's so virginal. It needs red earrings or something, put a little git in your giddyup." Gil was looking reborn these days. She was even scrambling up each morning to be on time for work. The new job had done wonders. Or maybe the ubiquitous Woody? "Listen, I've got the cutest red chiffon scarf with little rhinestones on it —"

"Sorry," Terra said, "but the only way I can dress around my sister is to keep it plain. She likes to apply her own taste in accessories." Dixie turned bilious at the word "cute."

"She sounds terrific. Can anybody go in this gallery of hers?"

"On weekdays, yes. I think she reserves

Saturdays for special showings. She's inclined to be dreadfully picky. Are my seams straight?"

"They're perfect. Good Lord you're skinny. You should eat more. Hurry on, you'll be late."

"I'm right on schedule." But to make sure, she took the subway, enduring the occasional curious stare, though most New Yorkers were immune to anomalies. Once she walked out onto 57th Street she felt more at home. Even on Saturday afternoon the clothing here was high-style. The glossy couples who strolled toward Broadway looked relaxed and expectant, heading for the theater district, an early cocktail, a show, a late supper afterward. Right now the sun was still high, showering the trees over in the park with a special luster in honor of their new leaves. There were moments like this, Terra thought, when you could almost pretend that the city was a modern paradise.

Climbing the stairs to the *Galerie* she found the waiting room deserted. Devoid of the usual large sketches around the wall, it stood spare and ready for enlivenment. Nothing but a delicate antique table and chair, to one side, and a chaise lounge from the Empire Period facing a row of easels.

"Make yourself comfortable, madam."

Dixie appeared in a striking sheath of black satin that fell from a high neckline straight to her knees and broke off short there. Her ebony hair was glued in short spikes that burst in a profusion all over her head — the word "Hottentot" came to mind. She set down a tray with two wine glasses and a tall bottle. "Fear not. It is pure sinless sarsaparilla. Or I could bring out my ginger ale, if you prefer."

"Sarsaparilla!" Terra marveled. "I haven't had a drink of that in years. Where do you even buy it these days?"

"Oh, my wine merchant is eager to please. He found me some when I told him I was entertaining a purist. Incidentally, thanks for wearing that white dress. It won't conflict with any of my doodles." She went off again, to return with a sheaf of sketches, which she began to set up on the easels. There were six of them, wild with color, jungle greens and oranges and purples. They were a riot of flowing skirts and wrapped bodices, blousy sleeves or no sleeves, just the suggestion of a bare shoulder, a long arm, the hard black outline of an ankle here, a spiked heel there — the strong strokes never faltered. And in the corner of each, the word ***DIXI***.

"Cancun must have been stimulating, to

say the least." Terra sipped her drink, reveling in the rampant color. "You've invented a whole new look."

"I hope so. I'm going all the way this fall, entering the big fashion shows, taking the plunge. Zoey says it's time." Dixie perched on the delicate chair next to the chaise. "You're supposed to recline on that thing, like David's nude. You can put your feet up. The needlepoint is only a hundred years old." She raised her glass, "So here's to my esteemed sister-in-law, our guest of honor today."

"I'm flattered to be the first to see your new line. The Cancun motif is very striking."

"Oh, that's just the beginning, to prepare the palate. These are the far end of the spectrum, the fun part. On the beaches I spent my mornings slashing around on big tablets of newsprint, trying to catch the feel of a tropical society and put it into a style that New Yorkers would accept. They're a conservative lot, you'd be surprised. Savage cultures scare them to death. Okay, enough of the gaudy." She was gone again, tripping across the floor on those deadly spike heels.

Dixie's nervous about something, her voice is pitched too high . . .

This time she brought a more mixed collection of styles which she placed on top of the first lot. "Watch out, these look conventional, but they aren't."

Looking over the new display, Terra instantly loved it. The kind of clothes that could be worn by ordinary women who didn't have salon hair styling and thousands of dollars, these dresses could be adapted to any reasonably shaped body, even though they had a distinctive flare.

"They're knock-outs," she proclaimed. "Every one of them. You're going to wow the style community."

"I call them my 'Terra Collection,' " Dixie went on rapidly. "I tried to do one for every mood. What you are to do is to pick out two, your favorite two. I'll make them up for you — we're still about the same height, I can use my own dress form. I want to get them to you by the first of June, because the day of mortality is approaching, and I want to give you a couple of months' use of the ones you pick."

"Day of — ?" Then she got it. Phin's letter had been dated August 21st. So this was the real purpose of the whole demonstration — Dixie was mounting a head-on assault against a situation that was scaring her. Terra struggled not to show any emotion. Calmly she said. "It's very thoughtful

289

of you, to want to help. I appreciate it. I just hope you're not going to try to talk me out of it."

Soberly Dixie said, "I wouldn't do that. In my chosen world we see many cases where life becomes too difficult to sustain. We understand. We try to respect others' choices, especially when it's not some rash impulse. You were inclined to rush off in all directions, back in the good old days, but now you seem different. Cool and deliberate, you don't make decisions lightly. I trust you to know what you're doing." Dixie spoke her little speech grimly, in spite of the smile on her tilted mouth. "So here's the deal: I want you to pick out one dress to get married in, and one to be buried in. Wear them for a month and see which feels right. Okay?"

This is a test. Don't blow it. "Interesting concept." Terra nodded gravely. "Of course, there isn't the faintest chance I would ever again go to the altar even if I lived to be a hundred. And the trouble with the alternative is, if they can't find the body I won't be buried. But the symbolism is valid. I appreciate the challenge, and I love the designs."

Her first pick was easy, a wide woolen skirt of tweed material, the swatch pinned to the bottom. Sleeves rolled to the elbow, the shirt was almost boyish, but the extra broad collar and the shirring in front were feminine. A few strokes of charcoal indicated a head thrown back to the sun — this was the way she had once felt and never would again.

For the second choice Terra pondered the other five sketches and settled on a party dress of lavender velvet — again a swatch of the material was provided — over which a delicate wrap of netting was delineated by fine red pencil lines, pin-pointed with small blue dots.

"Those are sequins," Dixie explained. "You should try drawing a sequin!"

"I know what they are," Terra said. "You are really a master of your medium, Dix. These sketches belong in an art gallery."

"Maybe next year." She flashed her rare child's smile, unblemished by mockery. "You really do like them, I can tell. And you don't willy-nilly around, I love that. If I were to pick out the two I'd like most to do for you, it would be those. I'm going to have such fun making them. Neither one is form-fitting, we won't need to do tedious try-ons. I'll have them finished in a couple of weeks."

"I don't know how to thank you."

"You already did. You took good care of

my crazy brother. You stuck by him all those years when you lived in solitary confinement out there in some wilderness. You made him happy. I know I come across as a fruit cake," she added wryly, "but I was serious about Phin. I adored him. Don't tell anybody, I'm sentimental."

"Your secret is safe, trust me."

"I do trust you," Dixie said earnestly. "I trust you will not elect an ill advised type of demise that will ruin one of my creations. No jumping off window ledges or diving in front of the subway."

Terra chose to laugh at that. "Good heavens, how I missed you all these years."

"Me too. You always were my best audience." Dixie's eyes brightened with tears and she began briskly to gather up the sketches. "Tell you what, let's go get obese on some chocolate cake at Brach's."

Too fast — all at once Terra felt as if her unreal slow-motion life had a plunged forward into reality. It was probably reaction to the fashion showing. When the dresses were delivered a week later they seemed to propel her headlong toward the ultimate decision she had avoided. Right now, with a glorious springtime breaking out all over the city, it seemed almost obscene to contemplate leaving the world, however imperfect.

She suddenly realized that she had found it in her heart to forgive Phin a little. It was not his fault that he had been born with a brilliance that dominated him. The driving force that quickened his mind from each scribble on the blackboard to the next was a thing she could only envy. In all great people, composers, painters, authors, you sensed it. The open agony of Steinbeck in The Grapes of Wrath, or the compulsion of Mozart — *"Amen, amen, amen"* — she had to admit there was something noble about investing yourself that totally. She had to absolve Phin of his own predestination.

But rather than stimulate her, it just contrasted with her own uninspired existence. *He thought I could handle it?* Great people never can imagine a life that's one long lonely trek, trying to dredge some meaning out of each day with no dream of achievement to look forward to. Surely there was no point in continuing to be useless. Even the improbable Higher Power could see that was a waste of time.

Uneasily she went to stand before the calendar on the wall of the office. Less than a week to go in May and then thirty days in June, plus another thirty in July. Followed by twenty-five in August — did the thought make her happy? She looked into an inner mirror. *Are you still bent on it, or is this just a vow you made that you're afraid to break? If so, you're going to be a long time dead. Think about it!*

"Don't tell me you're already making up a time-table for the fall mailings?" Manisch had paused to glance over her shoulder at the calendar. "I believe it's too soon to work on the list. We won't have our manuscripts in hand until mid-summer."

It was late afternoon. They were alone in the office, no pressing schedules for a while, nothing to prompt a lot of overtime. The new contract provided pay for that. Unless otherwise instructed, Terra was supposed to go home at five-thirty sharp.

"I'm off the clock," she told him. "Just trying to figure out where the year went. I've been here over ten months."

"And we have all benefited. I think that calls for a small celebration." He went over to the cabinet in the corner and unlocked it. Getting out a glass and a packet of powder, he added some vodka and a dash of tonic water. "Can't I persuade you to join me in a little relaxer? You look a bit down, my dear. There's nothing at all immoral about giving our psyches a slight chemical boost."

"Do you have any sarsaparilla?" she laughed, just joking.

"I'm sorry — of course, you don't partake of spirituous liquor. I'd forgotten. Plain tonic water, then, with a twist of lemon?" He fussed with the bottles, picked up another of the packets. "I do wish you'd try this. Nothing evil, it's just mildly euphoric."

"No thank you."

"I assure you, it's not at all like alcohol, which actually degrades the body and eventually provokes a worse depression. This is a stimulant. Great men have found the ancient tisanes to be quite beneficial. We drink tea, we drink Coke, both of them distilled from nature's secret pharmacy. The beauty of the poppy is only a variation on a theme."

Opium? He's offering me opium? Terra shook her head. "Thanks, but I'll pass."

With a sigh he poured her a glass of plain soda. "I'm glad to have this moment alone with you," he went on, pulling up his chair to face her across the desk. "I have a delicate matter to broach. It requires strictest secrecy, but then you know all about secrecy. In fact this subject is right down your alley. I wondered how you'd feel about helping us out, myself and some concerned friends whom I won't name at this point. We are troubled by the way the world has turned since the end of the war — as I'm sure you are. Your bereavement last year was only one symptom of a worsening of the environment, not just the scientific but the political."

Wary now, Terra waited for him to drop the shoe.

"To be plain, we're worried about the bomb. As everyone should be," he added. "Now that it has been turned over to the military, the people who built it are outside the picture. The Army has practically ostracized Oppenheimer, you know. He advocated a world organization to control the atom. It provoked all sorts of suspicion from our paranoid leaders."

"No, I didn't know that." When she left The Hill Terra had vowed grimly never again to have anything to do with that bunch of egomaniacs. Teller had gone kiting off with his militants to build a more horrible explosive, his "super bomb." Most of the others had gone into sack-cloth, like Phin. Half of them wanted to destroy all the technical data, others wanted to share it with every wild-eyed revolutionary country on earth. When Truman took The Gadget away and gave it to the military, he had good reason. You couldn't trust philosophers to harness the madness of a doomsday weapon.

"What the country needs is a sensible person in control. We believe Henry Wallace is the man to avert disaster," Manisch was going on. "He could be a broker for world peace. The problem is, to get him elected."

She shook her head. "Hasn't got a China-man's chance."

"Unless he can draw together some of the unaligned intellectuals in this country. There are undercurrents of dissatisfaction that could be channeled into a powerful force to create a society based on common sense, not hackneyed political parties. Think of it, Terra — a whole new philosophy of government."

"You mean socialism?" Terra asked mildly. *Does he expect to dazzle me with big words, after all the years I heard these sophistries kicked around Los Alamos?*

"Something akin to that. There are many good points to the socialist imperative. And many flaws in the republican form of government. What we need is a new amalgam of political thought, a different look for a different day and age. Terra, we aren't in Kansas any more."

She was amused at the thought of Manisch sitting in a theater watching "The Wizard of Oz."

"So we come to my proposal, which I hope you'll take as well-meant, even if you don't totally understand it. Agreed?"

"I always try to keep an open mind." She spoke the words automatically. They had served her well in years past.

"Frankly, we would like to enlist Robert Oppenheimer in our cause," he went on, blandly, as if he were proposing a day at the ballpark. "He must be smarting by now, his brilliance quenched by a cabal of his inferiors. They can't stand anyone who is a scientist and a philosopher as well. The problem is, we don't dare approach him openly. The man is under a close surveillance by the F.B.I., his phones undoubtedly tapped, his contacts observed. They're thirsting to call him a Communist and accuse him of selling atomic secrets to the 'enemy'." He scorned the word. "The media keep demonizing our Russian friends."

"Well, you can't blame the President for feeling Stalin has drawn a new line, with the Berlin blockade." She set down the untouched drink.

"And you can't blame the Communists for worrying, with the threat of the atom bomb hanging over the Soviet Union. You see, that is exactly why we need new management to convince the Russians that we are all in the same boat. We all want to stave off Armageddon. Oppenheimer could do that. He's the only one with the stature that they might respect. But he doesn't seem to realize what a leader he could be. What we need is an intermediary to take a message to him, somebody who wouldn't be seen by the Feds as a threat. So it occurred to me — since you already know the man — that you might be our go-between. Nobody would be suspicious if you dropped in on him. He's down there now at Princeton heading up their Institute for Advanced Study. If we could get him to join the cause of Wallace's party it might be enough to start a bandwagon toward a new political flowering in this country. Not to mention a new lease on world peace. Are you up for it?"

"Me?" Terra was struggling to process the real purpose behind this bizarre suggestion. Not that it was so crazy, she obviously could do it. But that Manisch should want her to? *He's a Communist himself.* The minute it crossed her mind it provided answers to several questions. Suggesting that she walk in the May Day Parade, placing his blessing on the union, the underlying subversive quality of his textbooks — it all came together. *That's why he can't approach Oppie himself. He's part of a subversive movement and doesn't want to reveal it publicly.*

"You would just be an old friend from The Hill, came by to say hello, the wife of a favorite protégé, the late Phineas Berensen, rest his soul. You could breeze in without raising suspicion from J. Edgar Hoover's flunkies."

And if they did draw a bead on me, I'd be expendable.

"We would be willing to compensate you for your good deed generously, pay for your ticket to Princeton and an overnight stay there. We would provide you with written documents to pass along, so you wouldn't have to make any arguments personally. Just the fact that you are the messenger should help impress Mr. Oppenheimer with the reasonableness of our proposal. After all, he has sat in your kitchen and broken bread with you. Obviously you aren't a wild-eyed radical."

Oppie once said I played a wild game of poker.

"I might add, Terra, that your personal future would be brightened by this small act of cooperation. I value team spirit highly, and I'm in a position to reward it, for better or worse. Will you think about it?"

Better or worse? He means he could make me pay, if I refuse.

Slowly she said, "Yes, of course I will. Think about it, I mean. I'm — flattered you'd ask me."

Manisch glanced at his watch. "Oh my, I'm late for a meeting. But I'm glad we had this talk. Let me know what you decide, and be sure that my personal gratitude can take many forms." He gave her his practiced smile.

After he had gone Terra searched around until she found a box — shoe box, she'd had to buy some new flats after that May Day walk. Rifling through her drawers she took out every small personal item she had brought in to the office, a folder of snapshots from home, a fountain pen her father had given her one birthday, a picture of Max Wolff taken at some school function she no longer remembered. She added a copy of her first brochure — the WPA book — she'd been so proud of it. Small bottle of sachet and a lipstick for touching up after lunch, an extra program from the last Carnegie Hall concert. Putting the shoebox in a shopping bag, she turned off the light.

Act normally, don't do anything to make the man mad. You need to figure a graceful way to make an exit from this place. But don't wait too long. Maybe right after the holiday?

Deus irae. The great Requiem Mass thundered in her head, a fitting thunder for Memorial Day. A day when graves were honored and salvos fired in cemeteries with their long geometric rows of crosses, and somewhere the ashes of a being once called Phin eddied in the waters of the Pacific. At least Terra had been told he was cremated and dispersed. Cold waters, deep seas, yes . . .

And yet here the sun was balmy. She sat on a bench in Central Park, watching the boaters out on the water, baseball games over on the playing fields. Kids and balloons and cops on horseback were everywhere. Somebody was cooking hotdogs, pigeons crowding around for crumbs. Nobody here was thinking about dead heroes. New York was agog with the glorious freedom of a day off-work.

The air was so free of fumes it felt almost medicinal, the light breeze better than the touch of a sympathetic hand. If she had ever believed in God it would be on a day like this. It kept returning, that curious moment a while back when she almost thought He had spoken to her. She kept wanting to test it.

"I know You don't approve of me Yourself, what I'm planning to do. But tell me: do You really like what the world is coming to?" She spoke in that conversational tone that Andy always used.

There were other times in olden days when society lost its way. There were times of chaos worse than this.

Terra was startled at the way the words flowed into her mind. Just random thoughts, and yet — she decided to continue the test. "Why didn't You stop it then?"

No answer, of course, but then — it was obvious, wasn't it?.

"Okay," she conceded. "I've read the story of Sodom and Gomorrah. And maybe you'll bring down our — hubris, was that the word? Meantime, is it so wrong for me to choose to get off the merry-go-round? What good am I doing here?" That was the question that always broke the connection. Maybe you were supposed to figure things out for yourself, when it comes to the totality of your value on earth.

Deliberately, she surveyed a montage of her life, at home, at the piano bench for long hours during high school days, at Gloucester College in the cottage with Max Wolff, at Annapolis with Tommy, graduation day December 12th, 1941, midshipmen's caps arching into the air, joy to a world at war. Then the grim train ride home to be there as her mother drifted away. The awful trip, conducting her distracted father back to his home in Iowa. Afterward a rush to get to Oak Ridge, to be married in a few minutes before a Justice of the Peace. It hardly seemed real now. She had worn one of her old recital dresses, made her look about twelve years old.

The few rare happy days of being a newly wed, with all the discoveries that implied, were gone too soon. She found herself in a place of muddy ruts and buildings smelling of green lumber amid tall locked fences in the high desert of New Mexico, a settlement with no name, but an aura of desperation about it. The months in the compound, amid a cacophony of intellectual brilliance, had intensified steadily up to that ear-splitting flash in the sky, a thousand times brighter than the sun. The Gadget had worked.

Terra was watching a ten-year-old trying to climb a huge boulder, throwing himself at it, scrambling and learning about toe-holds and finger grips. Experiencing great joy. *Watch out you don't fall!*

Her personal catastrophe had come crashing out of nowhere. Just when she'd thought the hard spell was over, there had been that long wretched night when Phin had sat like a man turned to stone as reports came in about the devastation of a city and most of its humanity.

"I've got to go there," he kept muttering. "I can help. There will be hot spots, and they don't have anybody who knows radiation like I do."

Arguments, pleading, then finally she had lost all pride and groveled to him in a spasm of anguish. "What about me?" she had sobbed.

"I'm sorry, but I have to try to undo some of the damage I caused." That stern hard set to his chin. They had both known then that he would not come back.

Wildly, "I swear, Phin, I will kill myself. I don't want to live in a world without you." The words glanced off him like paperclips. *So he didn't love me, much less admire me or even respect me. Not really.*

At least, she thought, she could try to do better, square things with the few people who cared about her. First and foremost Dixie. Her sister-in-law was proving to be more vulnerable than she had expected. *Got to do the thing with some kind of flare, so she won't be disappointed in me.*

Andrew. He could be hurt, and would be if she didn't prepare him for it. He must be aware that she was philosophically motivated, not just giving in to some weak spell of homesickness. She hadn't been over to the church in a while. Summer, the choir had disbanded temporarily. But he would still be there; some evening she would catch him. Explain to him. Maybe ask him to say a prayer to his God — that would comfort him.

Who else would be affected by her departure? Ari? He would probably give a silent cheer. And Gil would cry for ten minutes and then go to Klein's and buy a black dress for the funeral. No. No funeral. No corpse lying around for somebody to deal with, that's uncouth.

She had just about settled on a quick step off the Staten Island Ferry into the currents of the Harbor. Drift out toward the ocean beyond. Drowning, she had heard, was relatively painless and less stressful on others than the gorier demises. She would just to disappear . . .

Would that be a relief to Shanahan? With his brotherly sense of responsibility, surely he'd be just as glad not to have to shadow her home every night. She thought of the little carved rabbit and a moment of fondness came over her. If she still had the capacity for affection Terra would have been tempted to reach out to him, talk about it with him. He'd probably understand. The shadow of a similar weariness was in his own eyes at times. His Celtic blood streamed from a melancholy ancestry. Of all her present circle of acquaintances, he would take it in stride and go on with his life, adding another strand of sadness to his memories.

As for the rest of the world it could go to Hell. People could plot and lie and steal and despoil the land and debase their own heritage and get rich to their heart's delight. Only it would turn sour. Terra was as sure of that as she was sure there was a place of Damnation. What had the Devil said in Faustus? *Why this is Hell, nor am I out of it.* He meant the fires are right here and now. Amen.

Which reminded her — there was one small cloven-hoofed detail she still had to deal with. There was a certain inevitability about it — her final challenge, to face off against the man with the demonic smile and sulfurous aura. Oliver Manisch.

June, 1948

So far, so good. The first step in the process had been a success — the lunch with Dixie. Terra had worn the new outfit, the tweed skirt and frilly white shirt. She had added a cocky little straw boater that she chose to perch on the front of her head above the coil of braids.

"It would be smarter if you wore it back." Dixie was trying to hide how happy the sight made her, the way her own design looked on its intended model.

"I don't know," Terra said, dabbling with the vegetable plate. "I think this makes me look ready for a day at Saratoga."

"You're more the State Fair type," Dix informed her. "All you need is a prize loaf of bread or something." So it was plain that they were not going to talk about the future, and just as well.

Terra was ready to defend her course of action, but she didn't much want to dwell on it. The onset of summer was still breezy and bearable, as they sat in the sidewalk café on Lexington. She was sorry when the lunch hour was over.

"Got to get back to work. One more mailing to get out, for summer school programs — all it needs is to be proofed and printed. I'm trying to get my desk in order." She saw a shadow cross the homely sad little face across from her. "I should tell you, I'm going to be fired from my job. Soon, I think."

"Oh well, good for you." Dixie perked up. "Nothing invigorates the soul like giving the boss the well-known gesture." And if her bravado was a bit forced, still she stepped out briskly when they parted at Fourth Avenue.

Back at the office, Terra stopped by Ari's desk. He glanced up. "What's the occasion?" Looking her up and down, he added sourly, "Going to a funeral?"

"Yeah, my own," she said, flippantly. With a glance down the hall she lowered her voice. "I think I'll be looking for new employment any minute."

He reached out a foot and kicked the door closed. "I meant what I said to you. Give me as a reference on your next job. Don't mention this place, tell them you've been free-lancing. And if he does fire you, watch your back. Ollie doesn't like to lose a good employee."

"What about you?"

"I won't be advertising my departure ahead of time," he told her. "To you I will divulge it: by the 15th of the month I'll be gone. I'll start at Holt on the 1st of July. Going to take a couple of weeks off, except for night school."

"I thought that would be over now. Didn't they have a graduation last week?"

"They did. My entire class made it, which, considering their lack of enthusiasm, was a tribute to their teacher. But now comes summer school, time when you get the laggards who flunked regular day courses, the boneheads that I love so much. I'll be teaching three nights a week. Thank the fates — no, thank you — for getting me that room."

"Then I'll probably see you again. I'm glad of that."

"Lord knows why. I am not a barrel of laughs these days."

"When Manisch loses his favorite editor, what will he do?"

"He's already done his best to spread the word that I'm a traitor. Fortuately I have more friends than he does." He sobered into a frown. "But you will be on your own, and it concerns me. Thank goodness you've got a bodyguard to walk you home these evenings."

How did he know that?

Ari gave her a grin. " 'The Shadow knows.' I've seen our super hanging around the coffee shop, nights when I got home ahead of you. He's quite a guy, Cutter Shanahan, looks as though he could take on a whole crowd of muggers. But he's never met Manisch. You better warn him to watch for snakes in all that grass along Broadway."

Terra shook her head and left him to his work. She waved at Henny as she went past and took a seat behind her drafting table. The paste-up of the leaflet looked attractive, full color, 8″ × 10″, a reprise of their spring list, plus a preview of new titles for fall. She sat down and scanned the text for errors.

"I believe that's your crowning achievement," Manisch observed, moving in mysteriously to look over her shoulder. "You've really got the hang of this job. I'm quite impressed."

"Thank you," she said, without looking up. "This is ready for the printers. I thought I'd walk it over there, and then go on home if that's okay with you. Henny tells me I have too many hours of unauthorized overtime this week."

"Ah yes, our union girl. Well, this time it's perfectly all right. In fact you may want start packing for Princeton," he added. "I'm taking the train over this afternoon. I can make arrangements for your stay at the hotel near the campus. I would suggest that we travel together, but I think it best for you to be disassociated from any outside interest, even a small undistinguished press. You can plan to follow over tomorrow, we have to move quickly. Their campus is already in summer mode. I imagine Oppenheimer will be taking his usual safari out to the wilds of New Mexico. I understand he has a ranch there. I'm sure you don't want to trek that far to talk to him."

"Mr. Manisch." She turned to face him. "I thought about your idea — of me going to see Oppie — and I'd really rather not. Personal reasons. I'm sure you can find someone better to take a message to him. Actually you're persuasive, why don't you do it yourself? He's very approachable, and since it's not illegal to campaign for Henry Wallace I don't see why be so secret about it?"

"My dear child," he laughed. "You are delightfully unsophisticated. I was trying to be diplomatic when I described your mission, but I didn't mean to be ambiguous. The truth is, my offer to the Professor could be called into question by the flag-wavers who are so ardent to get us into a whole new war. How can our paranoid politicians resist the prospect of brandishing the H-bomb, with its tremendously greater destructive power? How tempting it would be to use it on, say, Moscow? I'm sure that's what the Russians are envisioning. Mr. Wallace and his followers are sympathetic to their fears. That may be construed as disloyal — I'm afraid the country has lost all sense of perspective. I really believe we would be better off with new leaders, no offense to your boy Harry Truman. He's doing the best he can, but the man was never groomed to be a President, I'm afraid."

"Maybe not," she said lightly, "but he's my neighbor from Missouri and I'm going to vote for him again next fall." *Or would if I were going to be around.*

Manisch was frowning. "Are you saying you don't want to help us out?" As if it were a betrayal of major proportions.

"Yes sir. I'm sorry, but I hope I never see Robert Oppenheimer again."

"Mmmm. Something personal, you said. About your husband?"

"Oppie encouraged Phin to go with the

observers to Hiroshima, right after the war. He could have kept him home. He knew how emotional it would be for Phin to see all that destruction. He knew how I felt about it. And he chose to say 'Go ahead, son. I'd like to read a report on the effects of radiation.' So Phin became a walking example of the effects of radiation." Of course, she wasn't being fair. Oppenheimer had vigorously opposed Phin staying on after the teams left. She didn't blame the Professor. But it was true, that she didn't ever want to see him again.

"Wouldn't your Phineas have wanted you to pursue his dream — world control of the bomb?"

Where did he learn the name "Phineas?" He's had us researched, got hold of the wedding license probably. Terra had to bear down hard to keep from revealing the tremor that went through her at the thought of snoops prying into her life that way.

"I don't know what Phin would think about that. I just know what *I* think, and I think I will stay 'way out of politics'."

"They can be scary, all right." Manisch indulged in a cheerful laugh. "But I could explain them to you in a manner that would prick your interest. Why are you shaking your head, dear child? I'm offering you a

314

world of opportunity."

"I've had enough secrecy and philosophical argumentation and all that to last a lifetime. I'm sorry." *You may now fire me.*

For an instant a glint of fury passed across his eyes, and then they were once more that clear, merry blue. It must be a trick that he'd practiced. "All right. Fine. We won't speak of it again. Go on with your work, my dear. I'll see you when I get back from my sales trip." And he was gone before she could adjust to the fact that she had crossed a master manipulator, refused to let him dominate her, and she still had a job. It seemed strange to walk out of work at the height of the afternoon. It brought a touch of euphoria, which worried her. *I shouldn't be feeling this good.* A breeze right off the harbor kept filling the skirt as she walked across town. It smelled of the sea and faraway places, like a drift of curiosity about the future. There was this odd temptation to take hope.

As she got off the subway at 86th she found herself amid the crowd of afternoon shoppers, strolling in and out of the small shops. Stopping at the grocery store to get an apple she heard an altercation between its owner and a tall woman with a bee-hive hairdo that gleamed with blue rinse.

"A can of coffee is only twenty-seven cents down at the A & P," she was scolding him. "That's a full penny less than yours."

The proprietor shrugged his shoulders sadly. "So take it, then. Vot's a penny?"

But the A & P is blocks away. She doesn't really want to walk that far. Don't let her bully you, Mr. Shuman. Terra had found herself forced to bite back words like that oftener all the time. She bought her seven-cent apple, gave him a dime and murmured, "Keep the change."

It won't be long, she thought, before the mom-and-pop groceries will be gone. The big Atlantic and Pacific Tea Company can buy cheaper in quantity and sell for less. It was the way the whole country was trending.

I'll bet their apples aren't hand-polished. Poor world.

With the sun in her face Terra stepped out briskly. When she got to the rooming house she came to a stop. Cutter was sitting on the stairs, as he had once before, except this time he was eating with a spoon straight out of a jar with the grim determination of a man who wants to get drunk on peanut butter. His hard-used face was downright ominous.

"Hi. What's up?" she asked cautiously.

316

"Nothing is up. Absolutely nothing is up."

"O-kay. Have a nice afternoon." She started past him, got almost to the front door, which was standing open.

"Quite a few things are down," he added through the peanut butter.

"Like what?"

"Like Gil. In case you should be interested, she's in the hospital."

In case I'm interested? Terra came back and joined him on the top step, tucking her skirt around her knees. "What happened?"

"Same guy, he's what happened. The Spalpeen." The word broke from him furiously. "Well, he's down. You could say he's down."

"Shan, please stop being cryptic and tell me from the beginning." *And why is he angry at me?*

"They came home together this morning — I guess they'd made a long night of it. Showed up right after you went off to work." He gave the words an accusing tilt, as if it were a flaw in her character. "I heard 'em go upstairs, both in their cups, talking loud. I heard him say 'Come on, one more time,' or some such. And she said, 'But I'm already late for work. I don't want to lose my job.' " He glowered off into space. "Should have known, should have followed 'em upstairs."

"You can't save the world, Shan. She made her choice." Then when he fell silent she prodded. "So go on, tell me what happened."

"I heard a ruckus and went up to see if she needed help. Too late. The door was open, I could see her on the floor, blood all over. He took one look at me and ran, I guess he figured I was going to clean his clock. And there was a time I would have, before the damned shoulder went. All I could do, as he ran past, was stick out a foot. He took that top flight of stairs head-first. I didn't chase him, I was more concerned for Gil. She was unconscious, lost a couple of teeth, I could see her arm was broken. What kind of mug would hurt a — ?"

"Good grief!" Terra gasped. "Did you call the police?"

"I called an ambulance," he said. "What good are the cops? The guy was long gone. He won't be back."

"How can you be sure?"

"I'm sure. I sent him a message as he departed, what I would do if I ever saw his ugly face again. He'd not be knowing whether I could carry it out. Anyway I didn't want to hang around and waste time filing a complaint. Let Gil make one later if she wants. I stuck with her, we took her to Belleview. She came to, enough to give me the name of an aunt. I called her up. She lives in Hoboken, she took the tunnel and got over pretty quick. Nice lady. Said she'd call me when they find out how bad the damage is. That's why I'm sitting here, don't want to miss the phone if it rings." He scraped the bottom of the jar angrily.

I've got to get over there. But she didn't say it to Shanahan. In his towering rage he seemed to be lashing out at anything that moved. Terra left him and went on up to the third floor. The door to Three-B was still open, the wreckage untouched. Chair overturned, mirror smashed, blood on the shabby carpeting. She straightened the room, searched the closet and found a cheap suitcase at the back, set it on the bed and began to pack it with overnight wear, gown and slippers and robe, toothbrush, comb and hair spray, pancake makeup and a lipstick. Gil of all people was a creation of her own. No matter how banged up, she would need the artificial façade, to feel halfway human.

As she folded in a skirt and blouse, something to wear home, she heard the phone ring downstairs. *Leave it for Shanahan. He's in his own place right now. Let him work his way out of it.*

A minute later he appeared in the door-way. "They've got her patched up," he said, stony-faced. "No internal injuries. Going to keep her overnight. Then the aunt is going to take her back to Jersey for a while. What do you think you're doing?"

"She'll need a few clothes," Terra said mildly. "I thought I'd take these to her."

"Not tonight. Visiting hours are over. But I guess you can pack the bag, I'll get it to her tomorrow morning."

"Shan, I don't need your permission. Gil's a friend of mine, remember? I owe her. And I owe you, the two of you were very good to me last Christmas when I was at death's door. All I want here is to help."

He slumped down in the rickety chair, as if the wind had gone out, leaving him deflated. "I should have known, the minute I saw the guy . . ."

"He was Gil's mistake, not yours."

"And you'll do the same," he said wearily. "You'll go stepping up the street in that skirt, looking like a rich debutante, inviting some thug to get the wrong idea and when you're lying dead in the gutter —"

"It won't be your fault," she finished. "Shanahan! You must never blame yourself for anything that happens to me." *Dear Lord, it gets complicated.* "If you ever do hear of me dying, know that I went in peace."

He looked at her startled, the tawny eyes rushing from rage to alarm. *How fast he picked up on the implications.*

Hastily she retreated. "It's just that you're too sympathetic for your own good. But thank heavens you were here for the poor girl."

"Feel so damned inadequate." He was back in the depths of Celtic depression, the guilt of a whole race weighing him down. "My mother used to say we must accept our lot in life. When I was five, I thought she meant a parcel of land. I wanted to know where mine was so I could start growing horseradish on it. Always did love horseradish. Later on, somebody set me straight about lots. They told me the word had to do with lotteries. In the old days everybody was dealt a ticket, some won, most were lucky to break even. And a lot of folks ended up in the poorhouse. The whole thing was just a matter of fate, they said. But I never believed that. I'd rather think we were each given a vacant lot, sort of spiritual homestead to work. Maybe some ground is better than others, some people try harder to make it grow crops. Some throw it away, as if it weren't worth a penny." He directed a look at her, so accusing it made her wonder if he had sensed something.

Terra felt her face suffused with heat. And nothing she could do about it, you can't argue with a blush. "Didn't you ever feel like giving up?" she wondered. "All you've been through."

"Bunny, what I have been through you don't know the half of. But I never considered tossing away the one thing anybody ever gave me that was valuable. I tell myself there'll come a day when it will all make sense. Maybe I'll grow some horseradish yet. Right now, I have to admit I've hit a rocky patch. Close that thing up and give it to me. I'll go over to Belleview in the morning." Briskly he added, "Sorry I snapped at you."

Back in her room, she changed out of the new clothes. Far from provoking admiration from Shanahan they had offended him, as if she were putting on airs, flaunting her good health and good mind and fair looks when Gil was crushed and suffering. Well, he was right. The skirt looked incredibly rich. And thoroughly out of place on West 88th Street. It looked like it should flirt itself around the grounds of some mansion out in the Hamptons.

In the name of humility she went into the office next morning, clad in her most conservative suit, a gray poplin with severe lines. Dixie would have hated it. Stopping by Henny's desk, she said, "Could you give me the number for that place where you got Gil her job? She's in the hospital. I thought I'd call them and explain why she wasn't at work."

"Sick?"

"Badly beaten up," Terra said, grimly.

"That boyfriend!"

"You've got it."

"I told the girl he was bad news. But she's so needy." The older woman underwent a remarkable softening, her hard-jawed face almost motherly. "I know. I was in her shoes once. Before I married Mike."

"The longshoreman?"

"Yep. Tough as a claw hook. I felt the back of his hand a few times, probably deserved it. But underneath he was decent. Gil's young bully is as ugly inside as he is outside. I'll be glad to call the folks over at the magazine and explain things. I don't want her to lose that job either. Was she badly hurt?"

"No, she's getting out today, going to her

aunt's to recuperate. Broken arm, lost some teeth."

"Lost more than that, I bet. The gumption. She's never had more than a smidgeon of self respect. It wouldn't take much to wipe the smile off her face permanently. Poor kid . . ." She turned away to the phone.

Terra went to her desk, sat down, and somehow lost a day of her life. The confusion of images, questions, emotions that raged through her was disturbing. *I can't check out with all these questions unresolved. You need to know where you are before you — aren't.* A year ago, she'd thought her personal decision was her own business, a commandment written in stone. Now . . . *Are my reasons legitimate? Am I planning to take my leave as some sort of revenge on Phin? Sort of a 'you'll be sorry' reaction? That would be stupid. I am not a dummy, I know nobody will give much of a hoot when I'm gone. I don't want them to. So why should I have second thoughts?*

And there was one place where, she thought, a little order might come out of her confusion. Her steps quickened that afternoon as she headed for the Church of the Master. No choir practice this evening. It would be deserted. At least she hoped so. She needed time in a quiet place, where her heart beat more slowly and her ears could almost hear those high harmonics overhead.

Past the fluttering candles she moved silently inside and stopped at sight of a dim figure up front, kneeling before the altar. Long and slim and dark-clad, it had to be Andrew. Reluctant to interrupt, she sat down in the rear pew. She puzzled over it — what it would feel like to pray. If Anybody was listening, He was the only one who could set her straight. *Is it a sin, what I am planning to do?* Right or wrong? The age-old question must have been lifted up a million times to the silence of those arching rafters overhead.

So try it. Just have a conversation, like Andy would. But the easy friendly discourse wouldn't come. You have to deserve God to talk to Him like a friend, which is exactly why she had always shied away from church. She had to admit that she lacked the faith.

After a while, the man up at the altar stood. Glancing around, he saw her and walked up the aisle to take a seat on the bench beside her. "It's remarkable," he said, "how you materialize just when I need you."

"You? Need me?"

"I think so. Just now I was asking guidance . . . it's a little different from the kind of prayers I make when the Lord and I are walking together down a well-known path. Then He's like a much-loved brother. But there are times when I am alone in the dark and needing a father's hand to guide me. Then I go through the ritual. It helps to observe the formalities, kneeling and supplicating. It's very good for reducing one's ego. You have to listen hard from deep inside, but the answer is always there. Just now He told me that someone was on the way to give me good counsel. Must be you."

"Oh, I doubt that," Terra smiled. "I'm the most confused person on earth right now. I came here looking for a clue or two myself. Not that I am hearing any. I'm the last one who could possibly give you advice."

"You're the only one I know who can relate to my problem. Terra, I think I want to get married. And yet I'm not sure what that kind of commitment means. For someone like me."

"Like you? How?"

"My own first allegiance will always be to Christ. Ever since I was a child I have dedicated myself to Him. It wasn't exactly a matter of choice, it was something I had to do. Now, I wonder if a marriage can be part of that."

"Does the church allow it?"

"Ours does, very much. They feel a man

can be a better pastor when he has experienced the family situations that others go through. He can minister better to the couples in his congregation if he's got a wife himself."

"You have one picked out?" she wondered.

Shyly he said, "I've grown very close to Mary Cordelia. She'd make a fine mother, a good mate for a man of the church — she's strong in her faith. She believes in everything I do."

"But — ?"

"The truth is, it sort of terrifies me — the responsibility of wedlock. I know what effort it takes to join two lives together, even in the most normal of marriages. And mine would be even more demanding. I remembered what you told me, of your late husband's dedication to his work. It's not unlike the priorities of a religion."

"Phin wasn't much of a believer," she told him. "He never went to the synagogue. He didn't practice the rituals that some of the others did."

"And yet he believed in the morality of his religion. And when he had to break the commandments as he saw them he atoned, or at least died trying to. This is the very essence of faith. I would feel that I had to do the same, in his circumstance. You have to answer to your Maker. It's a moral imperative that rises above personal relationships, and that's what concerns me. Do I have any right to take Mary as my wife if my first loyalty is to God and His son? Supposing I were called to serve the church in a way that separated me from her, would it be fair to leave her alone and saddened, as you are?"

"Sad," she said, "is all right. You expect to feel sad. People have to go to war. Men get drafted, they die in combat. Sadness is natural. What I feel is anger. I have been so furious with Phin, it seemed to me such a selfish thing he did, to put his own guilty conscience ahead of his duty to me — That's the worst part of it, to hate the man I loved. How does Mary feel about you?"

"I don't know. I haven't asked her yet. I know she's fond of me. I think she'd say 'Yes,' to a proposal. But love on a personal level is a kind of mystery to both of us."

"Well, let me tell you how it feels. If Phin had needed all of my blood I would have given it to him without a minute's hesitation. When he said we must not have children, I erased children from my mind. When he said we were going to live in isolation, maybe for years, I was glad to be by his side. When he told me he was going into the most deadly place on earth, I only wanted to go with him even if it killed me. He was part of me, the best part of me. Now I am incomplete, not just alone, but amputated. I'm crippled inside so that I sometimes wish I were dead. So I hope Mary Cordelia isn't that much in love, because it hurts like Hell. And I mean the word literally."

Andrew sat silent, battered by her words. Slowly he said, "What you have described is indeed a kind of Hell. One that I can't conceive. For a minister that's woeful. We're supposed to counsel people in pain, but how can we if we never have felt pain? It has to be the real reason — the one I never quite understood — why the Master needed to die that terrible death." For a while he stared off toward the front of the church appalled. Finally, he said, "Forgive me, Terra. I had no idea your despair went so deep. I've been so wrapped up in my music that I am truly a novice when it comes to the human condition, which is proof that I need to experience life a lot more profoundly. But you make a good case for the price being high. I'll have to think about it some more. Meantime, how can I help you?"

"Can you turn off this feeling of betrayal?"

"Your only antidote is to reawaken that dormant love — you obviously have a great wealth of it in you. Some philosopher once said something — I can't quote it exactly — but the gist of it was: Hell is the torment of not being able to love. Your mother is gone, I believe you said? And your husband that you adored, also erased from your life. Have you opened your heart to feel any affection for the people around you now?"

"I've vowed never to be that vulnerable again."

"But what kind of existence would that be for you?"

"Very unsatisfying," she agreed. "Probably unbearable."

He shook his head. "The only clue I can give you is to turn to a higher power than mine. If you give even a fraction of that kind of love to Jesus Christ He will never leave you for any reason. You couldn't pry Him loose, He will be at your side forever."

"Andy, I can't dream up a new soul. And I'll bet you will agree that it can't be faked."

He nodded unhappily. "That's the catch. You can only seek and hope. You can do the warm-up routine — to be generous and sympathetic and selfless in helping others. But you cannot evoke an emotion so deep and personal. It has to happen, like a revelation. Which it will, if you let it. If you keep an open heart with absolutely no skepticism, try to erase your doubts, it will come, but you have to have patience."

"I kind of wore my patience out in Los Alamos. I'm tired, I really don't relish being alone." *I want this inner ache to be over. I want the end to come quickly.*

"I pray you will dig down deep and find a way to ride it out. Maybe a few minutes at the organ, a brief sense of joy as we sing, a glimpse of God in the new leaves on a tree or a drift off the ocean. Or talking to someone — me — I'll be glad to discuss this again whenever you like."

"Thanks," she said. "I appreciate all your concern. But I have come to say goodby. I'm leaving the city."

It upset him visibly. "For good?"

"Oh yes. Very much for good."

"Where will you go?"

"I don't know," she said. "I truly don't know."

It was full twilight on Broadway by the time she came up out of the subway. The rush-hour commuters were gone. The coffee shop looked empty, no figure in a knit cap lurking around the taxi stand. And yet she suddenly felt a crawling of the hairs on the back of her neck, as if her sensors had picked up a predator. Walking briskly, she listened for footsteps behind. They were there, but softly, as if someone followed in the shadows.

As she crossed 87th she saw a couple of kids playing stick ball with an older man in a white jersey and baseball cap. She almost went to them for the safety of numbers. But they paid her no mind so she went on, impatient with herself. She'd never been one to borrow trouble. Besides, Manisch was out of town.

Ridiculous notion — the man wasn't a thug. He'd never visit physical harm on her. He was much subtler than that.

Violence always seemed unreal to her. And yet, there was nothing unreal about the blood on Gilda's floor. The newspapers were full of bad news. The movies, too — she had gone to a matinee of "The Kiss of Death," filmed on the streets of the city, where she walked daily. A different kind of picture than Hollywood used to produce, it had been like a rude wake-up call: We live in a world where death comes easily and danger wears a business suit. She began to quicken her pace even more.

All at once, the footsteps faded. Glancing back, she saw a man crossing the street, going into the deli. False alarm. She turned the corner and headed home.

July, 1948

Terra tore off the page of the desk calendar. July 3rd. That was the date she had received the first letter from Phin, telling her that he was in the hospital in Manila. The poison worked fast, toward the end. He was almost gone by then, but his orders had been firm: she must not come to the Phillippines. He didn't want her to be there through the final days of the illness. It probably hadn't occurred to him that rather than saving her misery he had added to it — the agony of imagination was far worse than the real thing. That was the point at which she had given up on the marriage. On him, on herself, on life.

This is the day I should end it all, this terrible anniversary, a kind of ugly celebration to finish a spent and useless existence.

The office was let off early and she headed straight for Battery Park. For a while she stood there, looking out over the waters that shuddered in the ebb of the tide, sucking at the embankment below the sea wall. It didn't bear too close examination, that back flow, where odds and ends of orange peel and paper bags and cigarette packages bobbed. You couldn't picture diving into that garbage. Out in the bay where the currents were cleansed by the ocean, she thought it would be all right.

But when the ferry came in, she immediately saw the difficulties of using it as a departure point. Much of the passenger space was enclosed by glass, and the open areas were surrounded by high safety walls, except the ramp where the cars were driven on. The whole vessel was crowded with people, too many by-standers. She would never be able to go over the edge without someone seeing and snatching her back. Horrified at the image of being restrained, possibly carted off to Belleview for observation as an attempted suicide, Terra turned away and marched grimly off to the subway.

She wasn't completely ready, she realized, or she wouldn't feel any pangs of reluctance. Words kept playing back in her head like a stuck phonograph full of the dogged sadness of another's hope: "Maybe I'll grow some horseradish yet." Cutter's talk about one's lot in life, maybe growing up in a religion gives you endurance. Somewhere he'd developed patience.

On an impulse she caught the bus and rode it up Broadway to 42nd Street. Walking east, she turned in at Bryant Park and headed for the back entrance of the New York Public Library. In the early days of her new job assignment she had spent a weekend here, delving into a variety of books on advertising techniques. Now she went to the central desk and enlisted the help of a librarian to choose a book on major deadly diseases. When it came up from the depths of the collection she took it to a table in the huge hushed reading room. When she turned to the chapter on tuberculosis Terra forgot, for a few moments, her own depression and entered into a new one. Finally, she thought, she understood Nehemiah Shanahan. It explained so much . . .

He wasn't around when she got home, hours ahead of her usual time. Just as well. She felt shy about talking to him now. How to offer the right words of reassurance, to admit she knew his secret? Maybe better left unspoken, now and forever. *I never learned the knack of consolation. He'd probably end up trying to comfort me I need to focus on my own problem — I need a new plan.*

■ ■ ■ ■

That next morning with the city gone silent under its holiday recess Terra got up, hesitated over the lilac dress which she hadn't worn yet. Then decided not to be hasty. She had hit on an alternative scenario, but it needed to be scouted first.

A nice day for a short walk through the deserted streets over to the riverfront, and a dock where she lined up for a tour on a sight-seeing boat. "Take A Ride Around Manhattan Island" the sign invited and hoards of holiday out-of-town visitors were crowded around the ticket office.

It was indeed a different perspective of New York, seeing it from the Hudson River. As the crowded craft pulled out, turning downstream past the docks, they passed a pier where a great liner was waiting to be boarded (Terra couldn't read the name). All up and down the waterfront tramp steamers waited to load cargo. At the foot of the Island the boat came close under the Statue of Liberty, impassive lady still welcoming the heavy laden to the golden shore, where all men are created equal.

They didn't mention anything about women. I want my money back.

From the railing of the boat it would be a straight fall into the water. Not a long jump actually if she were ever isolated long enough to climb over the rail. But once more she was repelled by the sight of trash, empty bottles, paper cups, condoms and horrid lumps of the unspeakable floating everywhere, gulls dipping over the obscene flotsam. Looking eastward, she could make out the delicate lines of the long and graceful bridge across the Narrows, and beyond, the whole Atlantic Ocean. Surely the water was cleaner out there . . .

But the boat turned away from the harbor and chugged up the East River, while tourist kids yammered and scrapped with each other and happily added to the trash in the waters with their hot-dog wrappers and half-finished sandwiches. More docks along this shore to the left, and on the right, stacked apartments, Brooklyn Heights and a faint aroma of raw sewage. It was so tremendous, the city with its huge populace massed, Terra could almost feel the maelstrom of needs and dreams and bathrooms all flowing together.

When they turned in west at the Harlem River, the waters grew surly. Here, she had heard, the tides were particularly lethal because they flowed into the river from both directions, creating a tumult of cross currents. Dirty water, and yet a few old men fished there, dragging in the occasional eel. The tidal flow eddied around hidden subsurface junk; it was a dumping ground, they said, for the detritus of the slums. But the docks were full of children, shrieking with laughter as they leaped into the oily water. How many went under and were hardly missed?

Terra was glad when they finished the circuit and docked again at the mid-town pier. As she headed for home, she had to rethink her new plan. For her grand finale she wanted no angry currents. She'd had enough of those lately. The office had seethed like a poisonous caldron since Ari had left.

It had happened so fast it was over before they could say good-bye. The 15th of June. Ari was gone and Manisch in a black mood that he didn't even try to lighten with his usual charm. The minute Terra came to work he sat her down at Ari's desk and instructed her grimly to go through it.

"Here's a master list of all the correspondence. We keep close track of every piece of communication," he told her between tight lips. "I want you to check this against Ari's files, see what's missing. Be very specific about it. As you go through, retrieve anything not on here — his conference notes, his rough drafts or handwritten memos or grocery lists. He's taken his address book with him, so you'll have to make a new one, using the signatures on the correspondence. Double reference it, name of school, name of contact there, official title and so forth."

"Yes, sir." *But there won't be anything missing. Ari made copies of everything important. While you were away on the trip he stayed late to run the machine.*

"You know, of course, that what he has done is unconscionable." Manisch eyed her fiercely. "To leave without notice, to abandon his post with the fall list coming on. It was just luck that we could find a replacement for him in such a hurry. I count on you to help the new man with the transition."

"Whatever I can do," she said automatically. *The new editor is a friend of Ari's, but I've been asked not to mention that — for his sake.*

"And I want this inventory done before tomorrow," Manisch had added as he paced back out the door.

Two days' worth of work, as he well knows. The man's just letting off steam, making me work overtime. Probably still sore at me for not agreeing to go see Oppie. She didn't mind, if that were the only retribution he tried to visit on her. She really didn't want any more warfare with only a month to go before her own departure.

Around noon Henny dropped by to lay a new stack of folders on the desk. "This is some back-log that Ari didn't get his mitts on," she said with a sneer. "It was locked in my desk."

"So far," Terra said, "I haven't found anything missing."

"Of course not. He probably copied everything important. That's what I'd have done. But then I'd never have jumped ship without notice. Ollie will see to it the word goes out across the publishing industry. No one will ever trust Ari again." Touch of mean gratification, Henny was her old arrogant self.

She's back on her pills!

During his absence, the woman had come to Terra and hinted, then suggested, then finally demanded that she open the locked cabinet. "You must know where Ollie keeps the key. You two are so klotchy, always conferring with the door closed. Long hours, weary nights, I know he's offered you pep pills."

"Oh, yes, he did," Terra told her carelessly. "I didn't take any. I don't like artificial pick-me-ups. Coffee is enough. Even that keeps me from sleeping."

"Well, there are times when I need something, and it's all right with him, I assure you. So just give me the key for a minute —"

"Henny, I truly don't have it. As far as I know he keeps it on his key ring. You'll just have to wait 'til he gets back, I'm afraid."

"But — oh, damnation." And for the next few days she jittered around like a woman possessed. Or addicted. Terra recognized the symptoms. When she was in that pressurized environment on The Hill she had seen what drugs could do — for you and to you.

Watching Henny squirm, she bumped into another thought: *I'll bet Manisch does it on purpose. It's why he kept after me. Once you start using, you become dependent on him. You can't leave, he's got you by the short hairs.* He probably took an acid delight in leaving her in need. *Show of power.*

Now since the boss had returned, the woman had settled down, returned to her own sour, hard-bitten self, gloating a little at Terra's enslavement over the files. It was almost nine o'clock when she finished them.

The subway home smelled of mildew and sweaty clothes and body odor, in spite of the ventilation system. Sharing her car was a drunk sprawled across three seats, snoring, occasionally rousing when the train stopped, to peer out at the station sign, then flopping back. *Is the rest of the world getting this bad?* she wondered.

During the year in San Diego she had seen plenty of drunken sailors, marines, broken warriors of all kind. It was a major discharge point. Being in the services could make you a little crazy. And New York always had been a pressure pot. But what about life in St. Louis? Is there still structure? Is Virginia continuing to run on its proud history?

Wearily she climbed the subway stairs at 86th Street, not a glimmer of sundown lingering. Broadway was dark, deserted, only a few isolated lights in the tobacco shop, the drugstore. Traffic was sporadic. In between the passing of cars an unnatural silence seemed to magnify small sounds — those footsteps again.

Quite a distance, but coming on fast and with a purpose. Her inner cognition lurched — she was sure this time. Someone was following her. When she glanced back he was just a dark figure in an overcoat and snap-brim hat.

"Hold on there, miss. F.B.I. We need you to talk to you . . ."

So you say. Terra had her keys ready, splayed between her fingers. When his hand came down on her shoulder she turned fast and attacked him, jamming the keys at his eyes and kicking his shin as hard as she could. He yelped, grabbed the hand with the keys. With her other she seized his thumb and ripped it backward. Cursing, he let go and slapped her across the face so hard she saw stars.

"You little . . ." He swung again and connected.

Stumbling sideways, she went down on hands and knees, her ears ringing from the blow. The menacing shadow loomed over her, and then was gone, spun hard aside and slammed to the ground with a force that drove the wind out of him in a *huff.* Someone was hauling her to her feet, a tall figure in a baseball cap, a loose jersey, pale in the dark — Shanahan shoved a key in her hand.

Softly he said, "My place. Lock the door. Don't go upstairs." Then he returned to the man on the ground who was gasping, trying to say something . . . groping inside his coat.

Cutter kicked his hand aside. "Don't you be tryin' to pull a gun on me, old son. No, you stay down there." Planting a foot on the man's back, he shoved him flat again.

"Ma'am, you trot on home while I make sure this varmint don't follow yuh." And as she turned to run she could hear him going on in that horrible fake western drawl, "We don't hold with no gangsters comin' up here in our neighborhood, muggin' folks, slappin' around nice women, and you can tell that to your pardners down in Hell's Kitchen."

As she turned the corner onto 88th Terra kept to the shadows. Her thoughts were scattered, but she clung to instructions. At the rooming house the street light in front had burned out. In perfect darkness she slipped down the stairs and fumbled with the lock on the basement apartment. From the parked cars up the street the sudden shaft of a spotlight speared the darkness, emanating from a black sedan. It zeroed in on the doorway of the house overhead. Crouching low, she scuttled inside the lower entry and closed the iron gate quietly. Fumbling in the pitch-black shadows she let herself into the cellar of the old house, aware of the spotlight above, still searching, prowling the fronts of the buildings on either side. Quietly shooting the bolt, she stood in the big basement room, breathing hard.

Leaning back against the door, Terra

stood, gripping her handbag, heart pounding, knees shuddering. Her face felt hot where the man had slapped her. F.B.I.? Terra couldn't believe a federal agent would strike a woman. This had to be Manisch, setting a hired thug on her. To do what? Beat her up? Kill her? *He made sure I worked late, until after dark.* Terra was shivering uncontrollably now, not just with shock, but with an unfamiliar sensation. She was afraid. She was terrified.

Why should I be this scared? My life doesn't mean anything to me, I shouldn't be concerned. You'd think I had a future, to care this much. If it really was the F.B.I. it meant going to jail. Federal prison, bars, trials, it all around in her head. *Of course I'm scared, who wants to be consigned to a cell? It's for certain they'd never let you take the long jump there.* That must be it — she was afraid her plans would be scuttled.

And yet the spasm of terror had done something odd to her, cracking the shell of all that cool independence, spilling the self confidence that she had stored. *Not so easy to down a man, not like the jujitsu class. If it weren't for Shanahan* — Her thoughts went black, and for a while she just stood there immobile, head beginning to throb, skinned knee smarting where she had gone down onto the pavement.

After a while he came. Almost noiselessly the sliding door to the rear courtyard opened and closed again, Shanahan pulled a drapery across it and turned on a light, just a pale glow from the lamp in the corner. Terra was grateful, tried to say something and couldn't. Her teeth were chattering. Still in shadows he came and caught her by the shoulders, felt her tremors and took her in his arms, held her tight a minute.

"Hey, it's okay, it's okay. You're safe here."

Instinctively Terra clung to him hard. Head against his chest, she could feel his heart beating, steady, tough. "Are you all right?" she asked thinly. "Did you hurt your arm?"

"There's nothing weak about my left," he told her. "Good thing I wasn't in top trim, b'gorrah, I'd have left the spalpeen with some broken bones. Which is probably why the Good Lord gave me the dislocated shoulder, to slow me down. I used to be a rare scrapper." Talking in a gentle, humorous murmur, he got her quieted down, walked her over to the sofa.

"How did you get away?"

"Turned the situation over to a cop. Squad car cruising down Broadway. I explained that I'd witnessed a mugging and detained the bum who did it, and while he was putting handcuffs on the guy who was still trying to get out his badge, I took my leave. Sort of casually strolled off down 87th. Friend of mine is super in that house behind us. He's dodging an ex-wife. We exchanged keys so that he could make a discreet exit across the courtyard. First time I've had occasion to use it — in the front and out the back, and where did that cowboy go?" He was talking to calm her down, his hard knuckles stroking her wounded cheek.

"Was the — the man — ? He wasn't really a — a —"

"A G-man? Seemed pretty insistent about it. I doubt he'd have claimed it to the police if he didn't have the credentials. And the backup. There's a car up the street with a spotlight — you dodged that? Good. But what really has to be considered is the other, the one upstairs in your room."

"What!"

"When I went around to collect the trash earlier there he was, poking in your apartment, bold as brass. I asked him — I did my Irish brogue that time — 'And what would y' be after doin' in one of me tenants' rooms?' At which point he flashed an I.D. at me, Federal Bureau of Investigation. It looked pretty genuine. He advised me to mind my own business, then asked me when did I expect the woman home? I told him 'Sure, and aren't oy mindin' me own business, then?' I think he's still up there. The light's on in your room."

"So you came to wait for me," she said, and for some reason she found herself trying to hold back the tears.

"Bunny girl, I always wait for you." His arm around her shoulders tightened and she buried her face in his jersey, fighting for control. Floundering for recognition. This was Terra Firma who could take care of herself, wasn't it? But she was confused, frightened, and his arms felt so good around her. It was what she had missed most, that protective embrace.

"I'm s-s-sorry," she stuttered. "Just all sort of caught me by surprise."

"Of course it did. Not to worry. It's over now."

"But it's not! There's a man upstairs and another on the street and one searching for you over on 87th and . . ."

He chuckled. "He'll need a lot of luck finding that cowboy in the baseball cap. I dumped it in the trashcan over there, and I will soon ditch this shirt. After a while we'll just slip back across the courtyard and go around the block. One of the guys at the taxi stand will take you to a good safe hotel for the night. Then tomorrow —"

"No!"

"No?"

"I don't want to — I can't — I just cannot spend this night alone in a strange place with no answers and —" Tears wouldn't be denied any more, they were streaming down her face.

"Aw-w-w damnation." He stroked her cheek with the back of his hand. "I wish I'd damaged the bully boy!" His voice was so quiet it vibrated with fury. "That eye is going to be a bit colorful tomorrow. We'd better put a cold pack on it."

"I've got a black eye?"

"It's getting there. Your nose is bleeding a little." He looked in her purse and got out a handkerchief with his free hand, the other arm still tight around her shoulders.

"Me and Gil." She blew her nose. "We ask for trouble."

"You think you provoked this?"

"I know I did. My boss, you know, Oliver Manisch? He asked me to do him a favor. Wanted me to go see a friend of mine and try to get him to endorse Wallace, but I think there's more to it than that. I bet he wants Oppie — you know, Robert Oppenheimer, the physicist? He was a friend of

Phin's — I bet he's trying to recruit him for the Communists. He expected me to be go-between, but I said 'No.' So what do you want to bet he's told the F.B.I. some lie to make them come after me?"

"What kind of lie?"

"Well, I was there, wasn't I? I was at Los Alamos and we knew that somebody was leaking information to the Russians. They developed their bomb too fast. The brass never did find out who, but Manisch could put them on my trail, just by suggestion. I couldn't prove I *wasn't* the spy. And all along, I think Manisch is the real Communist among us."

"That would give him a motive to set the hounds on you. Then if you ever pointed the finger at *him* you'd be discredited."

"That sounds like Manisch. The man's got more angles than one of Phin's diagrams." It was beginning to make sense. *He isn't just mad at me, he's scared of me.* "He can tell them I belong to a pinko union and how I marched in the May Day Parade. They've got those snapshots. They'll come after me like a dogs after a — rabbit."

"Well, now, have y' ever seen a snowshoe bunny outwit a hungry coyote? Down into the snow he goes, and comes up in a safe place."

Terra leaned into the shelter of his embrace. She didn't want to think any more — about anything.

Soberly Shanahan said, "Listen to me, girl. You are vulnerable, but not helpless. Those were some pretty good moves you made on the *federale*. You're here, you're safe for the moment, and we'll figure this thing out. Right now you need a hot shower. You're still partly in shock, I can feel you fluttering inside like an aspen leaf in the wind." He helped her up, took her over to the cubbyhole beyond the furnace room where a cement stall had been built with an overhead shower in it. "Watch out for the water, it comes out boiling. Be sure you tone it down before you step in." He pulled the curtain, and a moment later a hand came around holding a garment that looked familiar.

We always seem to be giving each other first aid with that awful flannel nightshirt. Terra felt a touch of hysteria.

A half hour later, adorned in the bedgown, which sagged almost to the ground, she had lost the desire to laugh or cry or explain. Her will power had retreated to a level that was almost primitive. She had one need, nothing else would satisfy it. Going over to Shanahan, who was making up the couch with fresh sheets, she put a hand on his arm.

"No couch."

"Right. You get the bed, I was just making up the sofa for me."

"Not you either." She took advantage of his confusion and put her arms around him, her head tight against his chest. "I want you to come be with me. Of course, if you would rather not . . ."

"Merciful Mother, I have wanted it so much all these months it's fair killin' me." The words burst from him painfully. "But Bunny, love, I have to be telling you a thing about me —"

Terra was ready. The book at the library — it had explained that in its aftermath tuberculosis can leave a variety of long-range problems, including loss of erectile capability. Impotence. So the man must feel he can't afford to be attracted to a woman. Such a monumental frustration — it explained his darkness. Saying the first prayer of her life she pleaded, *Dear Lord, please give me the right words.*

With her head tucked well down under his chin she said, "I think I already know. I read a whole chapter in a book about T.B. If it's the sex thing I don't care. This is what I want. This is all I want."

"You — read it in a book?"

"After you said I didn't know much I wanted to find out. And I did. And it doesn't matter to me. Shan, I'm so cold inside, I'll never be warm again, unless you lend me some of your good Irish heat." She could hear the thump of his heart and something else — an upheaval. Deep inside the shopworn body something broke loose, a sigh, or a laugh.

"She — read a book —"

For a while they hung there. Then, gently he released her. "Go on to bed. I'll be there in a minute. I have to go up and turn on the porch light. Somehow the bulb in the street lamp has got itself broken."

Again and again during that long night Terra started awake and roused up, only to be drawn down beside him again and folded in his arms, reassured by his hand stroking her hair. On some primitive level she was aware that this was more precious than any sex, this was kindness beyond the definition of the word. Unselfishness, generosity, but her mind wasn't up to words, she could only rest gladly in the safety of his warmth beside her.

In early morning Terra was dimly aware that he had roused up and left, with just a touch of a finger on her cheek, light as — a kiss? Half awake she heard the trash cans roll and the garbage truck picking up out front. *What happens now?* Didn't want to think about it. Didn't want to come back to the frigid loneliness of the real world. Pulling the sheet up she took refuge in oblivion.

It felt like a long time later when she was wakened by the smell of coffee. Someone was singing in a low clear Irish tenor . . . *"She rolled her wheelbarrow through streets wide and narrow . . ."* Secretly Terra stole a look and saw Shanahan over by the back window, working on his sculpture. With a small tool he was touching it lightly, sharpening some contour. Reminded her of the way his work-hardened hands had explored her face in the dark last night, so softly she almost thought she'd imagined it.

From the depths of the old brass bed she couldn't quite see the piece itself, just a vague impression. He had cast it in plaster, very clean white, about two feet high, the shrouded figure of a woman, possibly a saint. There had been that reference yesterday to "the good Lord," in the same familiar tone that Andy used. Being Irish, Shanahan probably was a proper Catholic. And right now he had a look on his face that she recognized. It was a kind of worship — and something else. The brightness, the intensity that came over Phin when he was working on an equation. The look she had come to think of as "obsessed."

So this was Cutter's secret, the one she had sensed all along. And it was good. He was committed to his craft. She was glad for him — all her life she had wanted something to absorb her, inspire her. Thought she had found it in Phin, but that had ended. *Let it go.*

When Terra sat up in bed Shanahan looked across at her with a smile, so boyish and unused it startled her.

"Hi," he said. "How does the eye feel? It's marvelously artistic."

She had almost forgotten about that. It hardly hurt now, but when she went into the bathroom and faced the mirror she was astounded. A whole palette of colors swirled around the left side of her face, from blue to green to purple. Her knee was swollen and stiff, and her hand hurt where she had hit the pavement and scraped it. She was suddenly aware of other smaller aches.

But the big transformation was stirring in a place so deep inside she had to hold still under the warm shower and focus, to isolate it. The ache of fatalism was gone. In the few seconds when she had feared for her life, somehow it had become valuable to her again. When she tried to retrieve her morose pessimism she couldn't summon the gloom. For some reason she felt — wonderful.

She came out of the shower to find Shanahan making breakfast, bacon in the pan, two pieces of toast in an odd little toaster with the wings that opened sideways. As she joined him he put the eggs on while she set two places at the kitchen table. It was clean of dust. She realized suddenly that the bucket of clay was gone. And when she looked more closely she saw that the sacks of raw materials had also disappeared. Floor scrubbed, shelves almost bare of tools. As if he were getting ready to leave?

NO!

The explosion of a new despair was so deep it frightened her. *Everybody leaves me.* Max had left her alone in a snowstorm. Tommy had sailed off to marry an Admiral's daughter. Poor Ozzie had shipped out to Pearl Harbor and vanished when the Arizona went down. Her mother had just faded away. Father escaped into a numbing world where no one could follow. And Phin — that had been deliberate.

Like this. The difference was that Shanahan didn't owe her anything. He had been kind. It was her own foolishness, to take him for granted. To assume he would always be there somewhere in time of need. *I swore*

I'd never need anyone that much again. Appalled she stood frozen by the table.

"Bunny, can you get the toast?" he roused her.

It was scorching. She grabbed it out of the funny little toaster and buttered it.

"Of course, I like burnt toast," he commented cheerfully, dishing out the eggs. "Gives it character — hey, are you okay?"

"Fine," she said weakly. Trying rapidly to retreat. *It's not that he doesn't care for me. Just the opposite — he doesn't want to complicate his life with a woman when he can't follow through.* And now embarrassment flooded through her, when she thought how she had used him last night. "Shan, I owe you an apology for going into spasms. It was awful, to back you into a corner like that."

"My pleasure," he told her cheerfully, "It was the best night I've spent in — shoot, best night of my life, I guess." He addressed himself to the plate.

Terra had lost her appetite. It was almost as if she had lost another whole world. *What an awful spot I've put him in, poor guy. It must have been painfully frustrating, if he does have feelings for me, to lie there all night and not be able to . . .*

He glanced across, saw her distress and

grew serious. "Bunny, everybody on earth needs to be held. Your skin gets hungry for it — you starve for some human warmth from someone who cares."

He's trying to make it easy for me. And for himself, so he can retreat without being unkind. She determined to be her old self, retreat with dignity, forsake all this maudlin sentimentality.

"You've been wonderful to me — to all of your tenants, but especially to me. I feel as if we're practically kinfolk. But I'm not your responsibility and I shouldn't have dumped my needy self on you that way. I will get out of here as soon as possible and you can — uh — go ahead with your plans. You are getting ready to move on?"

The early sun caught him squarely in the face as he looked across at her, his strange eyes as clear as a pool with autumn leaves deep at the bottom. "Not without asking you to come with me."

Terra sat stunned, mentally repeating the words in total confusion. "But — why?" she asked stupidly.

He came around the table, took her by the elbow and got her up, steered her over to look at his sculpture. With the morning light from the glass door full upon it, she saw the figure of a woman from the hips up. What she thought was a veil turned out to be a fall of hair, around the face, down over the shoulders, just hinting at the form below, the straight back, shoulders, curve of breasts. The features were stunningly simple, almost stylized, except for detail around the eyes, the mouth, the lift of the chin — the head was cocked upward. Not a portrait, but recognition struck her breathless. As she stared at it, a kaleidoscope of emotions scattered and rearranged themselves into a different pattern.

"You ask me why? Take a good look. There shouldn't be any doubt in your mind how I feel about you, or else I've blown it completely."

Yes. This was no tribute to a little sister, no pity for an orphan of the storm. This was a work of love. Beautifully committed, delicately shaped, as fine a piece of art as she had ever seen. It spoke more forcefully than words.

"I'm not that strong." She protested almost to herself. *This girl would never run away from life.*

He said, "You have so much courage I was hard-put to do justice to it. If I were wrong about that, I'd lay down my tools forever. So think hard what your answer is. Will you come with me?"

*He knows, somehow he knows all about —
death-day.* "How did you find out?"

"Back last Christmas when you were down with pneumonia, your sister-in-law called. She was frantic that she couldn't charge forth through the storm and be with you. She gave me some pretty hysterical instructions — namely, that I was to keep you alive, against your will if necessary."

"And you're still trying." She was glad he was standing behind her, hoped he couldn't tell how unnerved she was by the clattering collapse of old barriers, leaving unpredictable possibilities ahead. "Suppose I said 'no?' "

He was so close she could almost feel the turbulence in him, but he didn't touch her as he said, "Then I'd have to go on by myself. No way I could hang around and watch the biggest tragedy of my life unfold. I would go on living, as I always have. I know there has to be a reason that I'm here, and I wouldn't try to out-guess the Lord. For awhile now I've thought His purpose for me was — you."

"Shan . . . I have to be honest, I'm not ready yet for . . ."

"I know that. I don't expect you to have feelings for me. Just let me have mine for you, just go on being linked to you. So far it's panned out pretty well."

"But now it gets more complicated. I'm in big trouble. If I do — if I did stick around, if you tried to help you might get hurt."

"Then we'd better both get moving." Abruptly, his tone was light. His arms came about her and he spoke into her ear. "We'll make a run for it together."

Terra laughed, uncertainly. "Where? Where would we go?"

"Who knows?" He held her tighter. "We'll shuck this sorry city and wander off to look at our beautiful country. Have you ever seen Montana? We'll have fun, no strings attached. Bunny, how long has it been since you had fun?"

An odd thought struck her: *Would the Lord approve of me having fun?*

From somewhere came an answer: Why not? What do you have to lose?

"What do you think? Can you bring yourself to trust me?"

The possibility of beginning life all over was so foreign to her, Terra had to flounder a moment to orient herself. But she didn't back away. In fact a door seemed to be opening somewhere. And the sculpture on the table, caught in a slightly different light, almost took on the hint of a smile.

In a kind of anguish he burst out, "For the love of God say something!"

"Yes, for the love of God." Speaking slowly, she let a higher power supply the words. "This" — she reached toward the figure on the table — "it actually makes me want to live."

The Irishman drew a long breath. "Then I guess I got it right."

AUGUST, 1948

Terra stood before the statue, shadowed now under the overhead bulb, different from the girl in the sunlight. She could see that he had given her a touch of fear, but that was only human. Without fear there can be no courage. Who taught her that? Phin?

He was suddenly a long way off, as if she had released him to proceed to — wherever he was bound. Was the Lord with him, she wondered, still not quite comfortable with the idea of an all-powerful Companion. And yet when she thought about it she had to admit that there had been many times in her life when an unseen hand had turned aside disaster. Even permitted it — for Phin. Surely he had been fulfilling some destiny. She could accept that now. Incredible the relief she felt to be rid of that hurt. With a diffident thought upward she said, *Thank you.*

She owed Him that, for many reasons. For

guiding her steps this last year, for putting her together with Shanahan — if ever there was an unlikely match-up. *Only what comes next?* She actually listened as if there might be some magic answer telegraphed from Heaven. All she felt was a tentative sense of a future awaiting, and with it, an uneasiness. Because something was missing.

She was confident that the two of them would do well together. No doubt that Shan was in love with her. Or that she could give him enough of herself to make the relationship work, at least for now. Was that the catch? Just to go off with him without an unofficial commitment on both sides — it went against her whole upbringing, not to mention the old tried customs of society. Maybe that was to be the way of the new chaos, but she wasn't sure she could live a life "without strings," as Shan had put it.

Pacing the room, she wondered what was keeping him. To confound the watchers, one of whom still resided in her room upstairs, he had gone about his usual janitorial duties. Terra had spent the day trying to write a letter, working on it harder than she'd ever done before. After many drafts she thought she had it right, but she wanted to check it over with someone and . . . she realized she was about to get her wish.

They were coming downstairs, talking — that was Ari's voice, rasping with irritation. "I really am tired, Cutter. I need my sleep. I've just started a new job. What's so important — ?" And then he came in and saw Terra and his Semitic face was stricken with relief. The beam of gladness didn't sit right on that saturnine face.

"Terra Incognito!" He seized her hand, then retreated in a fluster of embarrassment. "I was hoping you had gone to ground in some appropriate place, after I heard you were missing. Oh yes, I know what's been going on. I have an inside source over at Paragon. The faithful Ruth is more observant than she looks. In fact she is driven by womanly curiosity, and Manisch's phone is linked to her desk. She overheard him besmirching you to the F.B.I. and it incensed her so that she spent one whole lunch hour informing me about it. By the way, if you did provide the secret of the atom bomb to the Russians, I'd say they were pretty slow on the uptake. They still don't have theirs perfected."

"It's no joke," she told him. "Someone on The Hill did give them inside information. It wasn't I, of course."

"Thank you, that was a lovely 'I.' Most people these days say 'me.' " Ari's right eye glittered like jet. "No, I never believed you'd rat on your own country. This smelled too much like Manisch getting even with you for something. Did you quit?"

"Not until he sicced the feds on me. It's only thanks to Shan that I didn't get ferreted away to some dungeon. No, what I did was refuse to help him with a little plan he had. He wanted me to drop in on Robert Oppenheimer and get him to sign up for Wallace's third party. I think Manisch is a full-fledged Communist himself."

"I know it for a fact," Ari said. "It's why I beat my hasty retreat from a very well-paying job. Even in a luxurious mansion, if you lie down with rats you get up with fleas."

Over on the far side of the room, Shanahan seemed to be suppressing a laugh.

"I figured he painted me red to the FBI so that anything I said about him would be discredited. But I have a question, Ari. What if I turned him in to the New York City Police?" She handed him her letter.

Ari read it swiftly, then again more slowly, his scrawny jaw ajar. "I can't believe this. Is it true? He keeps drugs in that locked cabinet in his office?"

"He tried to get me to join him more than once. Unless he's taken them out by now, but I'm betting he hasn't. He's so arrogant, it wouldn't occur to him. I think he's got poor Hennie hooked."

Ari began to smile, a grin that turned positively fiendish. "This is inspired! Your letter is well put, too. It makes sense, the way you have explained his lies about you in connection with the feds. This could create enough doubt to get you off the hook. If the NYPD can convince Hoover's boys that you've been framed to keep you from blowing the whistle on the narcotics, they may ease up on the hunt. Of course, you'll have to testify against him."

"They'll have to find her first," Shanahan mused retreating over to the glass doors in back. "We're on our way to the ends of the earth, or Montana, whichever comes first."

Ari frowned. "I hate to throw cold water, but the F.B.I. could track a fish through fast water. They'll be watching the railroads and airlines."

"I'm afraid they'll be disappointed then. We're sailing forth in a Buick convertible, lovely car I acquired from an old lady who only used it to go to church. Her boyfriend swore on the Bible, it's an honest two thousand on the speedometer. I named it The Beautiful Babe, parked right now over on 87th Street."

"All right, that's good. But Terra will still

have to change her identity. Costs a bundle to obtain false papers."

"About two dollars and fifty cents, in some courthouse. Ten bucks' donation to a preacher. Get a new social security card applied for under her maiden name, Miller, lots of Millers around the country. And her new married name won't ring any bells with the feds." Shanahan glanced over at Terra nervously. "I should have run this by you first. I'm sorry. I was going to wait a bit."

She reassembled her face rapidly. "It's okay. In fact I'll bet it would work."

Ari had already grasped the details. "It will certainly slow them down. Especially if you vanish into the wilderness — I've never been west of the Hudson River myself. Are there still marauding Indians in Montana?" It seemed to be a serious question.

Soberly Shanahan said, "You want to watch out for the Blackfeet."

"Better to fight redskins than yellow-bellies." Ari put the letter in an inside pocket. "I'll get this into the hands of the right people. My brother is one of New York's finest. He'll know how to handle it. Meanwhile, after you're gone who do I pay the rent to?" He dug into his pocket, but Shanahan shook his head.

"This week's on me. I've already squared

accounts with the owners of the building. The new super — name of Constantino — will be moving in by next Friday. Friend of mine over at the taxi stand, he got nailed for reckless driving and lost his medallion. He's taken over my contract — he'll be around to see you."

Ari turned toward the door. Then, almost shyly he said something in Yiddish. "That means, 'Go in good health,' Terra Mater."

"You, too," she returned, automatically. Her mind was still stumbling around the thought of that preacher, the implications. It was the missing piece. A promise of commitment. *Thank you, Lord.*

When they were alone, Shanahan came over to her diffidently. "I'm truly sorry. I meant to discuss it with you first. Dear little Bunny, I know you don't love me. But I can carry double for however long it takes. I promise —"

She put a hand on his mouth. "It's all right."

"You mean you would do it? Marry a loser like me?"

"Don't ever call yourself that! Please!"

"But I don't have anything to offer."

"Neither do I," she told him. "Shan, we're a couple of invalids, wounded veterans. The war has wrecked us, ruined the whole world, broken all the rules, turned our country upside down. I get the feeling this country is on a long skid to — somebody said 'chaos.' If we're going to survive it will take the two of us holding each other up through the rough spots. That's why I will go with you anywhere. But I have enough of the good old values left that I will be much happier if we make it official."

Looking stunned, he held her to him. "I was raised a good Catholic," he said. "But this is the first time I ever truly believed in miracles."

Next morning Terra waited in the furnace room, hardly breathing, as they came downstairs in a clump of boots, a rattle of voices. The vent behind the oil burner was like an open microphone. She couldn't make out the G-man's words, high and contentious, but Cutter's reply came clear and very Irish.

"And I'm tellin' yez, laddie, that it's the law: A puir landlord's got the right to hold the property of the de-linquent tenant until all rent is paid up, which amounts, in this case, to one-hundred-and-twenty-foive dollars, or ten weeks times fifteen, do the arithmetic, bhoyo. No, yez cannot pay me and take this stuff. It belongs to the tenant. I can't turn it over unless yez have an order from the court. Come back wi' a piece o' paper and the box is all yours. Meanwhile it'll be safe enough in storage. Nobody's going to lay a darlin' finger on it."

They were on the front stoop now. She eased back out of sight as Shanahan wrestled the door open, leaving the federal agent out on the sidewalk. The minute she heard the latch click Terra moved out of the shadows. Tacitly silent, they took the large cardboard box to the bed and she delved into it to get out the cashmere coat. Then searching deeper she found the little rabbit carving and set it on the night table. Cutter's face lit with pleasure. His smile was so new she still hadn't got used to it.

"It's starting to rain," he murmured in her ear. "I don't think he'll hang around long."

The pang of excitement was something she had almost forgotten, the precarious satisfaction of breaking the rules. It used to be the fuel that propelled her through those bad days at college. Only now, the stakes were so much higher. She had spent the last long hour envisioning what they would do if the authorities caught her: accusations of disloyalty to her country, of secret dealings with the Russians, prison even. How on earth do you prove that something didn't happen?

"I'm afraid they won't give up," she said, softly, though the basement was almost a fortress in its isolation. "I hate to put you in danger too."

"It's in a good cause," he said. "But I'm sorry to say they may have already cleaned out your private papers. I didn't see any letters or —"

"There's only one and I keep that with me." Which brought her to the last remaining chore. "I need you to do me a favor — find a safe phone and get in touch with Dixie. I can't just run off and leave her worrying."

By afternoon the rain was sheeting the city as if it were being shaken out of a blanket. Across the street the blue sedan which had been parked there for four days could be seen to turn on its wipers every time someone scuttled along the sidewalk under an umbrella.

"They think they're so invisible," Shan had remarked, "and all the while they're as obvious as a mule in a pony farm."

At least the agent was no longer stationed in her room, Terra thought thankfully. All quiet up there, as she paced the floor, first to the front door, then to the back, looking out onto the wet courtyard, splashing with the fall of rain. She paused before the statue.

"Shan, what are we going to do with her? I mean, as we travel? Plaster isn't all that impervious, is it?"

He had shellacked the piece to toughen the surface against nicks, and now was polishing it with wax, so that it took on the patina of old ivory. As she watched his hands working on it, she could almost feel them, as they caressed her in the dark at night. He always waited until he thought she was asleep. Still so shy, he had never asked to see her without her clothes.

Her own natural aloofness was vanishing as she began to taste the joy of life again. *I never was made to be independent. Neither was he.* The magnetic force with which they had come together proved that.

Phin knew. He wanted me to find somebody. The thought still brought its sadness. But she was becoming reconciled. *And that's what I need to tell Dixie. I don't want her to worry about me.*

He glanced at his watch. "The lady said she'd be here by two o'clock. I need to go to the bank."

"I've got money there too," Terra realized. "Almost five hundred dollars. How on earth do I get it out?"

"Write me a check for the balance. I'll put it into my account as back rent. Then I'll close the account later when we get somewhere that feels permanent for a while. Meantime I get a little windfall the first of every month, government check, full disability. At least the T.B. is good for something. Over three hundred bucks, it will cover expenses nicely. I've already put in a forwarding address to the homestead in Montana. Me old fayther's going to love you."

"I'll be glad when we're on our way. But I do wish Dixie would come."

A half hour later the knock at the front door was sharp and insistent, followed by a voice. "You, Heathcliff, I am here, as summoned."

He went to open up. "Come in, ma'am."

In the long flowing rain cape, the drops glittering like sequins, her hair caught up in a red turban, Dixie could have been trying out for the part of Wicked Witch of the West. Except that witches seldom look idiotically happy. "Gawd be praised!" She ran across and seized Terra in a hug that was entirely uncharacteristic. It even surprised Dixie. She stepped back and scowled ferociously. "You had me worried, girl. What's this he tells me, that you're being stalked by the F.B.I.?"

"I know. That's why I couldn't call you. We think our wire is tapped. And maybe even yours, if they show on their records that you're related to me. That's why Shan was so cryptic on the phone. He had to sneak out in the dark last night and find a pay booth over on Broadway."

"But what on earth have you done to get the United States government on your case?"

"I should have listened when you warned me about the Farcical Brainless Idiots being on the hunt." Hastily she sketched in the details.

Dixie began to nod. "I figured something had happened when I saw the piece in the paper about your boss getting arrested."

"What piece!"

Dixie dug inside the cloak, and from an inner pocket took a folded sheet from the New York Times. "What kind of people did you involve yourself with, you innocent child?"

It was a short column below the fold.

EXECUTIVE HEAD OF PARAGON PRESS CHARGED WITH DRUG DEALING.

The narcotics police had found not only the stuff in his office cabinet, but a quantity of marijuana and cocaine in his apartment on the upper East Side. Manisch was in jail and the Vice President of the company was wanted for questioning. The publishing house was closed until further notice.

"Sounds like your letter lit a fuse," Shanahan was reading over her shoulder.

"You were the one who blew the whistle?" Dixie was slightly awed. "I never figured you for a tightrope walker. We — my bunch — we're used to treading the edge. But you never did anything wrong except trust too easily and love too hard."

"And yet she brought the house down around their ears," Shanahan marveled in a tone that made Dixie give him a more critical look. She glanced around the room, so obviously in double residency. Studied the man and the joy as he stood with his arm around Terra. Then her eyes turned, as if instructed, and she saw the sculpture.

"Oh my stars and garters!" Slowly she moved toward it, transfixed.

Shanahan followed her over, trying not to show his pride.

"I want to buy it," Dixie spoke in awe. "I've got to have it! It's exactly what I need as a centerpiece for my new salon. The ultimate woman, mysterious, layers of complexity, suppressed emotion waiting to explode. Please Heathcliff, you can do another one. This I want. Charge me anything you like."

"It's not for sale." He told her gently. "But if you want it on loan for a while I'd be proud."

Terra was speechless. It was an ideal solution.

"Let me rent it, then. People rent museum pieces all the time. I'll pay you a year in advance —"

"You're Terra's sister," he said. "No rent."

"Is it okay with you?" Dixie turned to her fiercely.

Slowly she nodded. "It would be seen and appreciated in your gallery. That's what a piece of sculpture is all about. Right, Shan?"

"Not just seen. It will be coveted!" Dixie went back to hover over it, her hands reaching without touching. "Rich women come to my showings. They're going to want to commission you — *'an original Shanahan, my dear!'* No, you need a more Italian name. Who ever heard of an Irish sculptor? Never mind me, I'm running on, and I've got a taxi waiting outside — he'd better be waiting. I paid him a fiver. Can I take it with me?"

"I've got a piece of canvas somewhere. Hold on," the super disappeared back into the furnace room.

Dixie leaned close to Terra to speak into her ear. "I certainly hope you intend to marry this man!"

"That's the plan," Terra murmured.

"Wonderful. Here —" Dixie dug in her oversized handbag and pulled out a checkbook. "Don't tell Heathcliff, and don't you dare say no. This is a wedding present." She scribbled and signed and tore out a check, folded it and stuck it in Terra's shirt pocket.

Then he was back with a heavy scrap of tarpaulin. Draping the figure in blanketing, he wrapped it in the tarp and secured it with a piece of clothesline. "I'll carry it out for you. It's heavy. Is there someone at the other end to help you unload it?" Shanahan was moving quickly now, as if he dreaded what he was doing.

"Oh good grief, the boy is gone and I haven't said goodbye." Dixie seized Terra briefly. "Write to me. Don't let's get out of touch again *please!*" And she ran after him.

Terra understood why Shanahan had gone off in such a rush. The sculptor in him couldn't bear to part with his creation, even though it made ultimate sense not to cart the statue around on some uncharted journey. And yet, as she looked at the empty table she worried what it would do to him to come back and see that vacant spot.

On impulse, she began to strip. She took down her braids and combed the hair around her, imitating as nearly as she could recall the lines of the sculpture. *Lord, do me one more favor. Tell me if this isn't the right thing — I don't want him to be disappointed.* Feeling no negative vibrations Terra perched on the workbench, trying to get the pose right, head turned, chin up, hands at her sides. *And where is he? What's taking so long?*

She was starting to panic when she finally heard his step outside. He came in, slapping water off the broad-brimmed rain hat. "Taxi didn't wait of course. We had to go clear up to 86th Street . . ." He glanced over then and saw her.

The look on his face was well worth the wait.

The letter:

Red Lodge, Montana
August 21, 1948
Dear Dix:

D-day. As in 'dare to live' day. We were married this morning in a little church with the Beartooth Mountains outside its window and a trout stream running past just a block away. The lavender silk gown turned out to be the one to wear in honor of a new life.

It's a different world. The huge country we have come across is not all ruined — yet. People still have old-fashioned values. They run little diners and mom-and-pop grocery stores. They have barn dances and county fairs. They fly the flag.

In Kansas City we bought a small camping trailer so we could stay clear of cities. I find I am pretty good at cooking over a camp-fire. Even fresh trout. We bought some fly rods and I caught a fish while Shan whittled.

As we came through Missouri we saw a man cutting down a dead walnut tree. Shan stopped to help him, and was rewarded by a large segment of heartwood. He has already started carving a new sculpture (I keep telling him he should pick a better model.)

In the Clark's Fork Valley we went by his grandfather's homestead, a sod-roof house like something out of "Stagecoach." His father still lives there — we got along just fine. Tomorrow we're going over to look for remnants of the Oregon Trail.

To say we're happy is an understatement. I don't know where we'll eventually come to roost, but it doesn't matter. When we get there I'll write. As always, your sister,

Tess Shanahan

P.S. There is one development that worries me. I am falling in love again.

The employees of Thorndike Press hope you have enjoyed this Large Print book. All our Thorndike and Wheeler Large Print titles are designed for easy reading, and all our books are made to last. Other Thorndike Press Large Print books are available at your library, through selected bookstores, or directly from us.

For information about titles, please call:
(800) 223-1244

or visit our Web site at:
www.gale.com/thorndike
www.gale.com/wheeler

To share your comments, please write:
Publisher
Thorndike Press
295 Kennedy Memorial Drive
Waterville, ME 04901